TALES
FROM THE
CRYPT ®

PAPERCUT*Z* ™

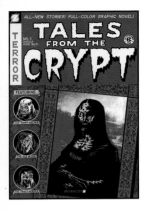

**Graphic Novels Available
from Papercutz**

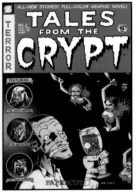

Graphic Novel #1
"Ghouls Gone Wild!"

Graphic Novel #2
"Can You Fear Me Now?"

Coming March 2008: Graphic Novel #3
"Zombielicious"

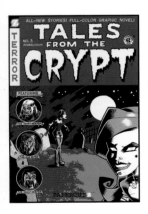

TALES FROM THE CRYPT®

NO. 2 – *Can You Fear Me Now?*

MORT TODD   STEVE MANNION
DON McGREGOR   JAMES ROMBERG
STEFAN PETRUCHA   DON HUDSON
FRED VAN LENTE   MR. EXES
JIM SALICRUP   RICK PARKER
Writers   Artists

MR. EXES Cover Artist

Based on the classic EC Comics series.

New York

"A MURDERIN' IDOL"
MORT TODD — Writer
STEVE MANNION — Artist
MARK LERER – Letterer

"CRYSTAL CLEAR"
DON McGREGOR — Writer
JAMES ROMBERGER — Artist
MARK LERER – Letterer
MARGUERITE VAN COOK - Colorist

"SLABBED!"
STEFAN PETRUCHA — Writer
DON HUDSON — Artist
MARK LERER — Letterer
DIGIKORE — Colorist

"THE GARDEN"
FRED VAN LENTE — Writer
MR. EXES — Artist
MARK LERER — Letterer

GHOULUNATIC SEQUENCES
JIM SALICRUP – Writer
RICK PARKER – Artist, Title Letterer, Colorist
MARK LERER – Letterer

PREVIEW OF "EXTRA LIFE"
NEIL KLEID – Writer
CHRIS NOETH – Artist
MARK LERER — Letterer

JIM SALICRUP
Editor-in-Chief

ISBN 10: 1-59707-084-X paperback edition
ISBN 13: 978-1-59707-084-3 paperback edition
ISBN 10: 1-59707-085-8 hardcover edition
ISBN 13: 978-1-59707-085-0 hardcover edition
Printed in China.

10 9 8 7 6 5 4 3 2 1

THE CRYPT OF TERROR

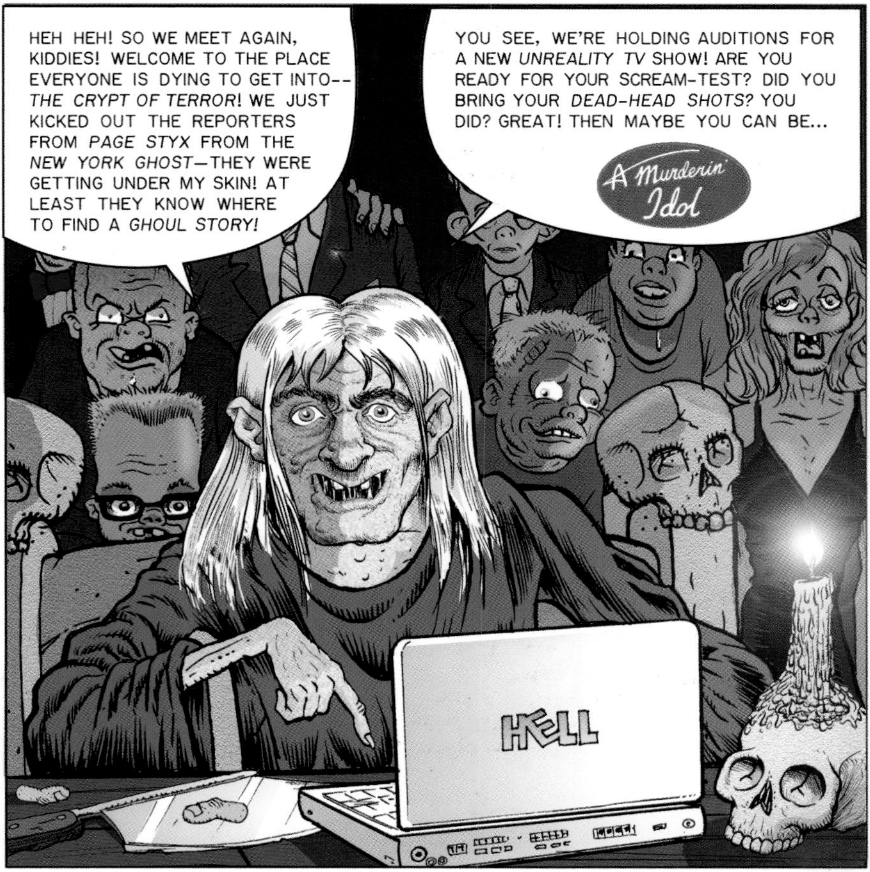
HEH HEH! SO WE MEET AGAIN, KIDDIES! WELCOME TO THE PLACE EVERYONE IS DYING TO GET INTO-- *THE CRYPT OF TERROR*! WE JUST KICKED OUT THE REPORTERS FROM *PAGE STYX* FROM THE *NEW YORK GHOST*—THEY WERE GETTING UNDER MY SKIN! AT LEAST THEY KNOW WHERE TO FIND A *GHOUL STORY!*
YOU SEE, WE'RE HOLDING AUDITIONS FOR A NEW *UNREALITY TV* SHOW! ARE YOU READY FOR YOUR SCREAM-TEST? DID YOU BRING YOUR *DEAD-HEAD SHOTS?* YOU DID? GREAT! THEN MAYBE YOU CAN BE...
A Murderin' Idol
HELL

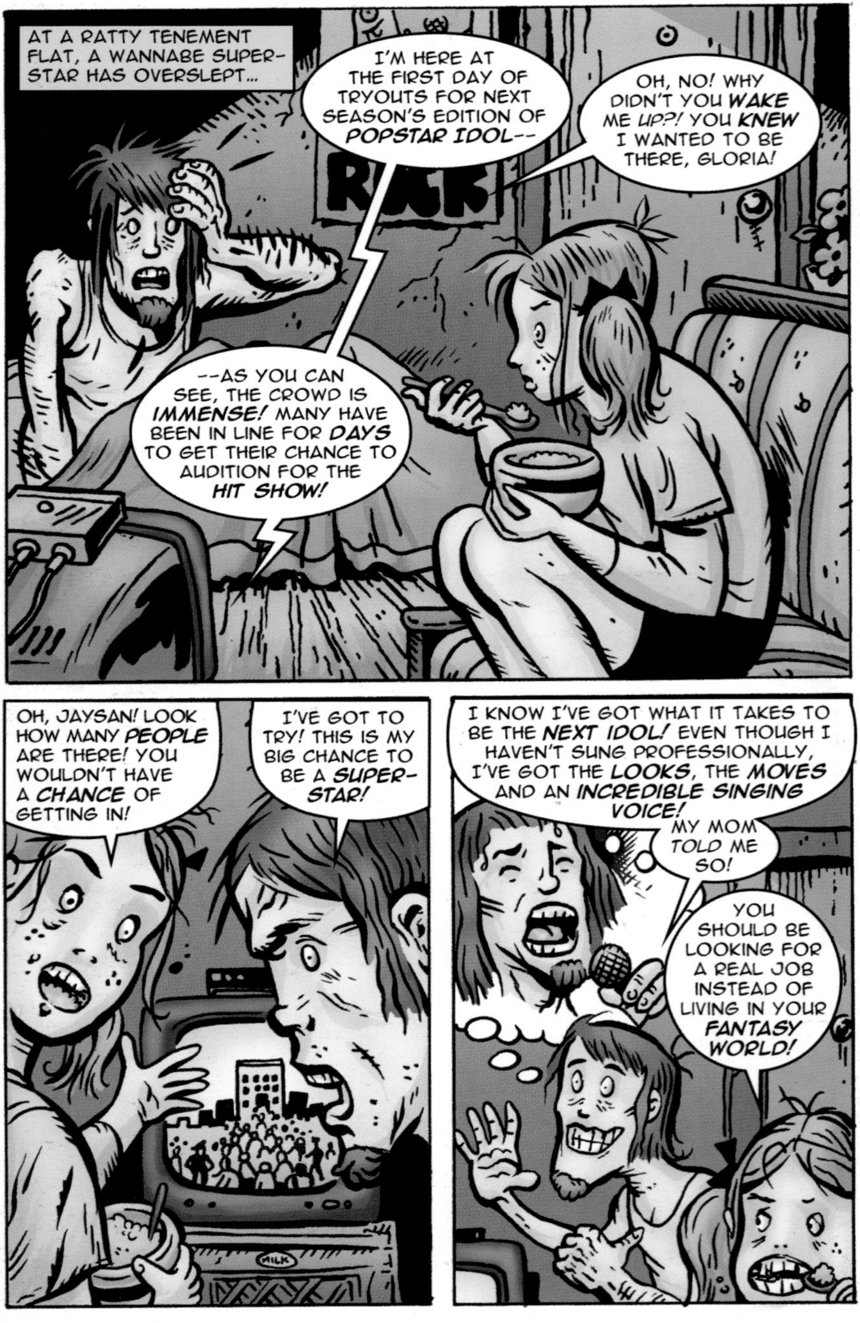
AT A RATTY TENEMENT FLAT, A WANNABE SUPER-STAR HAS OVERSLEPT...
I'M HERE AT THE FIRST DAY OF TRYOUTS FOR NEXT SEASON'S EDITION OF POPSTAR IDOL--
OH, NO! WHY DIDN'T YOU WAKE ME UP?! YOU KNEW I WANTED TO BE THERE, GLORIA!
--AS YOU CAN SEE, THE CROWD IS IMMENSE! MANY HAVE BEEN IN LINE FOR DAYS TO GET THEIR CHANCE TO AUDITION FOR THE HIT SHOW!
ROCK
OH, JAYSAN! LOOK HOW MANY PEOPLE ARE THERE! YOU WOULDN'T HAVE A CHANCE OF GETTING IN!
I'VE GOT TO TRY! THIS IS MY BIG CHANCE TO BE A SUPER-STAR!
MILK
I KNOW I'VE GOT WHAT IT TAKES TO BE THE NEXT IDOL! EVEN THOUGH I HAVEN'T SUNG PROFESSIONALLY, I'VE GOT THE LOOKS, THE MOVES AND AN INCREDIBLE SINGING VOICE!
MY MOM TOLD ME SO!
YOU SHOULD BE LOOKING FOR A REAL JOB INSTEAD OF LIVING IN YOUR FANTASY WORLD!

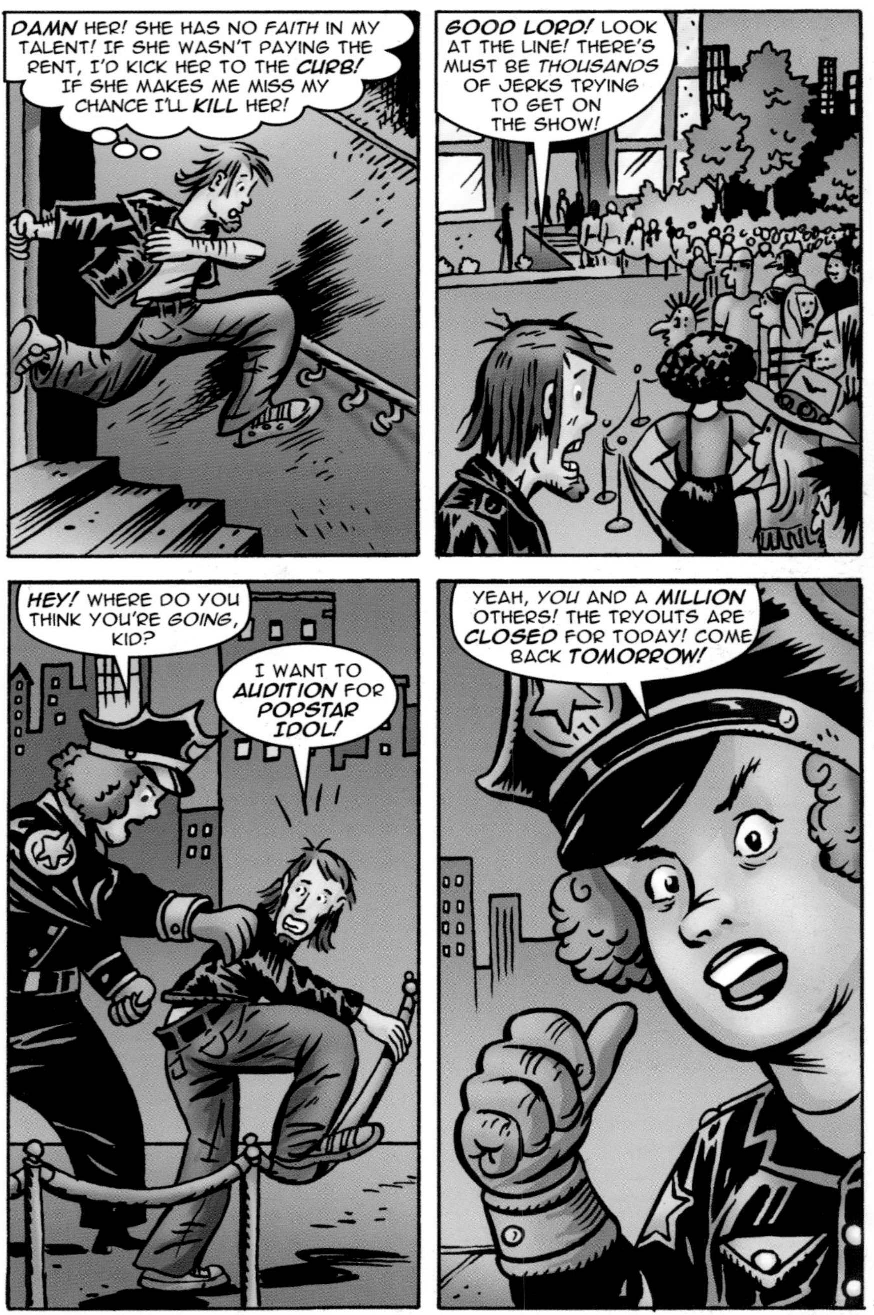

DAMN HER! SHE HAS NO FAITH IN MY TALENT! IF SHE WASN'T PAYING THE RENT, I'D KICK HER TO THE CURB! IF SHE MAKES ME MISS MY CHANCE I'LL KILL HER!
GOOD LORD! LOOK AT THE LINE! THERE'S MUST BE THOUSANDS OF JERKS TRYING TO GET ON THE SHOW!
HEY! WHERE DO YOU THINK YOU'RE GOING, KID?
I WANT TO AUDITION FOR POPSTAR IDOL!
YEAH, YOU AND A MILLION OTHERS! THE TRYOUTS ARE CLOSED FOR TODAY! COME BACK TOMORROW!

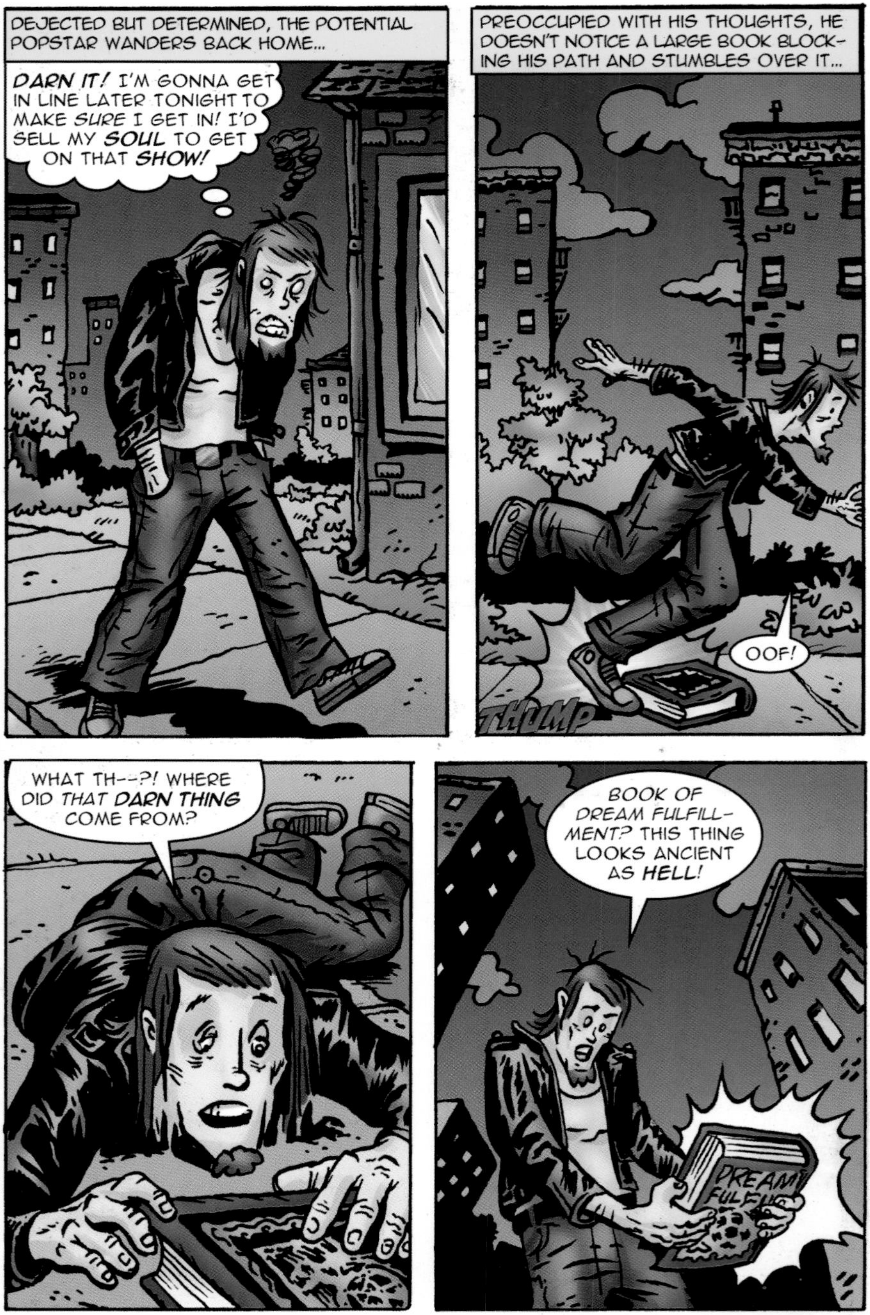
DEJECTED BUT DETERMINED, THE POTENTIAL POPSTAR WANDERS BACK HOME...
DARN IT! I'M GONNA GET IN LINE LATER TONIGHT TO MAKE SURE I GET IN! I'D SELL MY SOUL TO GET ON THAT SHOW!
PREOCCUPIED WITH HIS THOUGHTS, HE DOESN'T NOTICE A LARGE BOOK BLOCKING HIS PATH AND STUMBLES OVER IT...
OOF!
THUMP
WHAT TH--?! WHERE DID THAT DARN THING COME FROM?
BOOK OF DREAM FULFILLMENT? THIS THING LOOKS ANCIENT AS HELL!
DREAM FULFIL

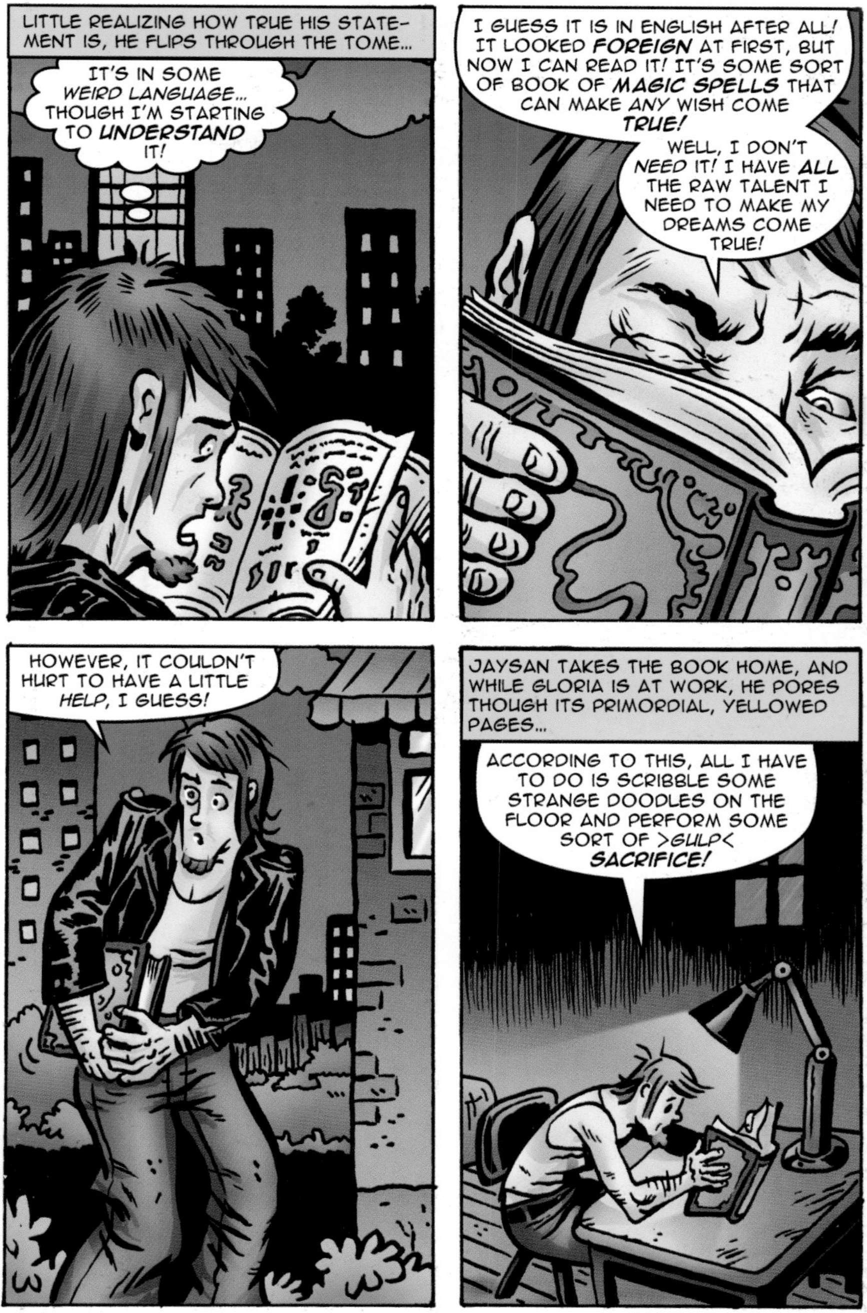
LITTLE REALIZING HOW TRUE HIS STATEMENT IS, HE FLIPS THROUGH THE TOME...
IT'S IN SOME WEIRD LANGUAGE... THOUGH I'M STARTING TO UNDERSTAND IT!
I GUESS IT IS IN ENGLISH AFTER ALL! IT LOOKED FOREIGN AT FIRST, BUT NOW I CAN READ IT! IT'S SOME SORT OF BOOK OF MAGIC SPELLS THAT CAN MAKE ANY WISH COME TRUE!
WELL, I DON'T NEED IT! I HAVE ALL THE RAW TALENT I NEED TO MAKE MY DREAMS COME TRUE!
HOWEVER, IT COULDN'T HURT TO HAVE A LITTLE HELP, I GUESS!
JAYSAN TAKES THE BOOK HOME, AND WHILE GLORIA IS AT WORK, HE PORES THOUGH ITS PRIMORDIAL, YELLOWED PAGES...
ACCORDING TO THIS, ALL I HAVE TO DO IS SCRIBBLE SOME STRANGE DOODLES ON THE FLOOR AND PERFORM SOME SORT OF >GULP< SACRIFICE!

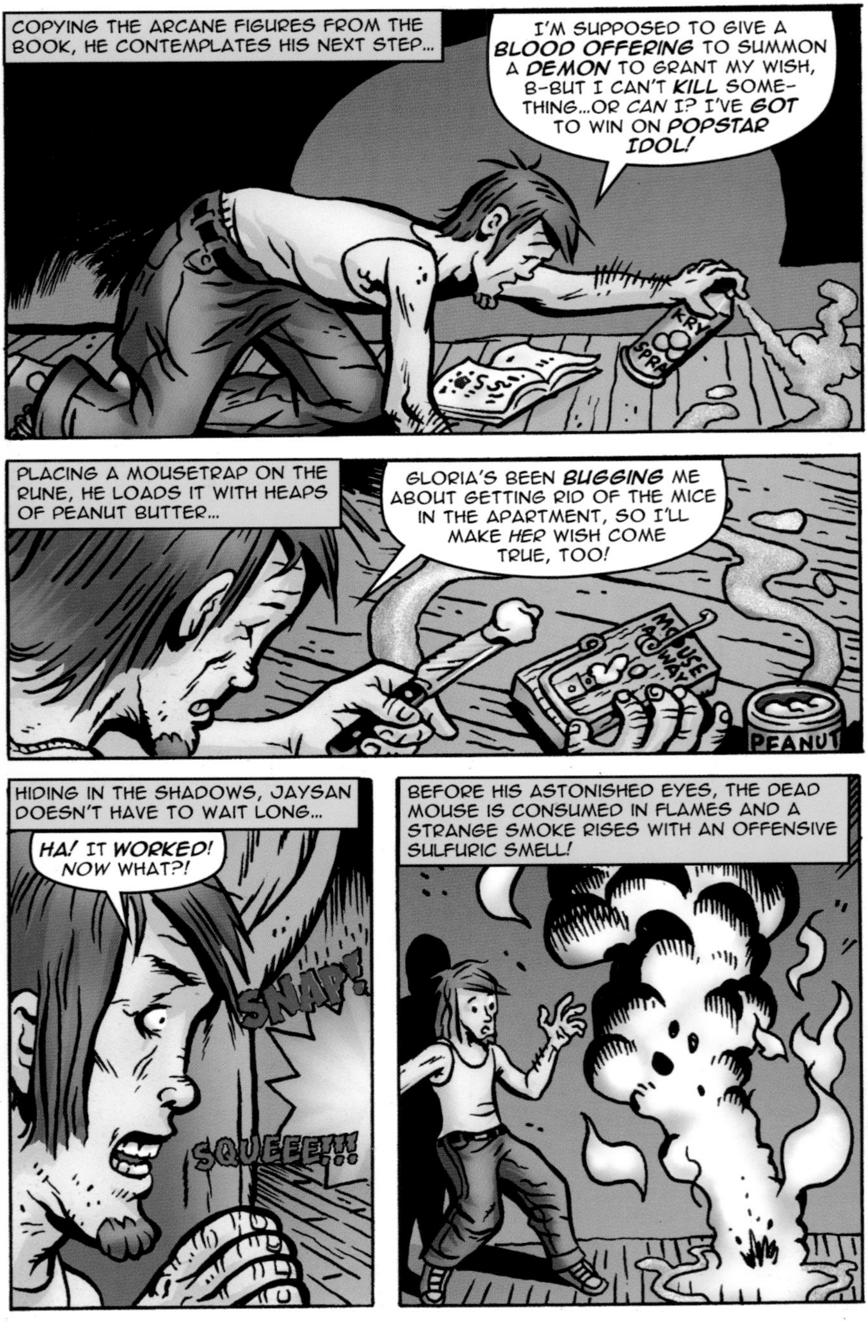
COPYING THE ARCANE FIGURES FROM THE BOOK, HE CONTEMPLATES HIS NEXT STEP...
I'M SUPPOSED TO GIVE A BLOOD OFFERING TO SUMMON A DEMON TO GRANT MY WISH, B-BUT I CAN'T KILL SOMETHING...OR CAN I? I'VE GOT TO WIN ON POPSTAR IDOL!
KRY SPRA
PLACING A MOUSETRAP ON THE RUNE, HE LOADS IT WITH HEAPS OF PEANUT BUTTER...
GLORIA'S BEEN BUGGING ME ABOUT GETTING RID OF THE MICE IN THE APARTMENT, SO I'LL MAKE HER WISH COME TRUE, TOO!
MOUSE AWAY
PEANUT
HIDING IN THE SHADOWS, JAYSAN DOESN'T HAVE TO WAIT LONG...
HA! IT WORKED! NOW WHAT?!
SNAP!
SQUEEEE!!!
BEFORE HIS ASTONISHED EYES, THE DEAD MOUSE IS CONSUMED IN FLAMES AND A STRANGE SMOKE RISES WITH AN OFFENSIVE SULFURIC SMELL!

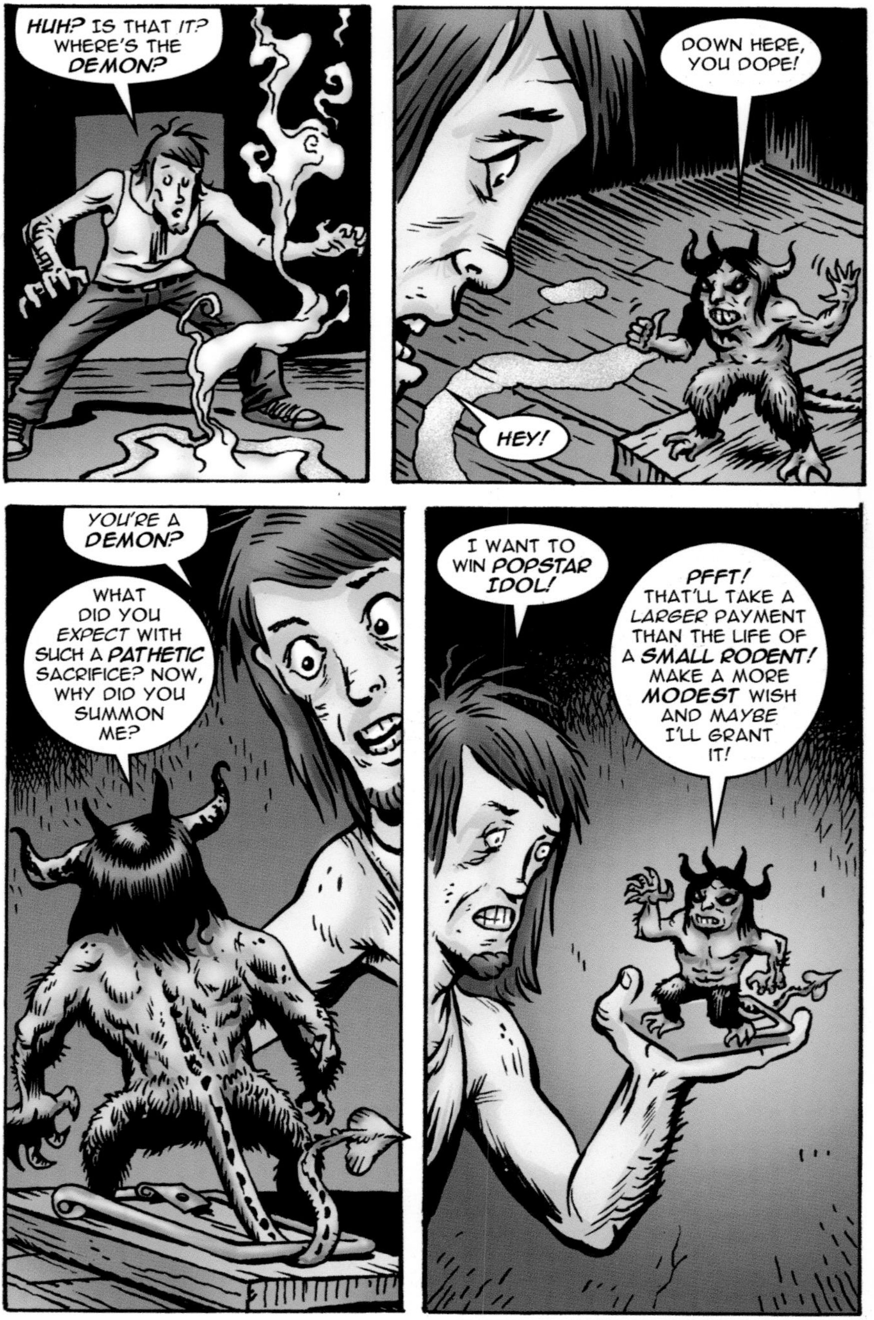
HUH? IS THAT IT? WHERE'S THE DEMON?
DOWN HERE, YOU DOPE!
HEY!
YOU'RE A DEMON?
WHAT DID YOU EXPECT WITH SUCH A PATHETIC SACRIFICE? NOW, WHY DID YOU SUMMON ME?
I WANT TO WIN POPSTAR IDOL!
PFFT! THAT'LL TAKE A LARGER PAYMENT THAN THE LIFE OF A SMALL RODENT! MAKE A MORE MODEST WISH AND MAYBE I'LL GRANT IT!

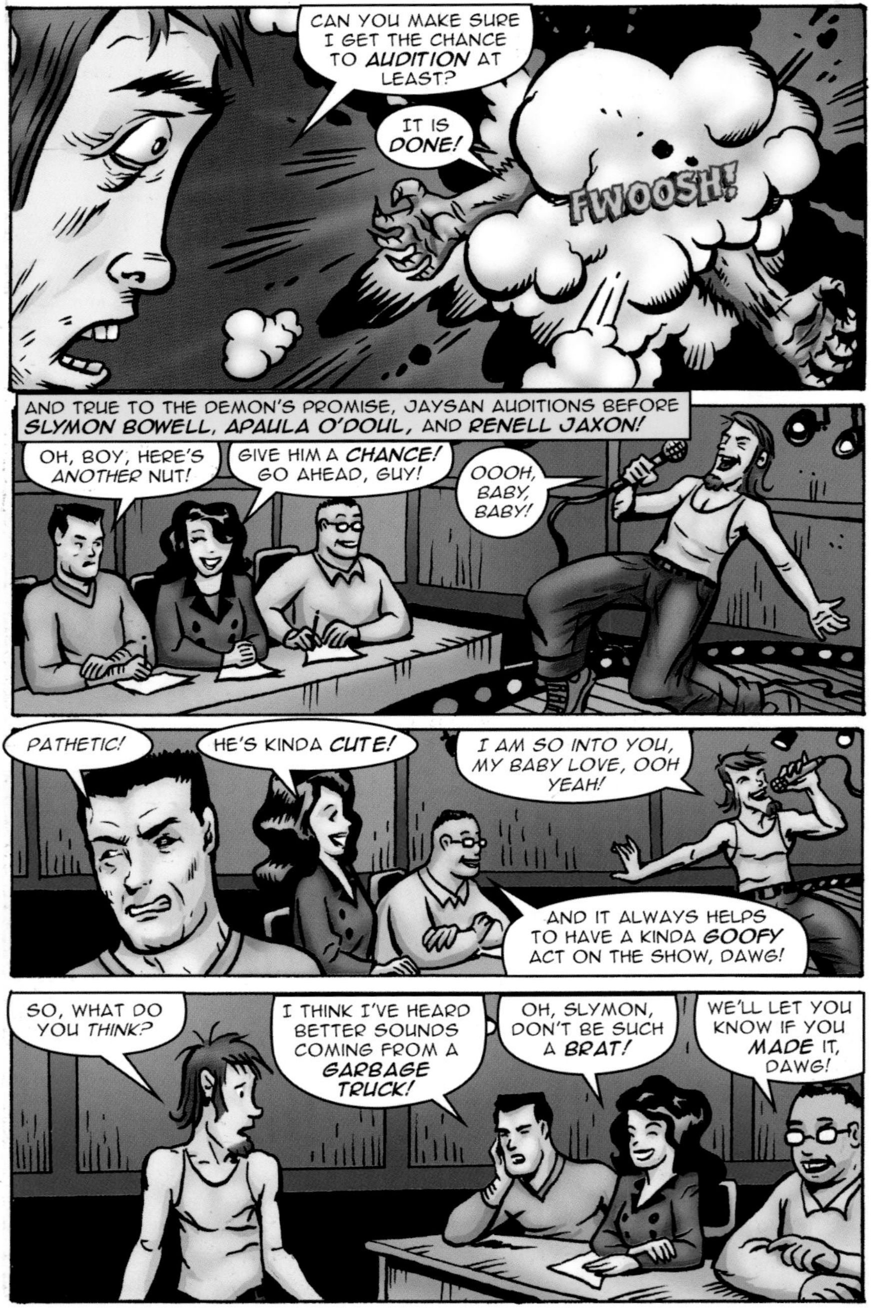
CAN YOU MAKE SURE I GET THE CHANCE TO *AUDITION* AT LEAST?
IT IS *DONE!*
FWOOSH!
AND TRUE TO THE DEMON'S PROMISE, JAYSAN AUDITIONS BEFORE *SLYMON BOWELL*, *APAULA O'DOUL*, AND *RENELL JAXON!*
OH, BOY, HERE'S ANOTHER NUT!
GIVE HIM A *CHANCE!* GO AHEAD, GUY!
OOOH, BABY, BABY!
PATHETIC!
HE'S KINDA *CUTE!*
I AM SO INTO YOU, MY BABY LOVE, OOH YEAH!
AND IT ALWAYS HELPS TO HAVE A KINDA *GOOFY* ACT ON THE SHOW, DAWG!
SO, WHAT DO YOU *THINK?*
I THINK I'VE HEARD BETTER SOUNDS COMING FROM A *GARBAGE TRUCK!*
OH, SLYMON, DON'T BE SUCH A *BRAT!*
WE'LL LET YOU KNOW IF YOU *MADE* IT, DAWG!

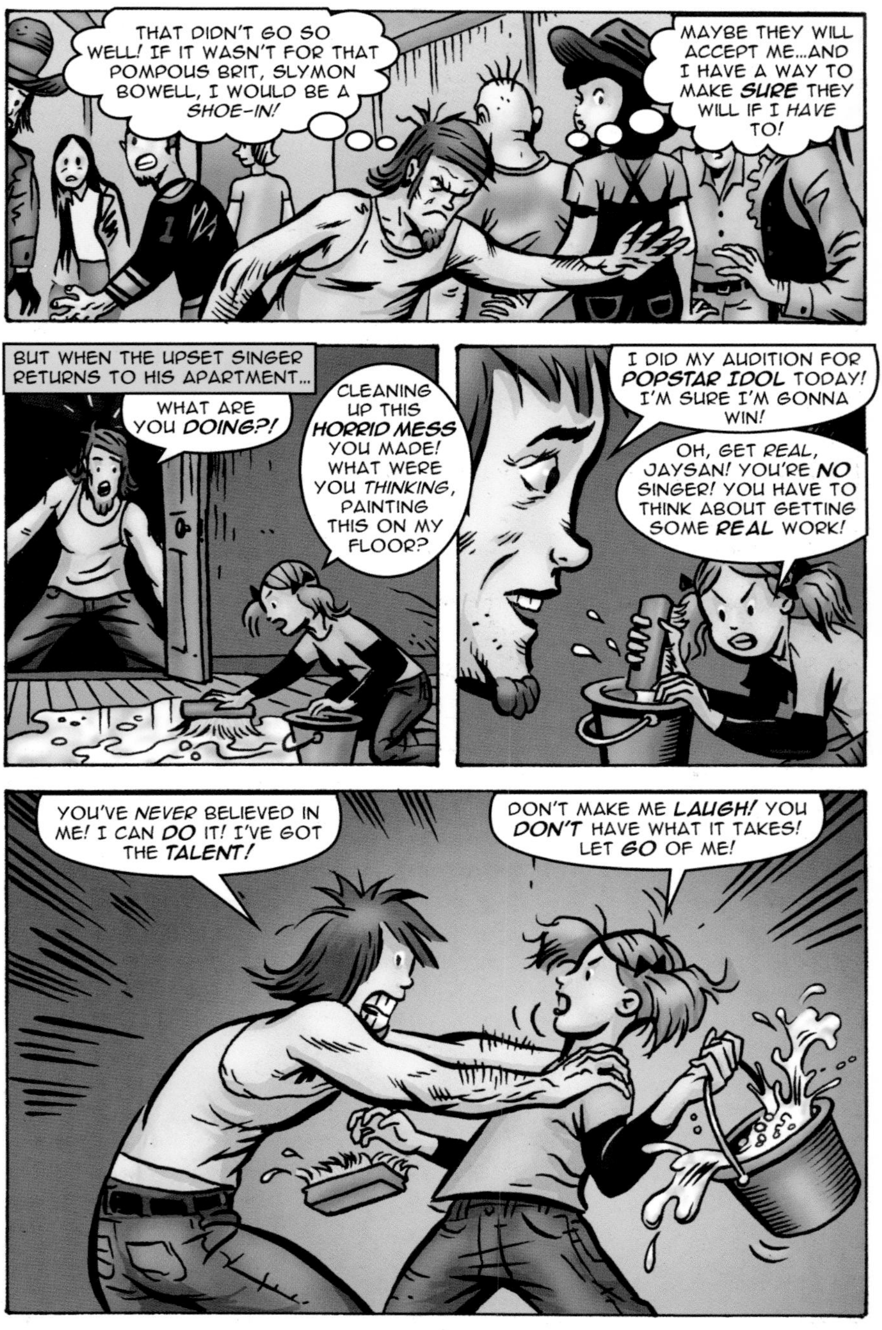
THAT DIDN'T GO SO WELL! IF IT WASN'T FOR THAT POMPOUS BRIT, SLYMON BOWELL, I WOULD BE A SHOE-IN!
MAYBE THEY WILL ACCEPT ME...AND I HAVE A WAY TO MAKE SURE THEY WILL IF I HAVE TO!
BUT WHEN THE UPSET SINGER RETURNS TO HIS APARTMENT...
WHAT ARE YOU DOING?!
CLEANING UP THIS HORRID MESS YOU MADE! WHAT WERE YOU THINKING, PAINTING THIS ON MY FLOOR?
I DID MY AUDITION FOR POPSTAR IDOL TODAY! I'M SURE I'M GONNA WIN!
OH, GET REAL, JAYSAN! YOU'RE NO SINGER! YOU HAVE TO THINK ABOUT GETTING SOME REAL WORK!
YOU'VE NEVER BELIEVED IN ME! I CAN DO IT! I'VE GOT THE TALENT!
DON'T MAKE ME LAUGH! YOU DON'T HAVE WHAT IT TAKES! LET GO OF ME!

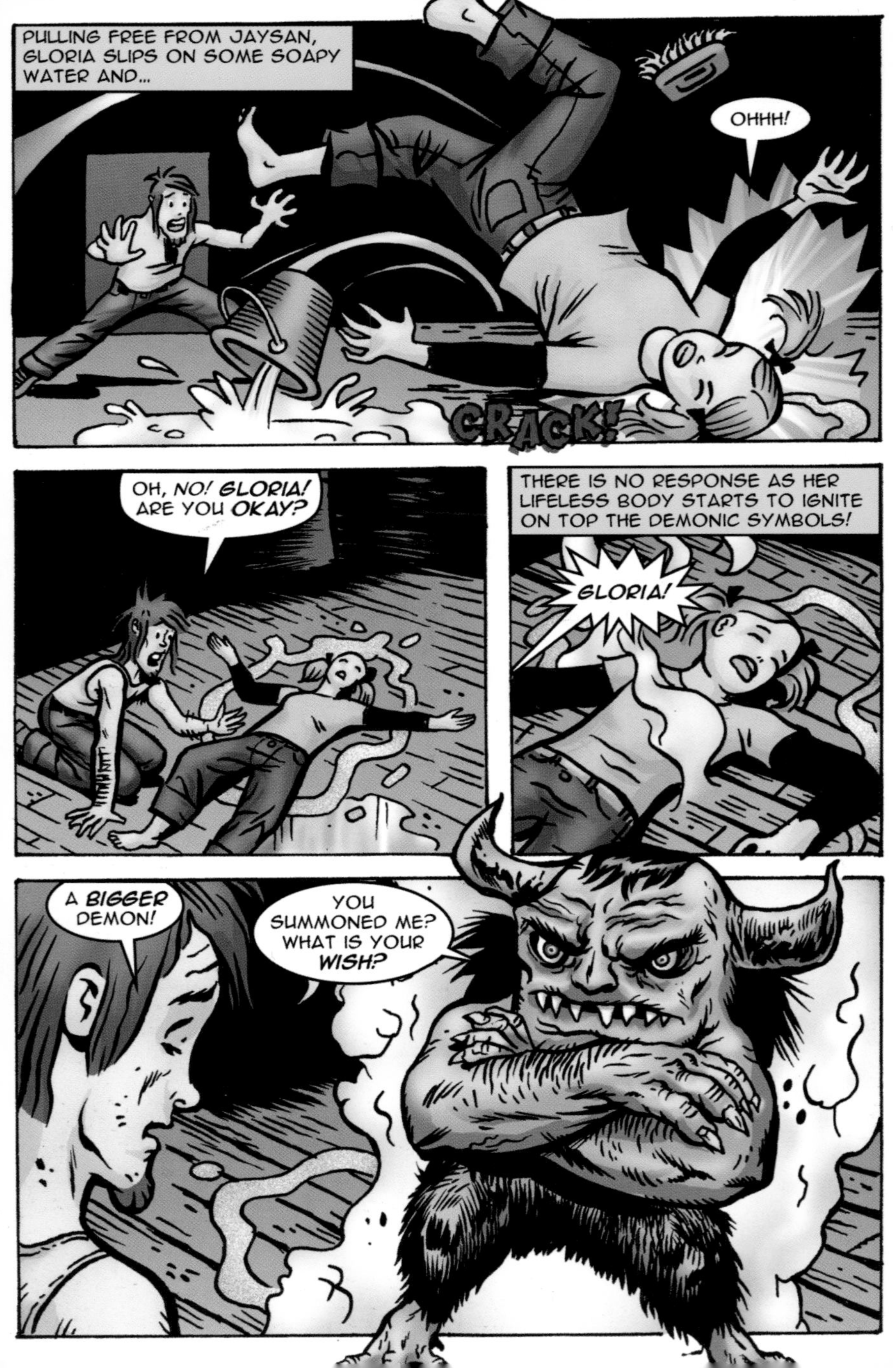
PULLING FREE FROM JAYSAN, GLORIA SLIPS ON SOME SOAPY WATER AND...
OHHH!
CRACK!
OH, NO! GLORIA! ARE YOU OKAY?
THERE IS NO RESPONSE AS HER LIFELESS BODY STARTS TO IGNITE ON TOP THE DEMONIC SYMBOLS!
GLORIA!
A BIGGER DEMON!
YOU SUMMONED ME? WHAT IS YOUR WISH?

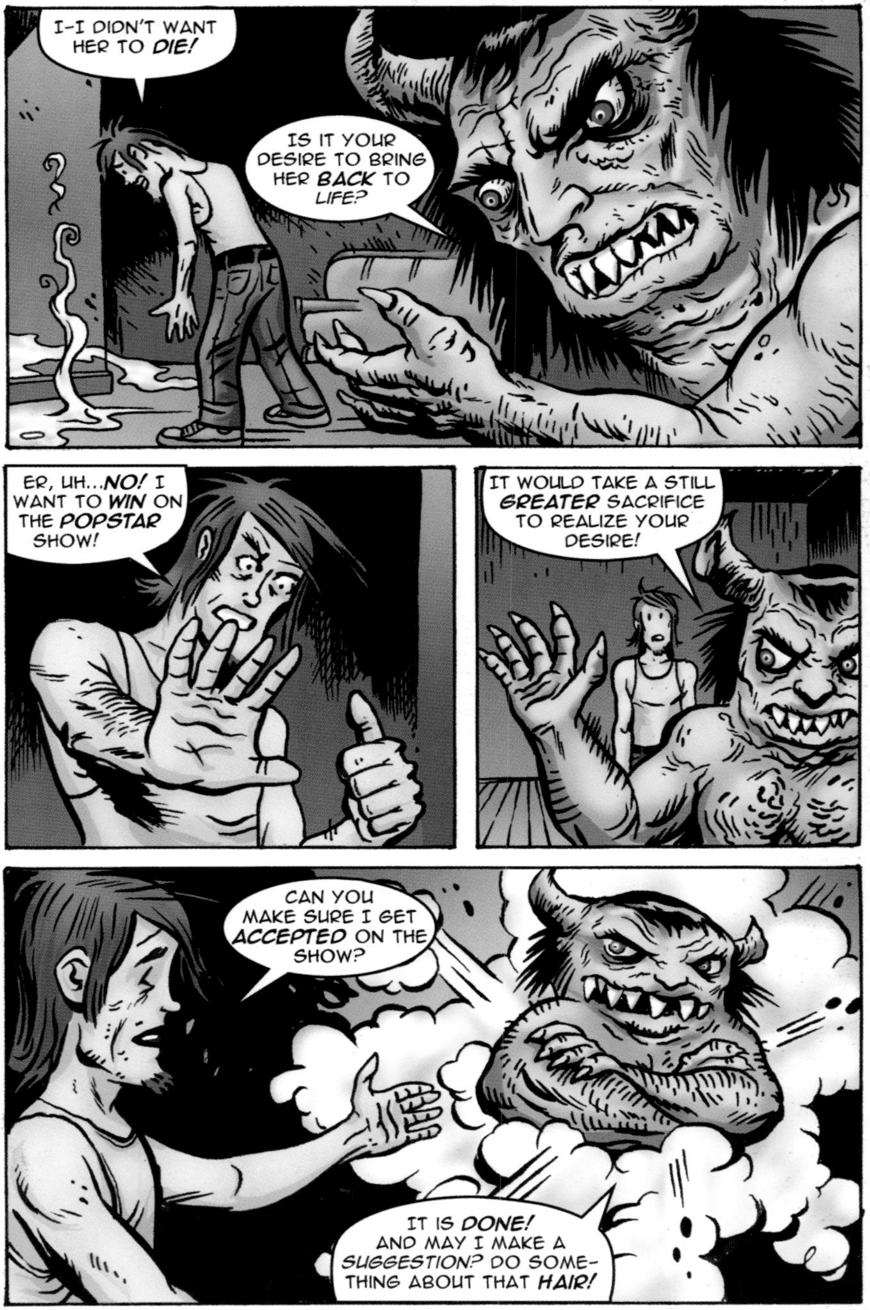
I-I DIDN'T WANT HER TO DIE!
IS IT YOUR DESIRE TO BRING HER BACK TO LIFE?
ER, UH...NO! I WANT TO WIN ON THE POPSTAR SHOW!
IT WOULD TAKE A STILL GREATER SACRIFICE TO REALIZE YOUR DESIRE!
CAN YOU MAKE SURE I GET ACCEPTED ON THE SHOW?
IT IS DONE! AND MAY I MAKE A SUGGESTION? DO SOME-THING ABOUT THAT HAIR!

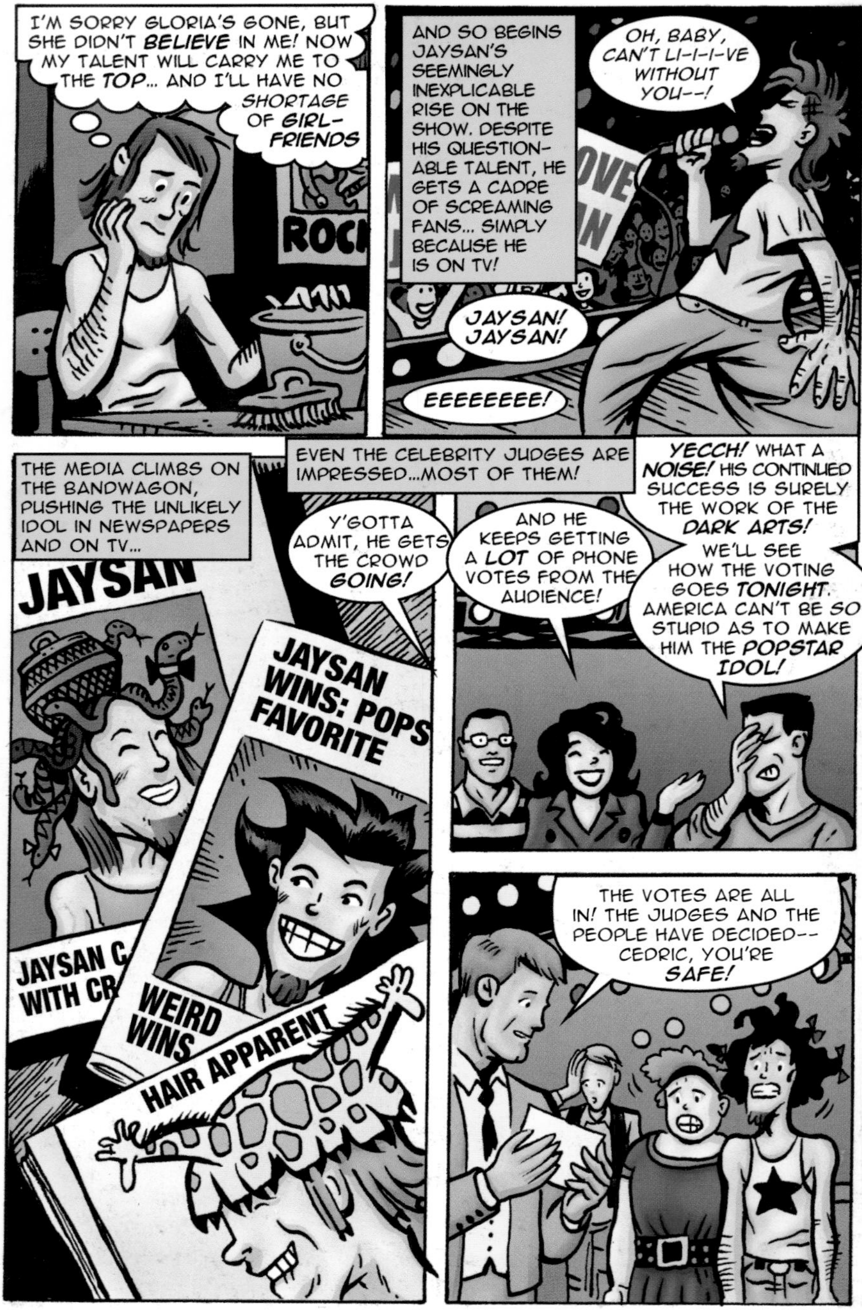

I'M SORRY GLORIA'S GONE, BUT SHE DIDN'T BELIEVE IN ME! NOW MY TALENT WILL CARRY ME TO THE TOP... AND I'LL HAVE NO SHORTAGE OF GIRL-FRIENDS
ROCK
AND SO BEGINS JAYSAN'S SEEMINGLY INEXPLICABLE RISE ON THE SHOW. DESPITE HIS QUESTION-ABLE TALENT, HE GETS A CADRE OF SCREAMING FANS... SIMPLY BECAUSE HE IS ON TV!
OH, BABY, CAN'T LI-I-I-VE WITHOUT YOU--!
JAYSAN! JAYSAN!
EEEEEEEE!
THE MEDIA CLIMBS ON THE BANDWAGON, PUSHING THE UNLIKELY IDOL IN NEWSPAPERS AND ON TV...
EVEN THE CELEBRITY JUDGES ARE IMPRESSED...MOST OF THEM!
JAYSAN
Y'GOTTA ADMIT, HE GETS THE CROWD GOING!
JAYSAN WINS: POPS FAVORITE
JAYSAN C
WITH CR
WEIRD WINS
HAIR APPARENT
AND HE KEEPS GETTING A LOT OF PHONE VOTES FROM THE AUDIENCE!
YECCH! WHAT A NOISE! HIS CONTINUED SUCCESS IS SURELY THE WORK OF THE DARK ARTS!
WE'LL SEE HOW THE VOTING GOES TONIGHT. AMERICA CAN'T BE SO STUPID AS TO MAKE HIM THE POPSTAR IDOL!
THE VOTES ARE ALL IN! THE JUDGES AND THE PEOPLE HAVE DECIDED-- CEDRIC, YOU'RE SAFE!

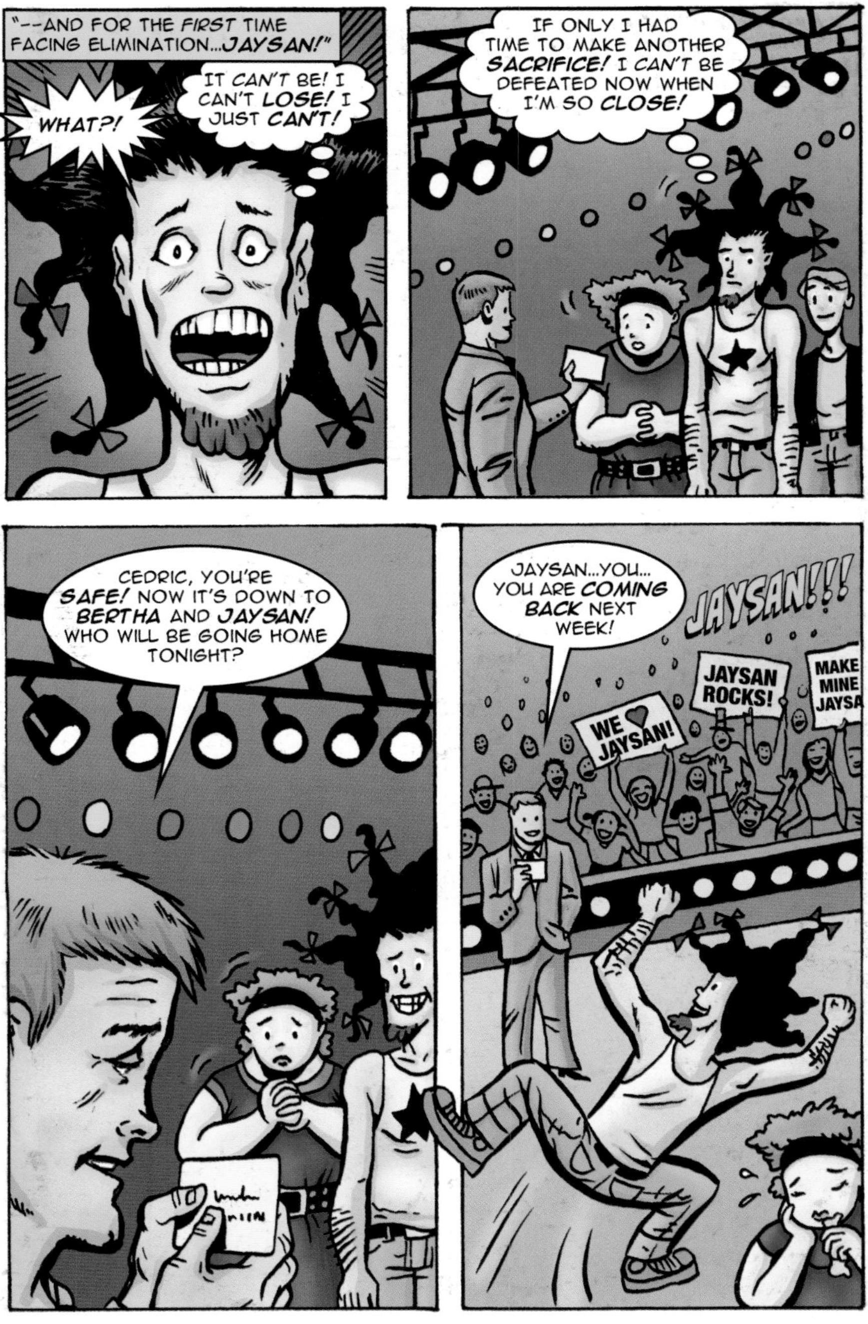
"--AND FOR THE FIRST TIME FACING ELIMINATION...JAYSAN!"
WHAT?!
IT CAN'T BE! I CAN'T LOSE! I JUST CAN'T!
IF ONLY I HAD TIME TO MAKE ANOTHER SACRIFICE! I CAN'T BE DEFEATED NOW WHEN I'M SO CLOSE!
CEDRIC, YOU'RE SAFE! NOW IT'S DOWN TO BERTHA AND JAYSAN! WHO WILL BE GOING HOME TONIGHT?
JAYSAN...YOU... YOU ARE COMING BACK NEXT WEEK!
JAYSAN!!!
JAYSAN ROCKS!
MAKE MINE JAYSA
WE ♥ JAYSAN!

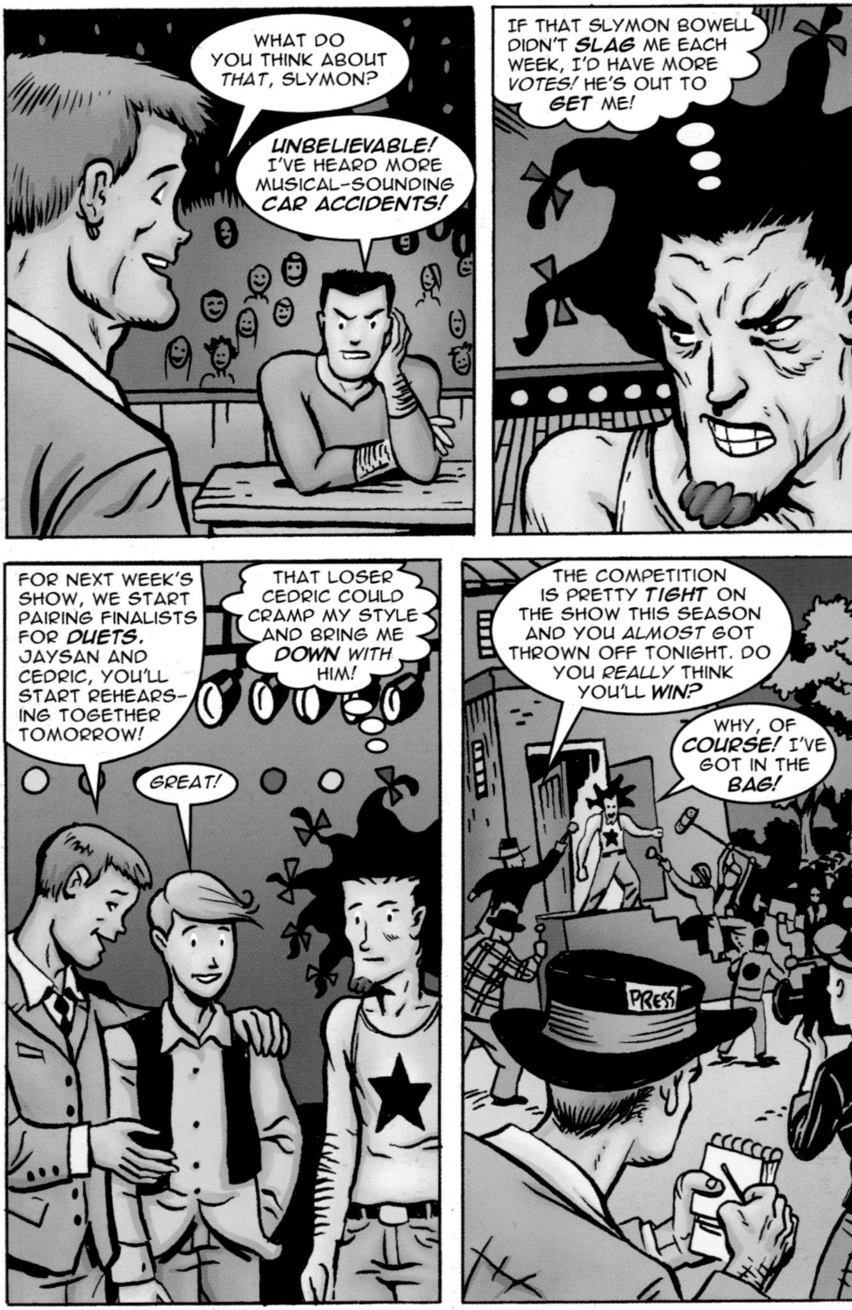
WHAT DO YOU THINK ABOUT THAT, SLYMON?
UNBELIEVABLE! I'VE HEARD MORE MUSICAL-SOUNDING CAR ACCIDENTS!
IF THAT SLYMON BOWELL DIDN'T SLAG ME EACH WEEK, I'D HAVE MORE VOTES! HE'S OUT TO GET ME!
FOR NEXT WEEK'S SHOW, WE START PAIRING FINALISTS FOR DUETS. JAYSAN AND CEDRIC, YOU'LL START REHEARSING TOGETHER TOMORROW!
THAT LOSER CEDRIC COULD CRAMP MY STYLE AND BRING ME DOWN WITH HIM!
GREAT!
THE COMPETITION IS PRETTY TIGHT ON THE SHOW THIS SEASON AND YOU ALMOST GOT THROWN OFF TONIGHT. DO YOU REALLY THINK YOU'LL WIN?
WHY, OF COURSE! I'VE GOT IN THE BAG!
PRESS

BUT JAYSAN DOES HAVE HIS DOUBTS...

I'LL HAVE TO MAKE *SURE!* I'LL MAKE ANOTHER OFFERING *SO* BIG I'LL *HAVE* TO WIN!

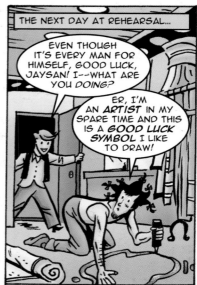

THE NEXT DAY AT REHEARSAL...

EVEN THOUGH IT'S EVERY MAN FOR HIMSELF, GOOD LUCK, JAYSAN! I--WHAT ARE YOU *DOING?*

ER, I'M AN *ARTIST* IN MY SPARE TIME AND THIS IS A *GOOD LUCK SYMBOL* I LIKE TO DRAW!

HEY, WHATEVER! IT'S KINDA *ODD*, BUT IF IT WORKS FOR YOU--

WHOMP!

ACCGK!

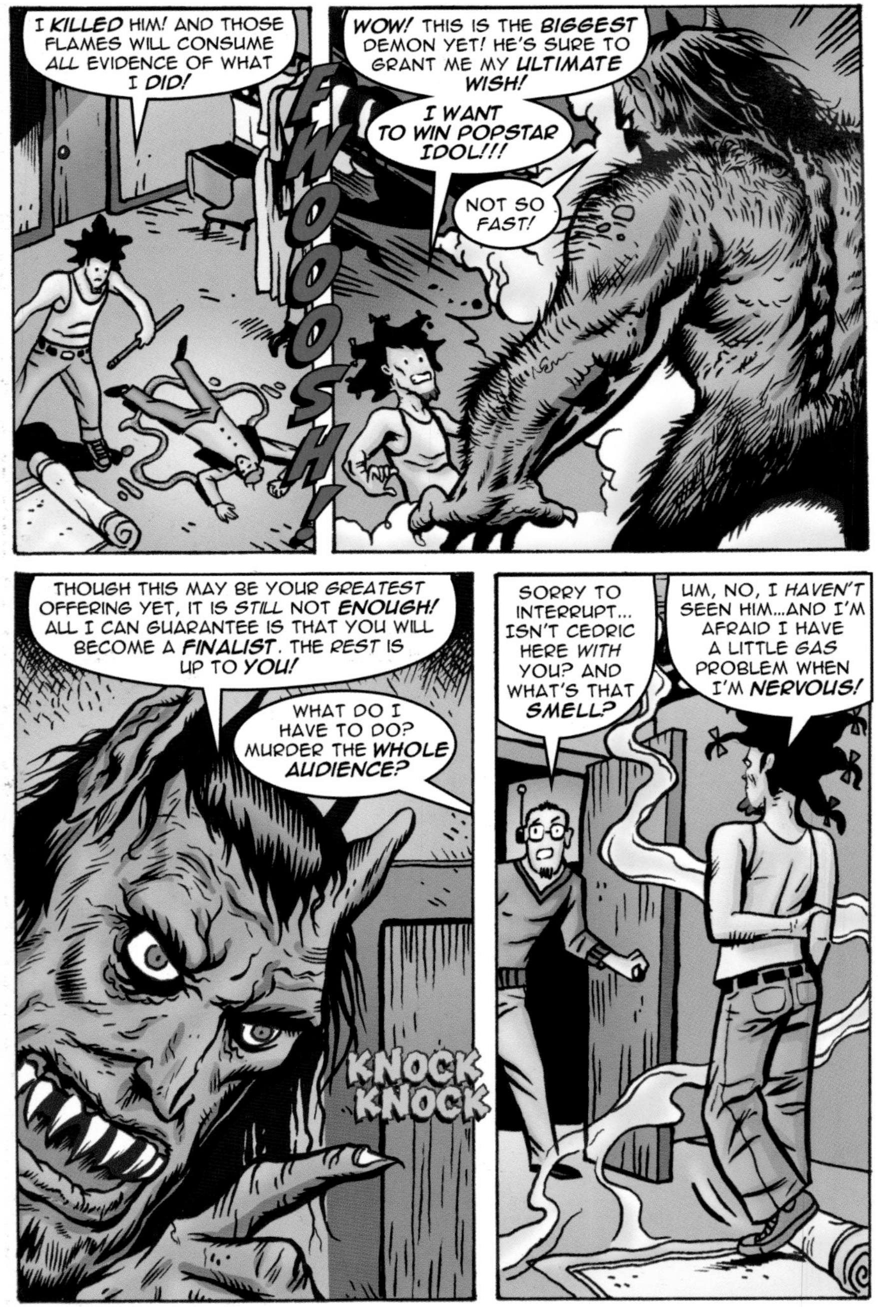
I KILLED HIM! AND THOSE FLAMES WILL CONSUME ALL EVIDENCE OF WHAT I DID!
FWOOOOSH!
WOW! THIS IS THE BIGGEST DEMON YET! HE'S SURE TO GRANT ME MY ULTIMATE WISH!
I WANT TO WIN POPSTAR IDOL!!!
NOT SO FAST!
THOUGH THIS MAY BE YOUR GREATEST OFFERING YET, IT IS STILL NOT ENOUGH! ALL I CAN GUARANTEE IS THAT YOU WILL BECOME A FINALIST. THE REST IS UP TO YOU!
WHAT DO I HAVE TO DO? MURDER THE WHOLE AUDIENCE?
KNOCK KNOCK
SORRY TO INTERRUPT... ISN'T CEDRIC HERE WITH YOU? AND WHAT'S THAT SMELL?
UM, NO, I HAVEN'T SEEN HIM...AND I'M AFRAID I HAVE A LITTLE GAS PROBLEM WHEN I'M NERVOUS!

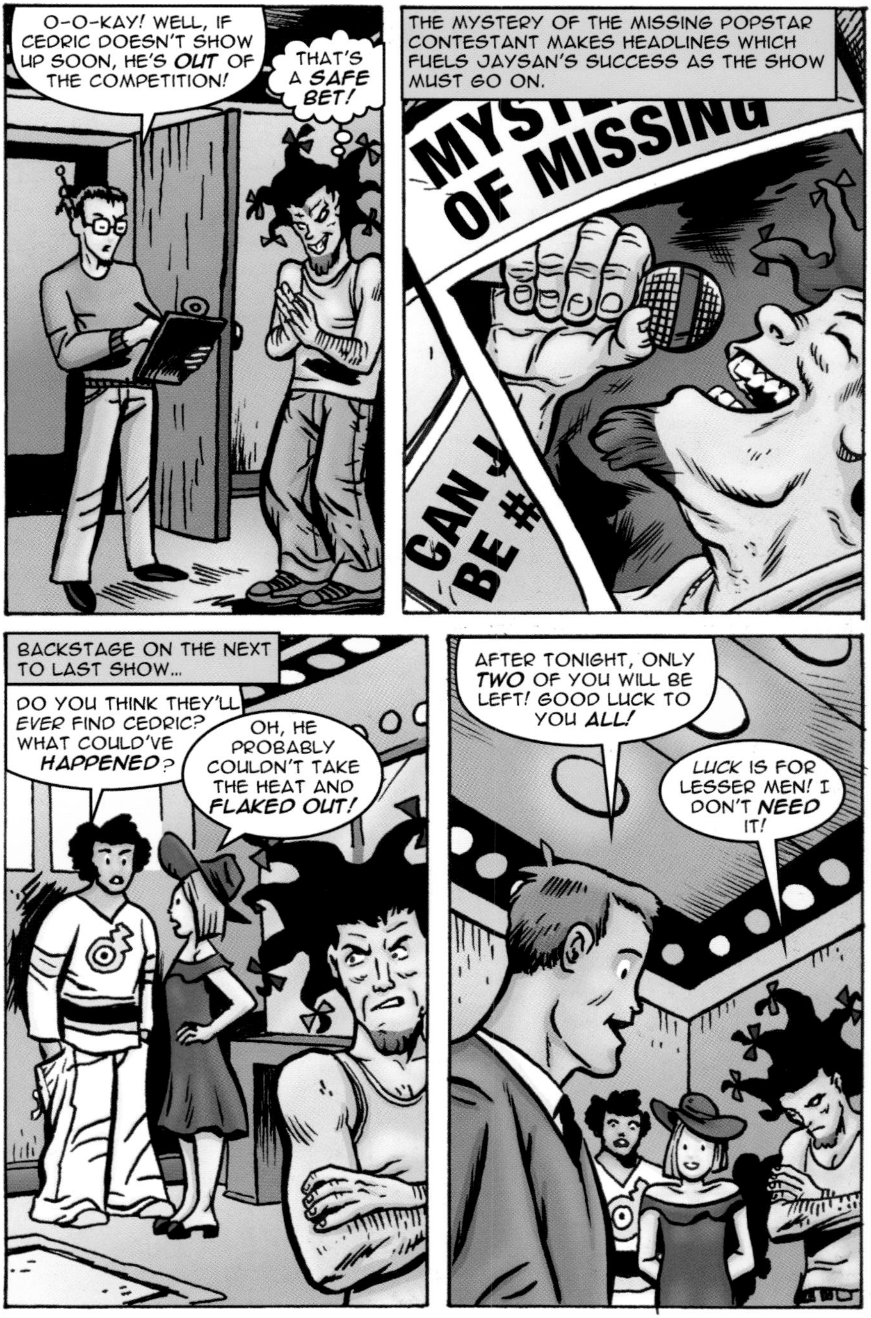
O-O-KAY! WELL, IF CEDRIC DOESN'T SHOW UP SOON, HE'S OUT OF THE COMPETITION!
THAT'S A SAFE BET!
THE MYSTERY OF THE MISSING POPSTAR CONTESTANT MAKES HEADLINES WHICH FUELS JAYSAN'S SUCCESS AS THE SHOW MUST GO ON.
MYST
OF MISSING
CAN J
BE #
BACKSTAGE ON THE NEXT TO LAST SHOW...
DO YOU THINK THEY'LL EVER FIND CEDRIC? WHAT COULD'VE HAPPENED?
OH, HE PROBABLY COULDN'T TAKE THE HEAT AND FLAKED OUT!
AFTER TONIGHT, ONLY TWO OF YOU WILL BE LEFT! GOOD LUCK TO YOU ALL!
LUCK IS FOR LESSER MEN! I DON'T NEED IT!

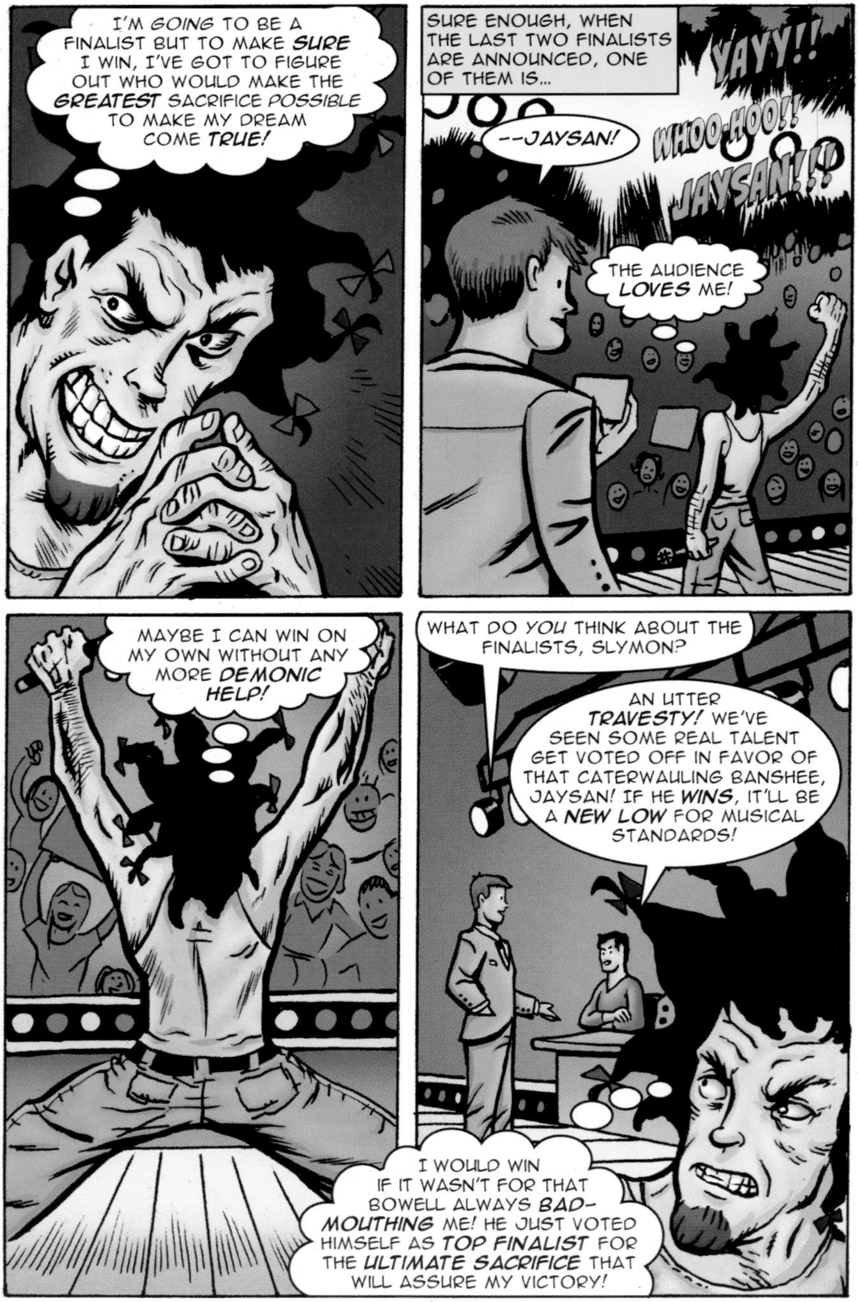
I'M GOING TO BE A FINALIST BUT TO MAKE SURE I WIN, I'VE GOT TO FIGURE OUT WHO WOULD MAKE THE GREATEST SACRIFICE POSSIBLE TO MAKE MY DREAM COME TRUE!
SURE ENOUGH, WHEN THE LAST TWO FINALISTS ARE ANNOUNCED, ONE OF THEM IS...
YAYY!!
WHOO-HOO!!
JAYSAN!!!
--JAYSAN!
THE AUDIENCE LOVES ME!
MAYBE I CAN WIN ON MY OWN WITHOUT ANY MORE DEMONIC HELP!
WHAT DO YOU THINK ABOUT THE FINALISTS, SLYMON?
AN UTTER TRAVESTY! WE'VE SEEN SOME REAL TALENT GET VOTED OFF IN FAVOR OF THAT CATERWAULING BANSHEE, JAYSAN! IF HE WINS, IT'LL BE A NEW LOW FOR MUSICAL STANDARDS!
I WOULD WIN IF IT WASN'T FOR THAT BOWELL ALWAYS BAD-MOUTHING ME! HE JUST VOTED HIMSELF AS TOP FINALIST FOR THE ULTIMATE SACRIFICE THAT WILL ASSURE MY VICTORY!

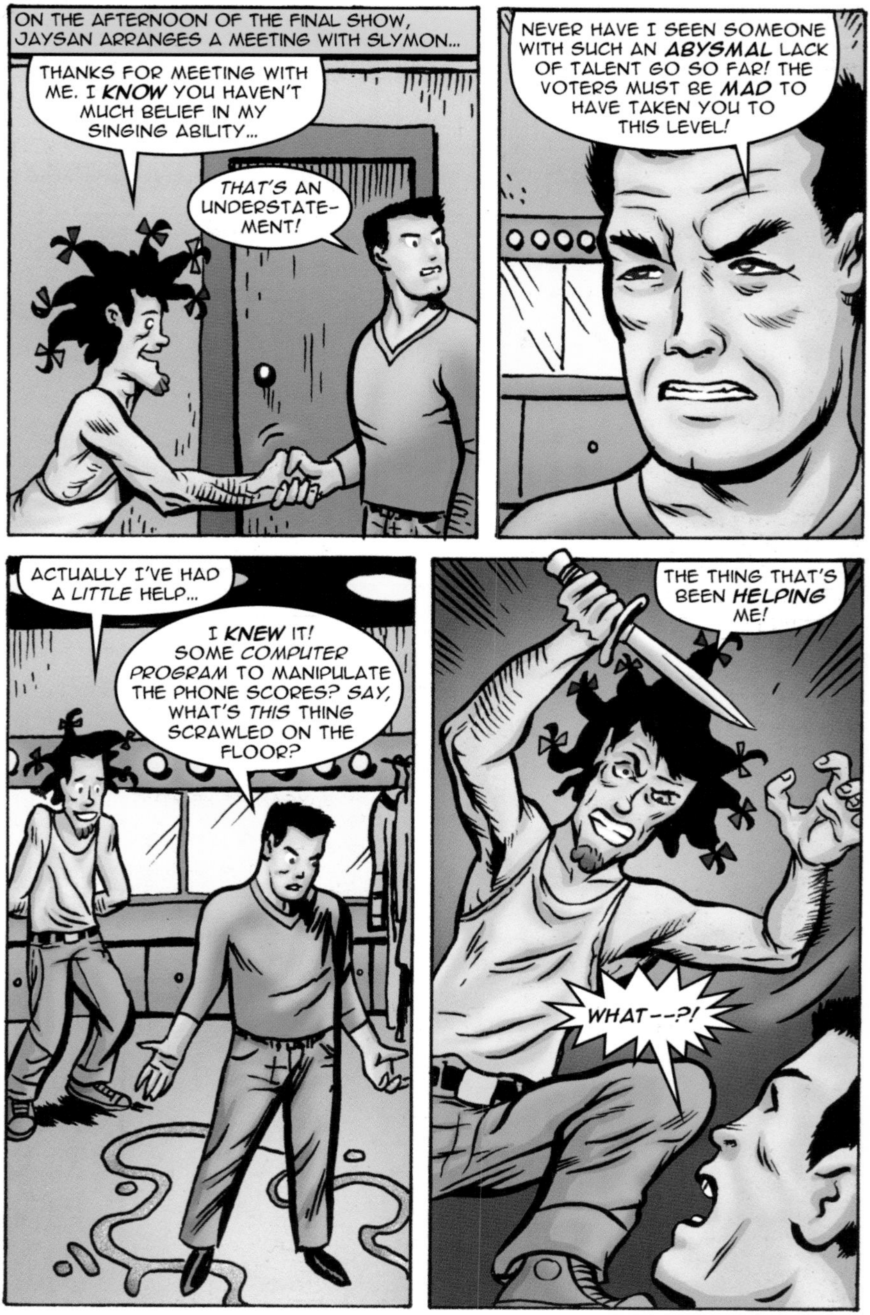
ON THE AFTERNOON OF THE FINAL SHOW, JAYSAN ARRANGES A MEETING WITH SLYMON...
THANKS FOR MEETING WITH ME. I KNOW YOU HAVEN'T MUCH BELIEF IN MY SINGING ABILITY...
THAT'S AN UNDERSTATEMENT!
NEVER HAVE I SEEN SOMEONE WITH SUCH AN ABYSMAL LACK OF TALENT GO SO FAR! THE VOTERS MUST BE MAD TO HAVE TAKEN YOU TO THIS LEVEL!
ACTUALLY I'VE HAD A LITTLE HELP...
I KNEW IT! SOME COMPUTER PROGRAM TO MANIPULATE THE PHONE SCORES? SAY, WHAT'S THIS THING SCRAWLED ON THE FLOOR?
THE THING THAT'S BEEN HELPING ME!
WHAT--?!

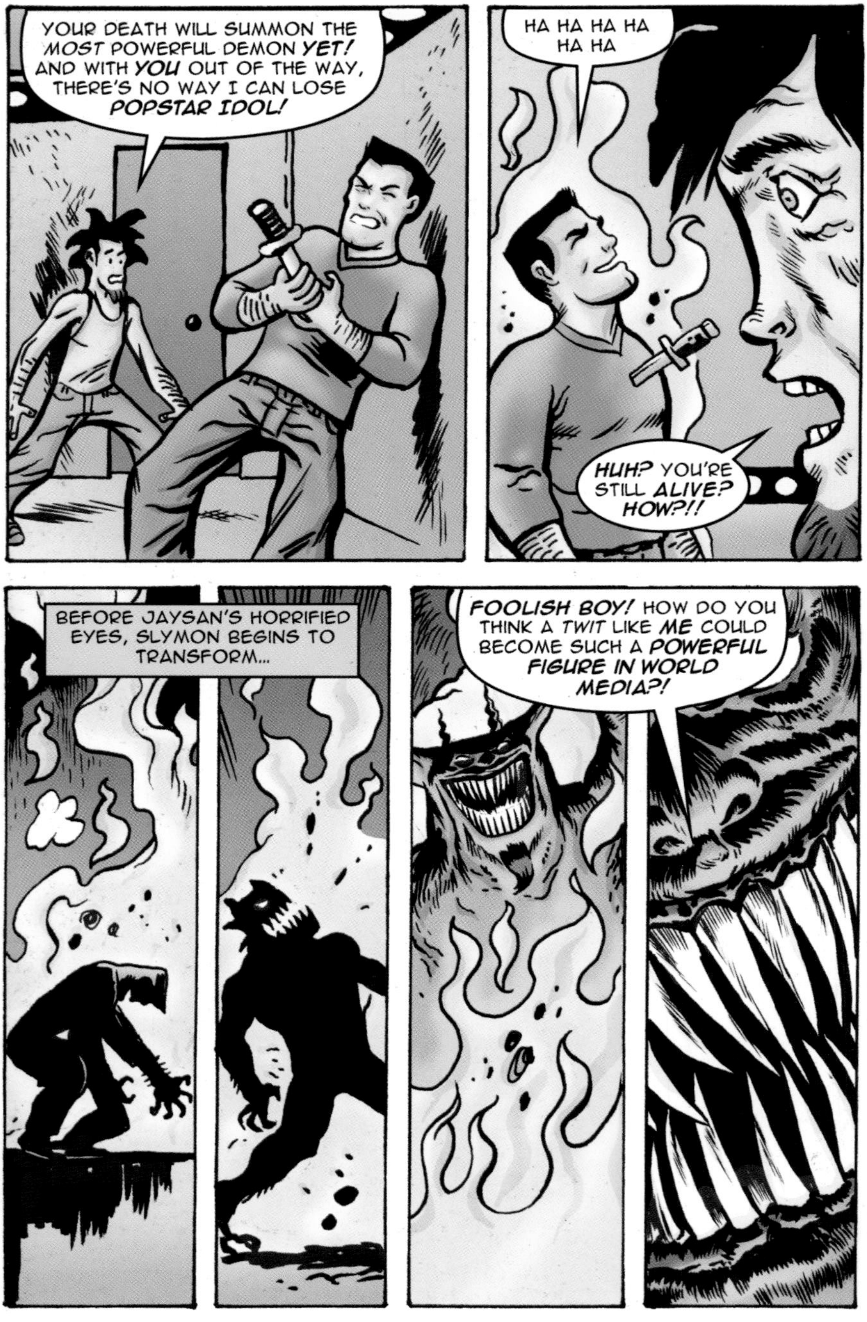

YOUR DEATH WILL SUMMON THE MOST POWERFUL DEMON YET! AND WITH YOU OUT OF THE WAY, THERE'S NO WAY I CAN LOSE POPSTAR IDOL!
HA HA HA HA HA HA
HUH? YOU'RE STILL ALIVE? HOW?!!
BEFORE JAYSAN'S HORRIFIED EYES, SLYMON BEGINS TO TRANSFORM...
FOOLISH BOY! HOW DO YOU THINK A TWIT LIKE ME COULD BECOME SUCH A POWERFUL FIGURE IN WORLD MEDIA?!

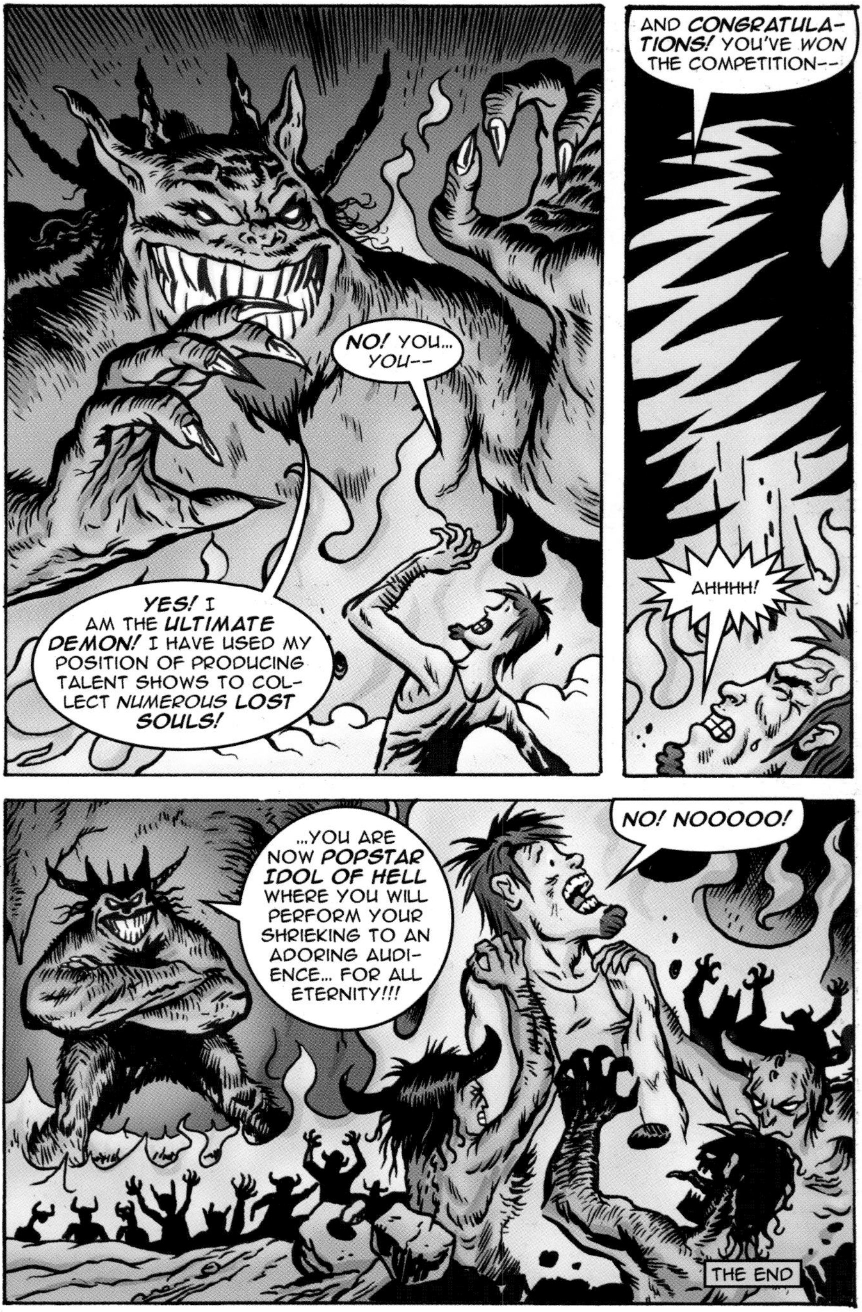
NO! YOU... YOU--
YES! I AM THE ULTIMATE DEMON! I HAVE USED MY POSITION OF PRODUCING TALENT SHOWS TO COLLECT NUMEROUS LOST SOULS!
AND CONGRATULATIONS! YOU'VE WON THE COMPETITION--
AHHHH!
...YOU ARE NOW POPSTAR IDOL OF HELL WHERE YOU WILL PERFORM YOUR SHRIEKING TO AN ADORING AUDIENCE... FOR ALL ETERNITY!!!
NO! NOOOOO!
THE END

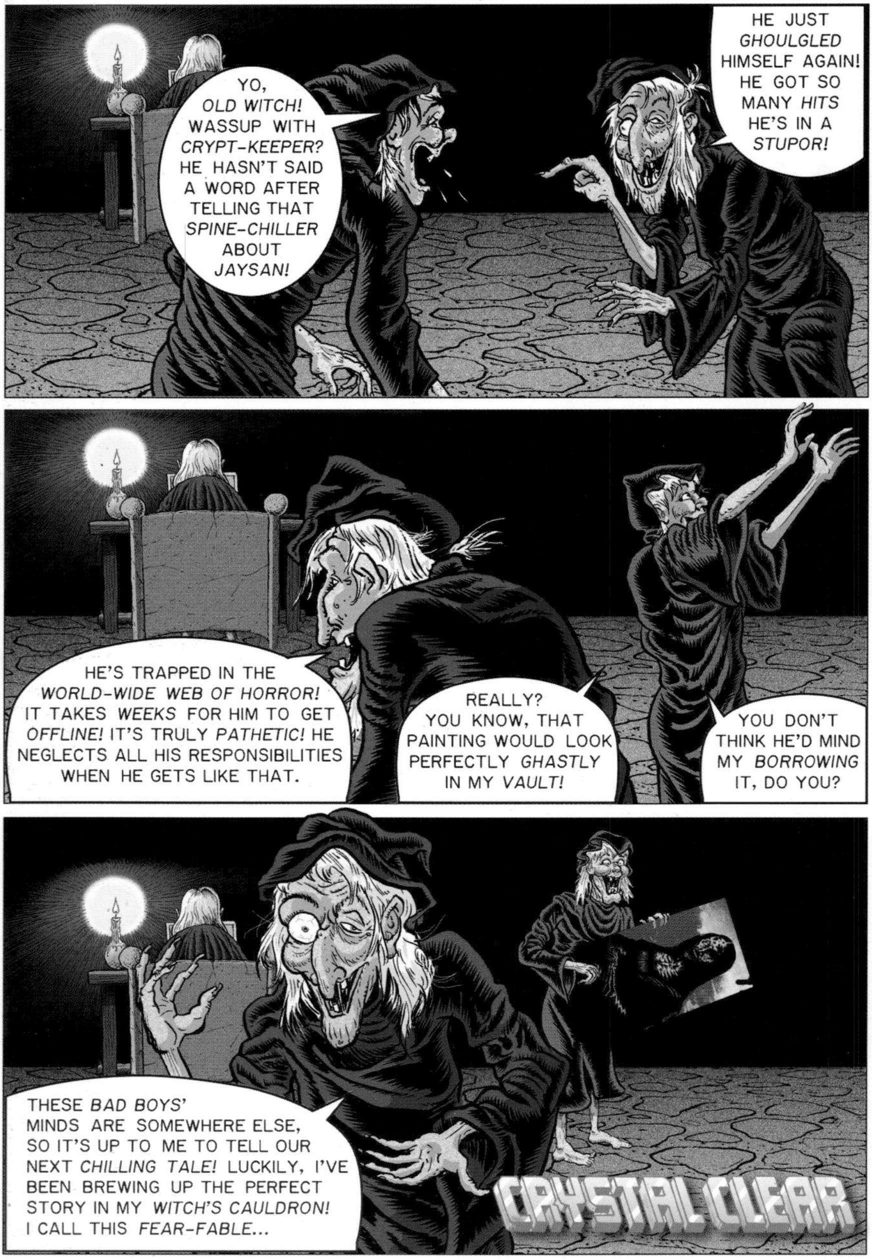
YO, OLD WITCH! WASSUP WITH CRYPT-KEEPER? HE HASN'T SAID A WORD AFTER TELLING THAT SPINE-CHILLER ABOUT JAYSAN!
HE JUST GHOULGLED HIMSELF AGAIN! HE GOT SO MANY HITS HE'S IN A STUPOR!
HE'S TRAPPED IN THE WORLD-WIDE WEB OF HORROR! IT TAKES WEEKS FOR HIM TO GET OFFLINE! IT'S TRULY PATHETIC! HE NEGLECTS ALL HIS RESPONSIBILITIES WHEN HE GETS LIKE THAT.
REALLY? YOU KNOW, THAT PAINTING WOULD LOOK PERFECTLY GHASTLY IN MY VAULT!
YOU DON'T THINK HE'D MIND MY BORROWING IT, DO YOU?
THESE BAD BOYS' MINDS ARE SOMEWHERE ELSE, SO IT'S UP TO ME TO TELL OUR NEXT CHILLING TALE! LUCKILY, I'VE BEEN BREWING UP THE PERFECT STORY IN MY WITCH'S CAULDRON! I CALL THIS FEAR-FABLE...
CRYSTAL CLEAR

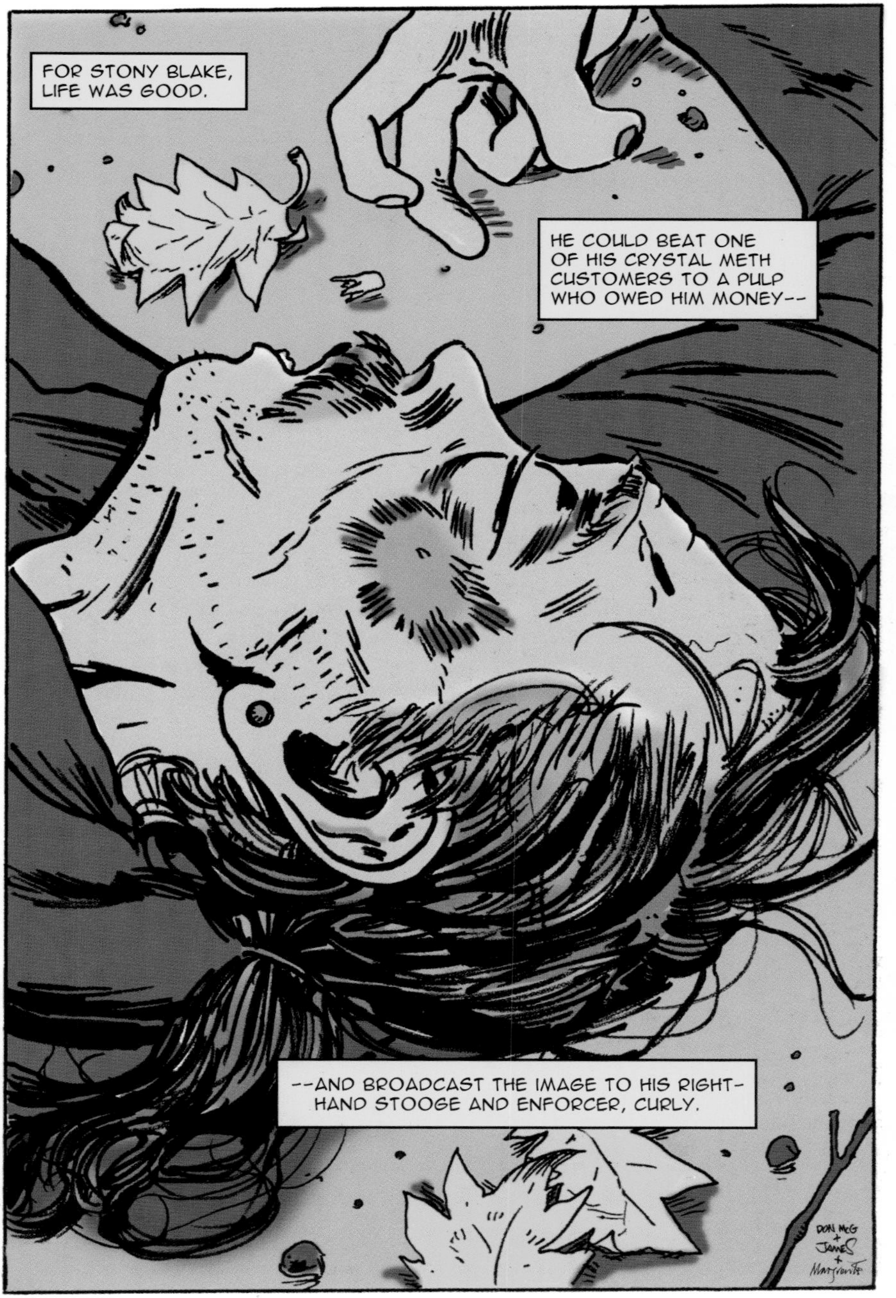
FOR STONY BLAKE, LIFE WAS GOOD.
HE COULD BEAT ONE OF HIS CRYSTAL METH CUSTOMERS TO A PULP WHO OWED HIM MONEY--
--AND BROADCAST THE IMAGE TO HIS RIGHT-HAND STOOGE AND ENFORCER, CURLY.
DON McG + JAMES + Margreiter

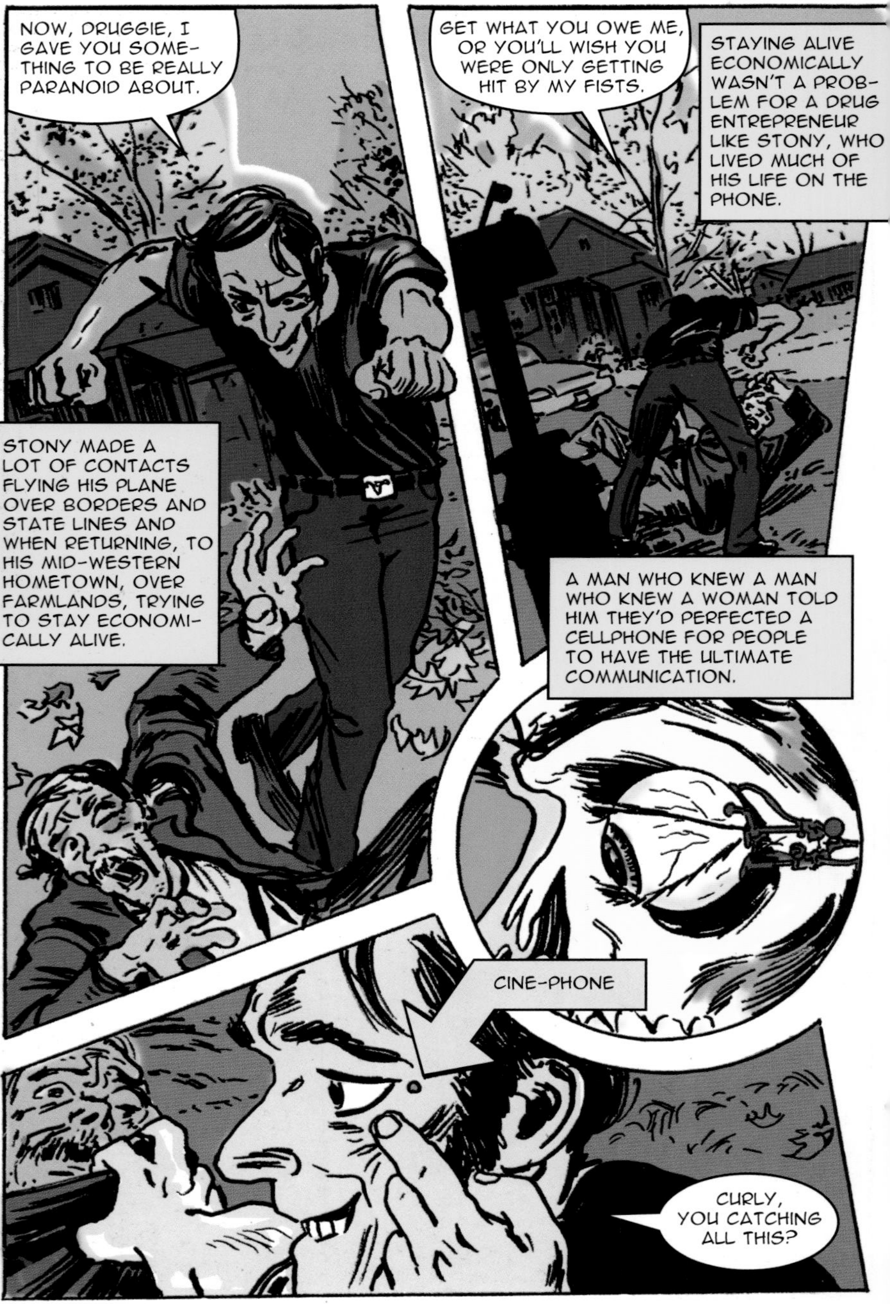
NOW, DRUGGIE, I GAVE YOU SOME-THING TO BE REALLY PARANOID ABOUT.
STONY MADE A LOT OF CONTACTS FLYING HIS PLANE OVER BORDERS AND STATE LINES AND WHEN RETURNING, TO HIS MID-WESTERN HOMETOWN, OVER FARMLANDS, TRYING TO STAY ECONOMI-CALLY ALIVE.
GET WHAT YOU OWE ME, OR YOU'LL WISH YOU WERE ONLY GETTING HIT BY MY FISTS.
STAYING ALIVE ECONOMICALLY WASN'T A PROB-LEM FOR A DRUG ENTREPRENEUR LIKE STONY, WHO LIVED MUCH OF HIS LIFE ON THE PHONE.
A MAN WHO KNEW A MAN WHO KNEW A WOMAN TOLD HIM THEY'D PERFECTED A CELLPHONE FOR PEOPLE TO HAVE THE ULTIMATE COMMUNICATION.
CINE-PHONE
CURLY, YOU CATCHING ALL THIS?

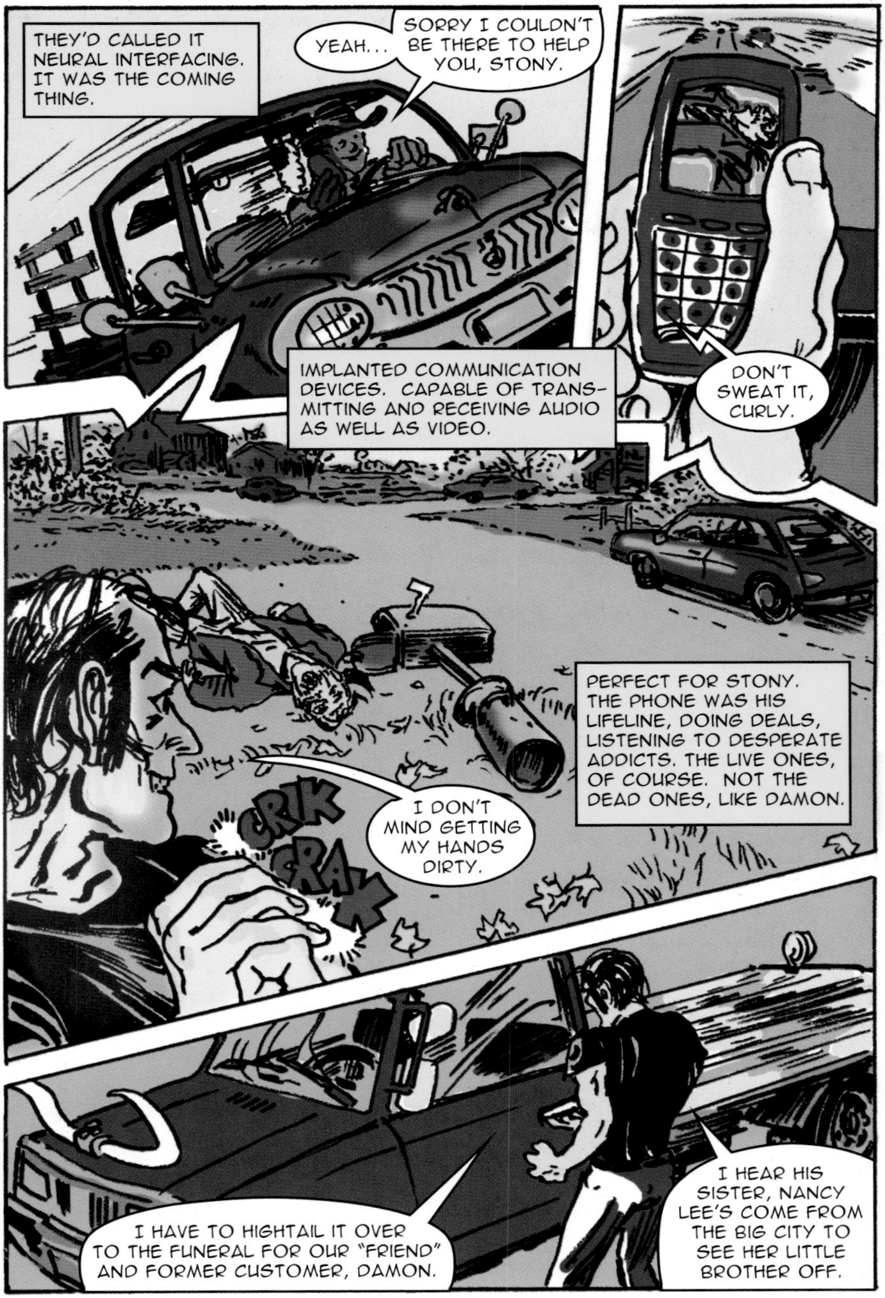
THEY'D CALLED IT NEURAL INTERFACING. IT WAS THE COMING THING.
YEAH...
SORRY I COULDN'T BE THERE TO HELP YOU, STONY.
DON'T SWEAT IT, CURLY.
IMPLANTED COMMUNICATION DEVICES. CAPABLE OF TRANS-MITTING AND RECEIVING AUDIO AS WELL AS VIDEO.
PERFECT FOR STONY. THE PHONE WAS HIS LIFELINE, DOING DEALS, LISTENING TO DESPERATE ADDICTS. THE LIVE ONES, OF COURSE. NOT THE DEAD ONES, LIKE DAMON.
I DON'T MIND GETTING MY HANDS DIRTY.
CRIK
CRAK
I HAVE TO HIGHTAIL IT OVER TO THE FUNERAL FOR OUR "FRIEND" AND FORMER CUSTOMER, DAMON.
I HEAR HIS SISTER, NANCY LEE'S COME FROM THE BIG CITY TO SEE HER LITTLE BROTHER OFF.

STONY LOVED IT. HE DIDN'T HAVE TO FREEZE HIS FINGERS OFF IN THE COLD, HOLDING A CELL-PHONE TO HIS NUMB EAR.

KEEP TUNED, CURLY.

A PHONE CALL DIDN'T STOP HIM FROM USING HIS HANDS FOR WHATEVER ELSE HE MIGHT BE DOING AT A GIVEN MOMENT.

I SEE NANCY LEE NOW. STILL LOOKING PRETTY GOOD.

WAY I REMEMBER HER--

--FROM WHEN SHE WAS GROWING INTO A WOMAN. I'LL TEACH YOU SOMETHING HERE.

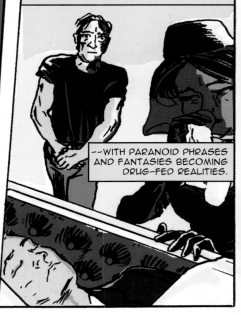

STONY HAD THE STRAY THOUGHT THAT DAMON HAD HEARD VOICES IN HIS HEAD AT THE END, MAYBE SOME OF THE VOICES CRYSTAL METH-FED--

--WITH PARANOID PHRASES AND FANTASIES BECOMING DRUG-FED REALITIES.

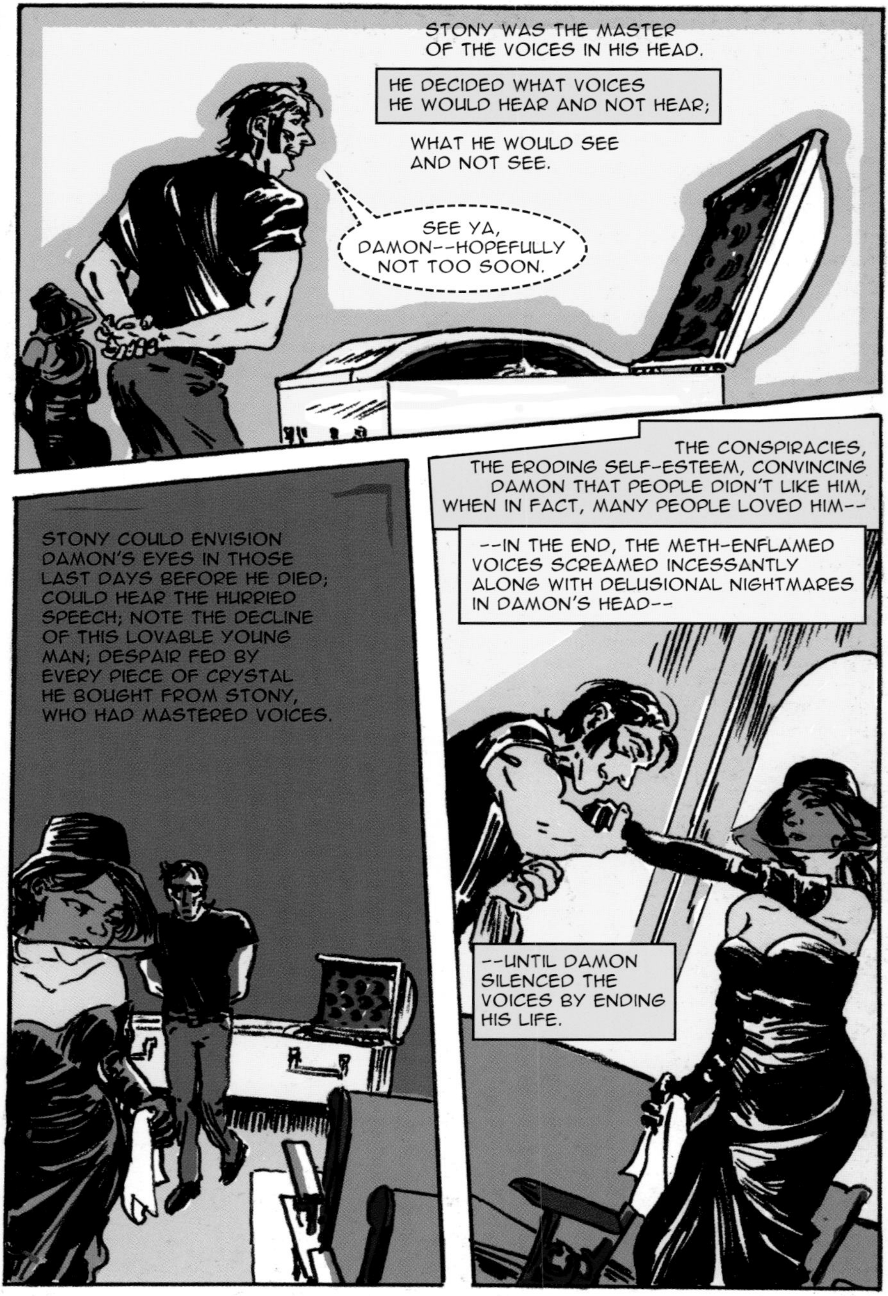
STONY WAS THE MASTER OF THE VOICES IN HIS HEAD.
HE DECIDED WHAT VOICES HE WOULD HEAR AND NOT HEAR;
WHAT HE WOULD SEE AND NOT SEE.
SEE YA, DAMON--HOPEFULLY NOT TOO SOON.
STONY COULD ENVISION DAMON'S EYES IN THOSE LAST DAYS BEFORE HE DIED; COULD HEAR THE HURRIED SPEECH; NOTE THE DECLINE OF THIS LOVABLE YOUNG MAN; DESPAIR FED BY EVERY PIECE OF CRYSTAL HE BOUGHT FROM STONY, WHO HAD MASTERED VOICES.
THE CONSPIRACIES, THE ERODING SELF-ESTEEM, CONVINCING DAMON THAT PEOPLE DIDN'T LIKE HIM, WHEN IN FACT, MANY PEOPLE LOVED HIM--
--IN THE END, THE METH-ENFLAMED VOICES SCREAMED INCESSANTLY ALONG WITH DELUSIONAL NIGHTMARES IN DAMON'S HEAD--
--UNTIL DAMON SILENCED THE VOICES BY ENDING HIS LIFE.

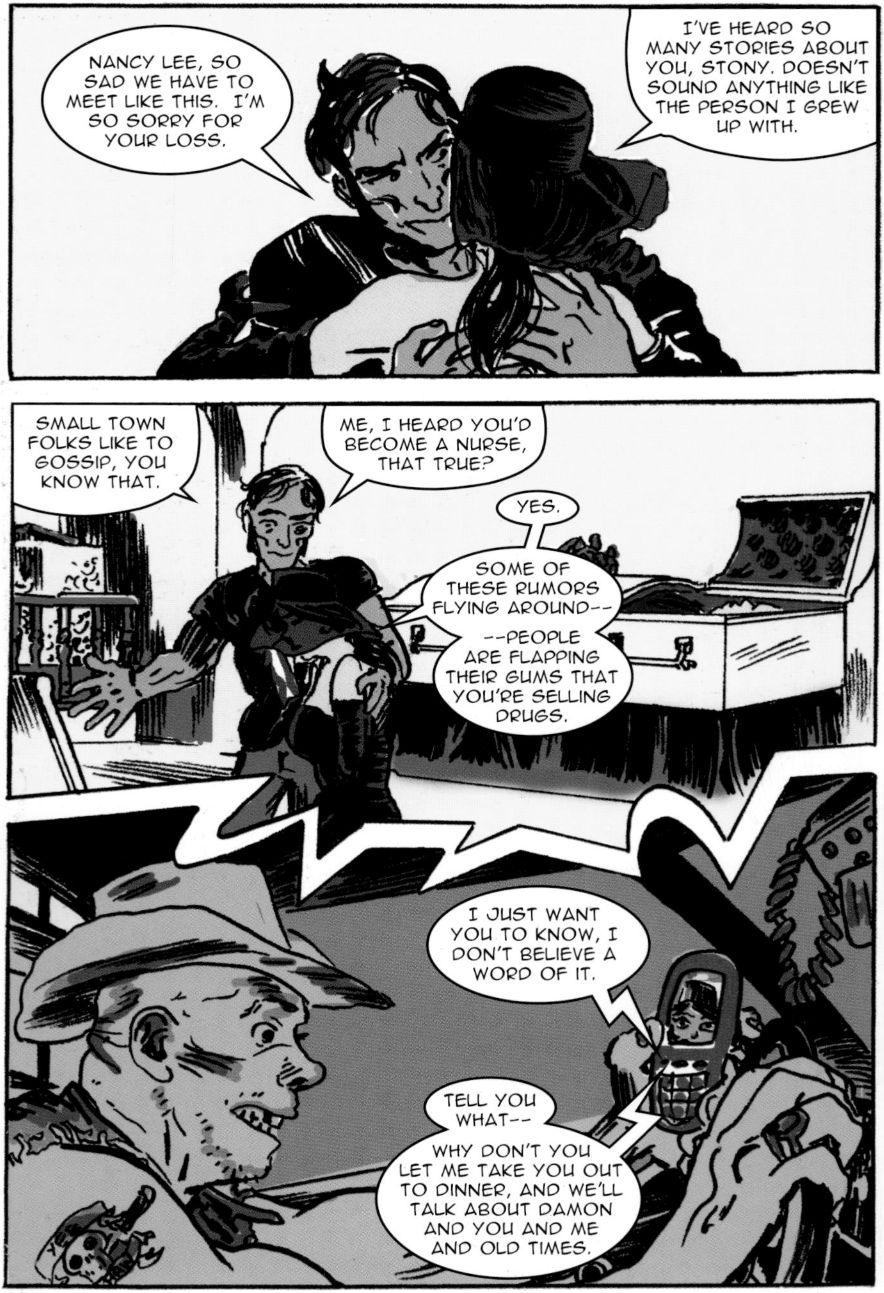
NANCY LEE, SO SAD WE HAVE TO MEET LIKE THIS. I'M SO SORRY FOR YOUR LOSS.
I'VE HEARD SO MANY STORIES ABOUT YOU, STONY. DOESN'T SOUND ANYTHING LIKE THE PERSON I GREW UP WITH.
SMALL TOWN FOLKS LIKE TO GOSSIP, YOU KNOW THAT.
ME, I HEARD YOU'D BECOME A NURSE, THAT TRUE?
YES.
SOME OF THESE RUMORS FLYING AROUND--
--PEOPLE ARE FLAPPING THEIR GUMS THAT YOU'RE SELLING DRUGS.
I JUST WANT YOU TO KNOW, I DON'T BELIEVE A WORD OF IT.
TELL YOU WHAT--
WHY DON'T YOU LET ME TAKE YOU OUT TO DINNER, AND WE'LL TALK ABOUT DAMON AND YOU AND ME AND OLD TIMES.

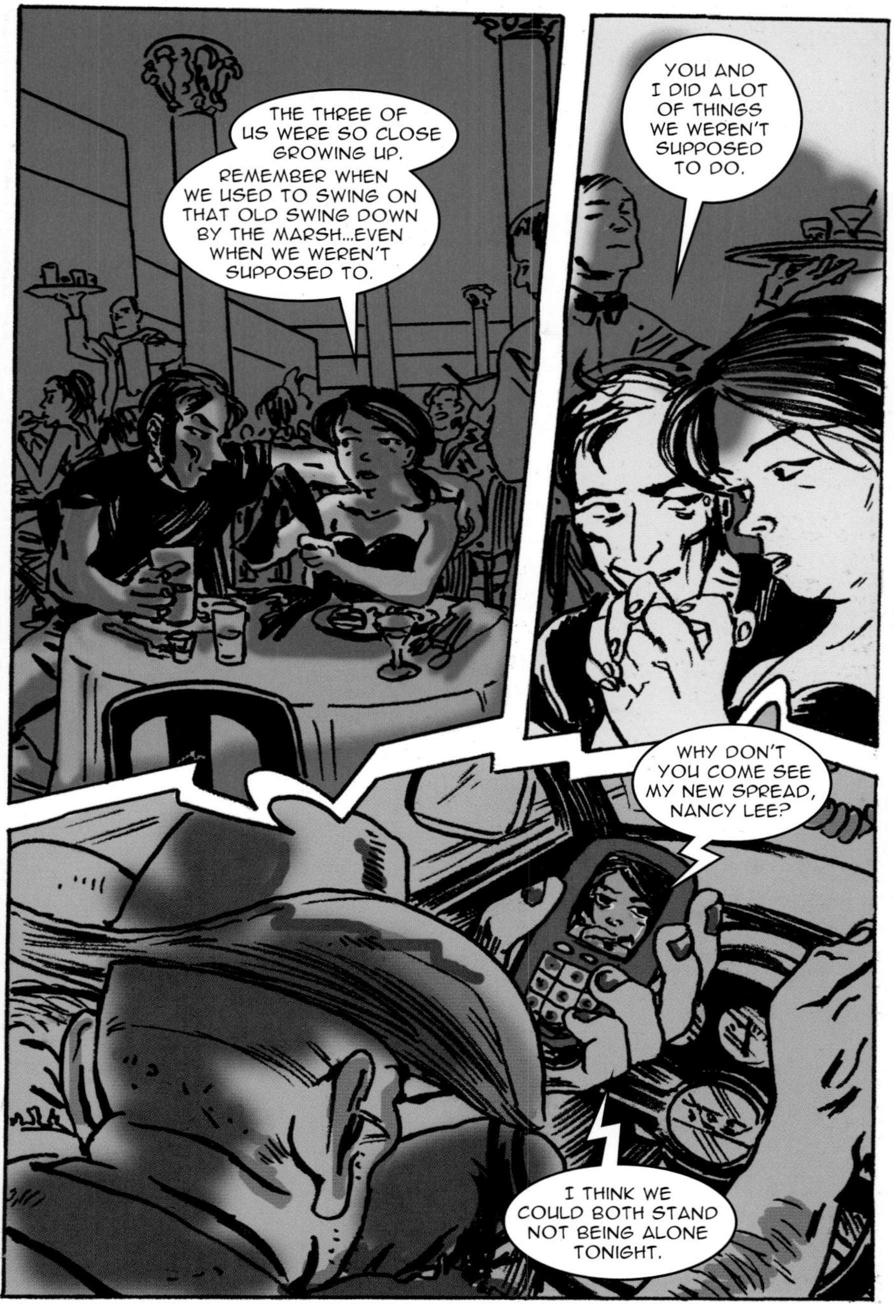
THE THREE OF US WERE SO CLOSE GROWING UP.
REMEMBER WHEN WE USED TO SWING ON THAT OLD SWING DOWN BY THE MARSH...EVEN WHEN WE WEREN'T SUPPOSED TO.
YOU AND I DID A LOT OF THINGS WE WEREN'T SUPPOSED TO DO.
WHY DON'T YOU COME SEE MY NEW SPREAD, NANCY LEE?
I THINK WE COULD BOTH STAND NOT BEING ALONE TONIGHT.

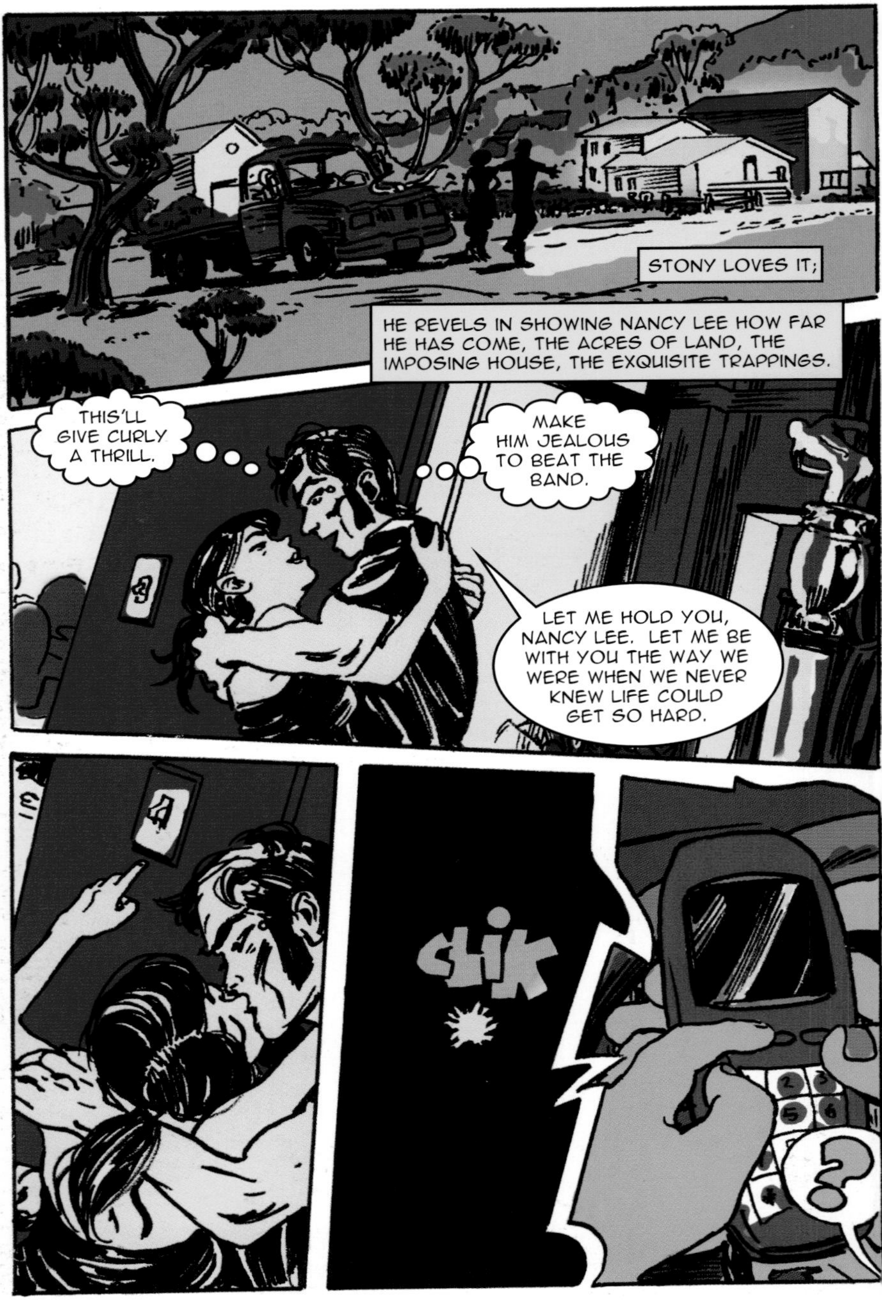
STONY LOVES IT;
HE REVELS IN SHOWING NANCY LEE HOW FAR HE HAS COME, THE ACRES OF LAND, THE IMPOSING HOUSE, THE EXQUISITE TRAPPINGS.
THIS'LL GIVE CURLY A THRILL.
MAKE HIM JEALOUS TO BEAT THE BAND.
LET ME HOLD YOU, NANCY LEE. LET ME BE WITH YOU THE WAY WE WERE WHEN WE NEVER KNEW LIFE COULD GET SO HARD.
CLIK
?

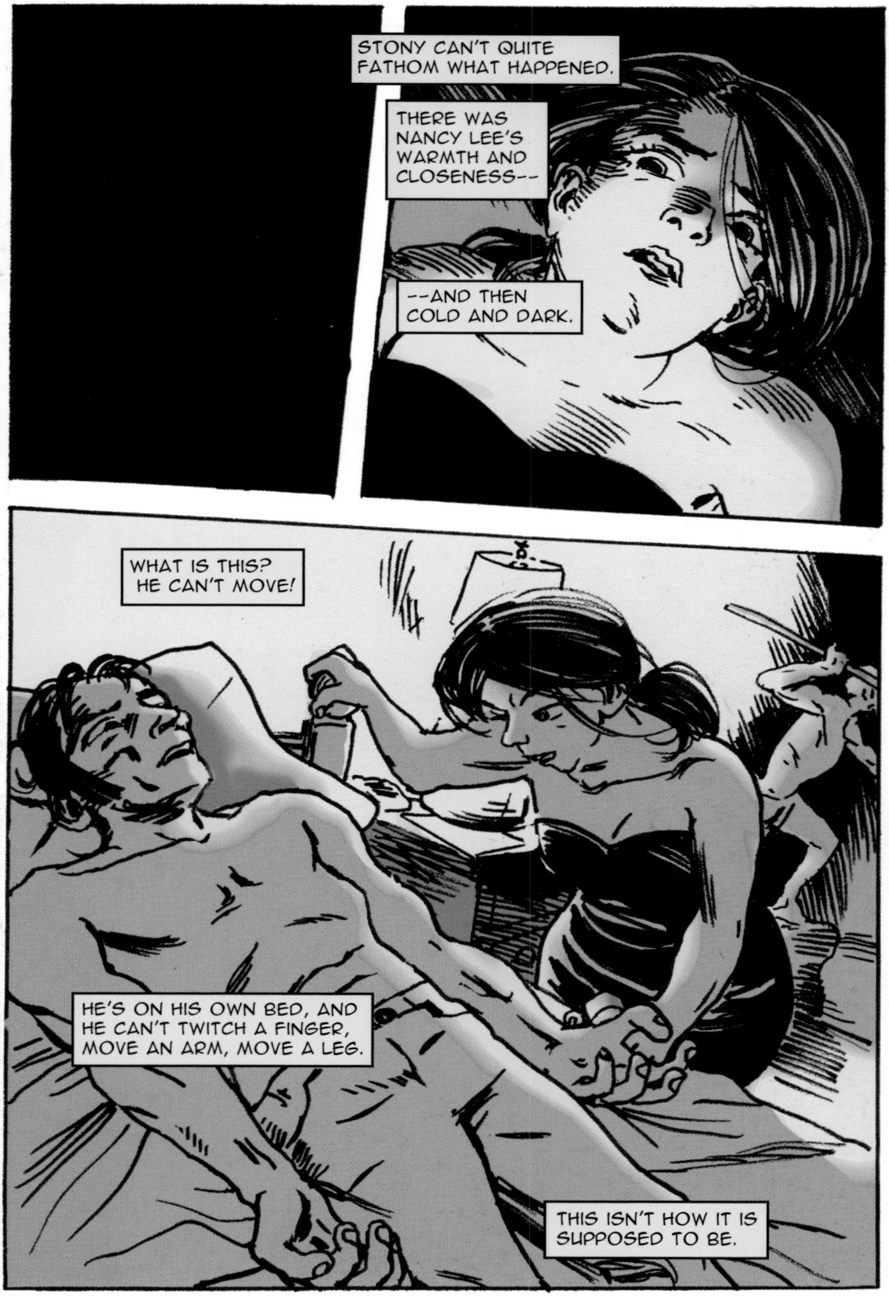
STONY CAN'T QUITE FATHOM WHAT HAPPENED.
THERE WAS NANCY LEE'S WARMTH AND CLOSENESS--
--AND THEN COLD AND DARK.
WHAT IS THIS? HE CAN'T MOVE!
HE'S ON HIS OWN BED, AND HE CAN'T TWITCH A FINGER, MOVE AN ARM, MOVE A LEG.
THIS ISN'T HOW IT IS SUPPOSED TO BE.

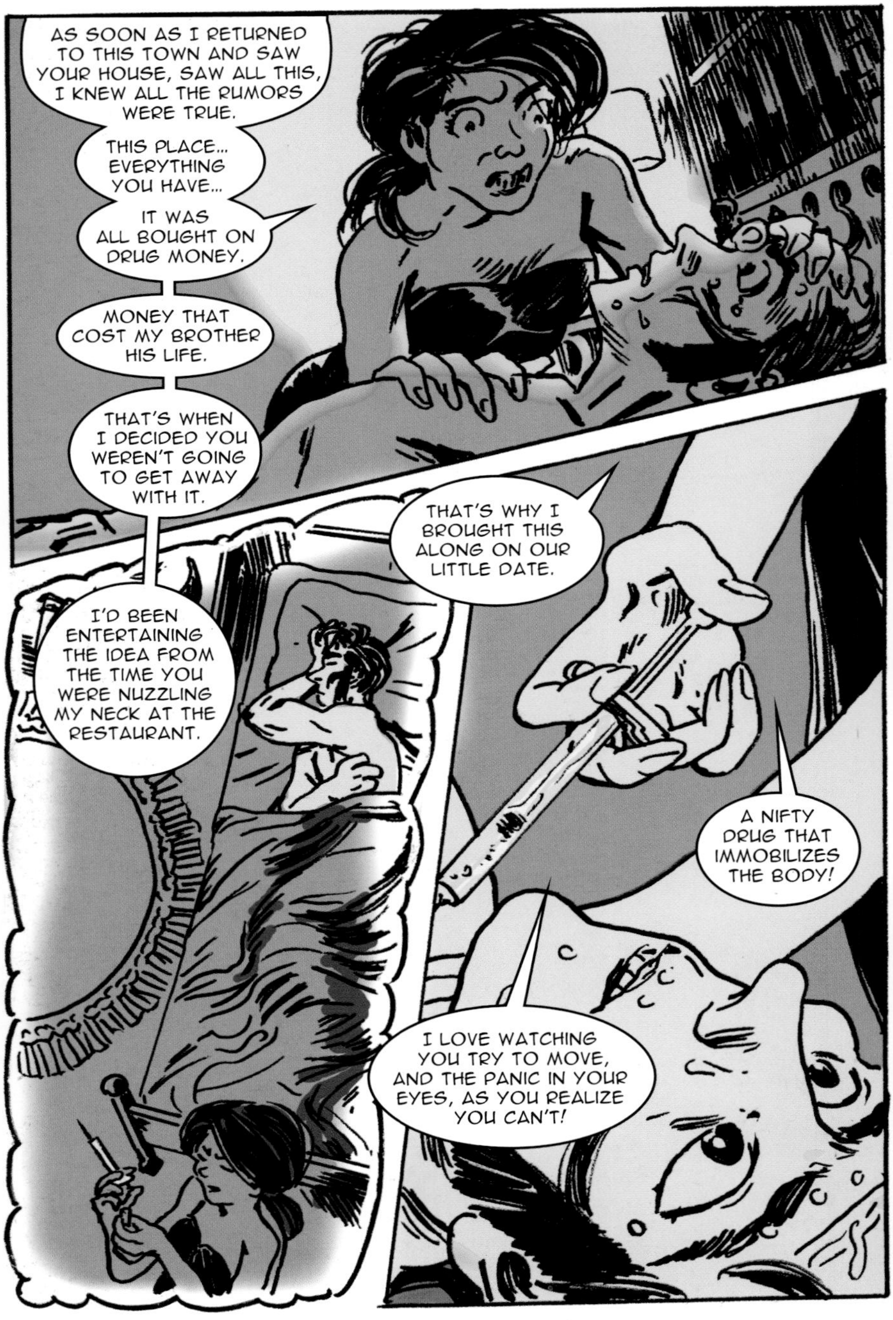
AS SOON AS I RETURNED TO THIS TOWN AND SAW YOUR HOUSE, SAW ALL THIS, I KNEW ALL THE RUMORS WERE TRUE.
THIS PLACE... EVERYTHING YOU HAVE...
IT WAS ALL BOUGHT ON DRUG MONEY.
MONEY THAT COST MY BROTHER HIS LIFE.
THAT'S WHEN I DECIDED YOU WEREN'T GOING TO GET AWAY WITH IT.
I'D BEEN ENTERTAINING THE IDEA FROM THE TIME YOU WERE NUZZLING MY NECK AT THE RESTAURANT.
THAT'S WHY I BROUGHT THIS ALONG ON OUR LITTLE DATE.
A NIFTY DRUG THAT IMMOBILIZES THE BODY!
I LOVE WATCHING YOU TRY TO MOVE, AND THE PANIC IN YOUR EYES, AS YOU REALIZE YOU CAN'T!

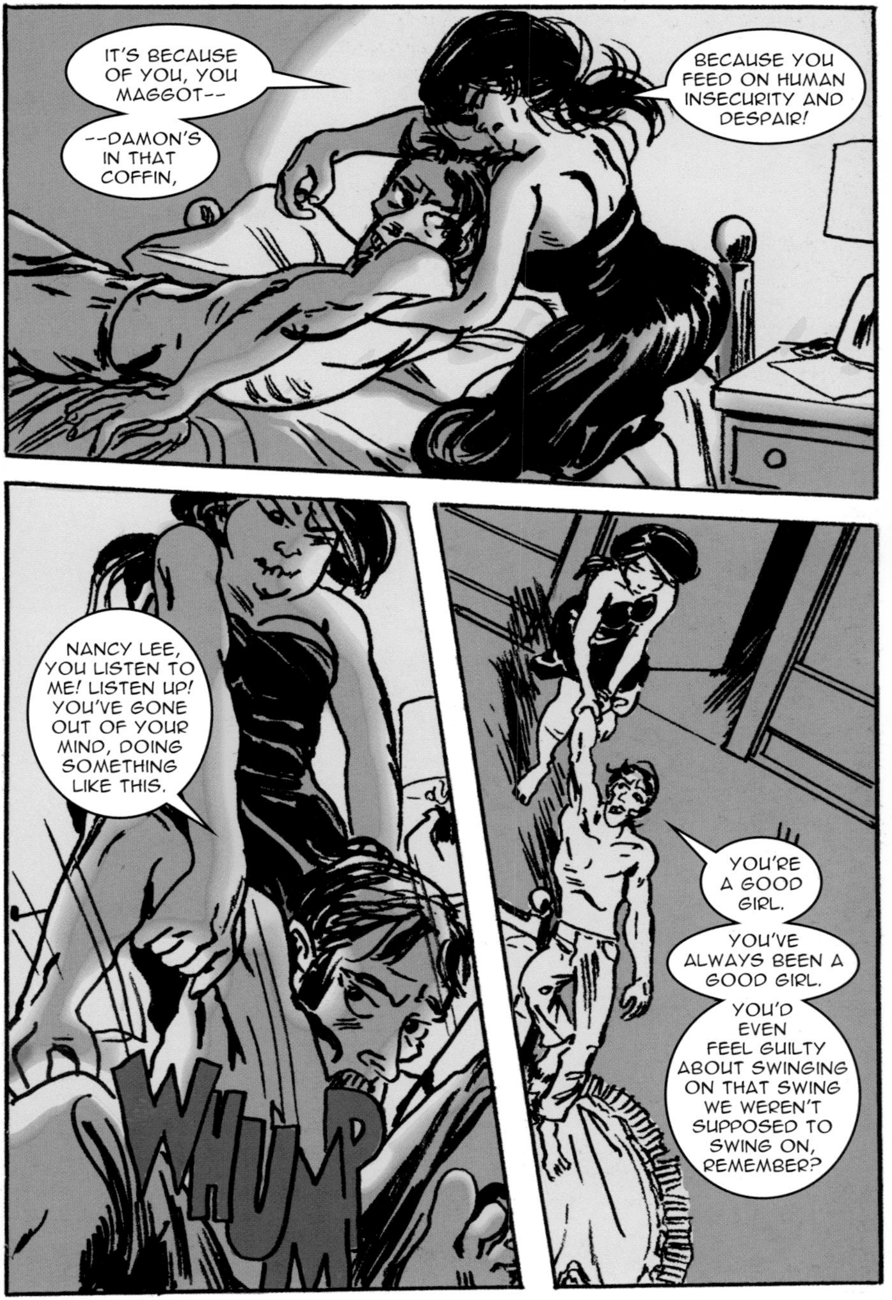
IT'S BECAUSE OF YOU, YOU MAGGOT--
--DAMON'S IN THAT COFFIN,
BECAUSE YOU FEED ON HUMAN INSECURITY AND DESPAIR!
NANCY LEE, YOU LISTEN TO ME! LISTEN UP! YOU'VE GONE OUT OF YOUR MIND, DOING SOMETHING LIKE THIS.
WHUMP
YOU'RE A GOOD GIRL.
YOU'VE ALWAYS BEEN A GOOD GIRL.
YOU'D EVEN FEEL GUILTY ABOUT SWINGING ON THAT SWING WE WEREN'T SUPPOSED TO SWING ON, REMEMBER?

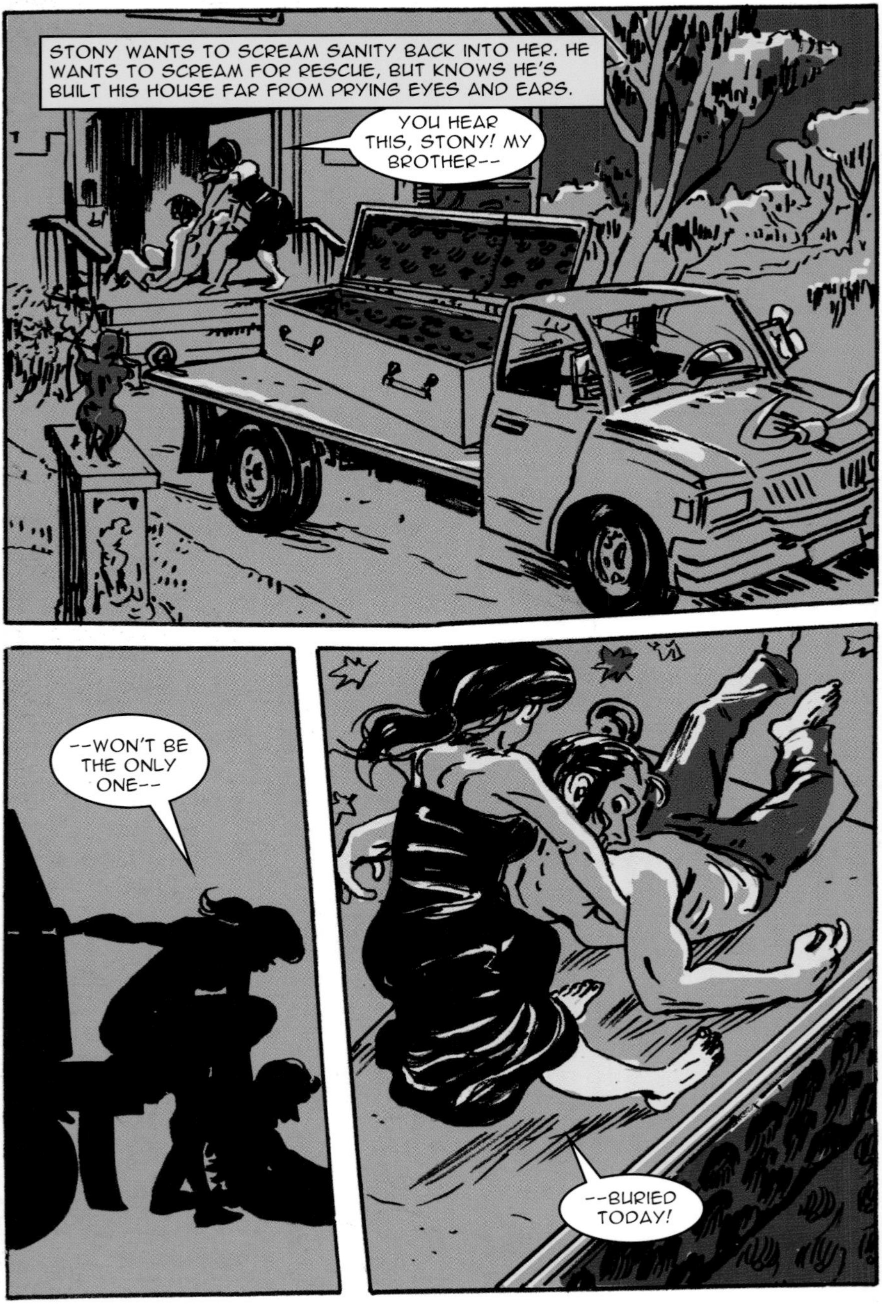
STONY WANTS TO SCREAM SANITY BACK INTO HER. HE WANTS TO SCREAM FOR RESCUE, BUT KNOWS HE'S BUILT HIS HOUSE FAR FROM PRYING EYES AND EARS.
YOU HEAR THIS, STONY! MY BROTHER--
--WON'T BE THE ONLY ONE--
--BURIED TODAY!

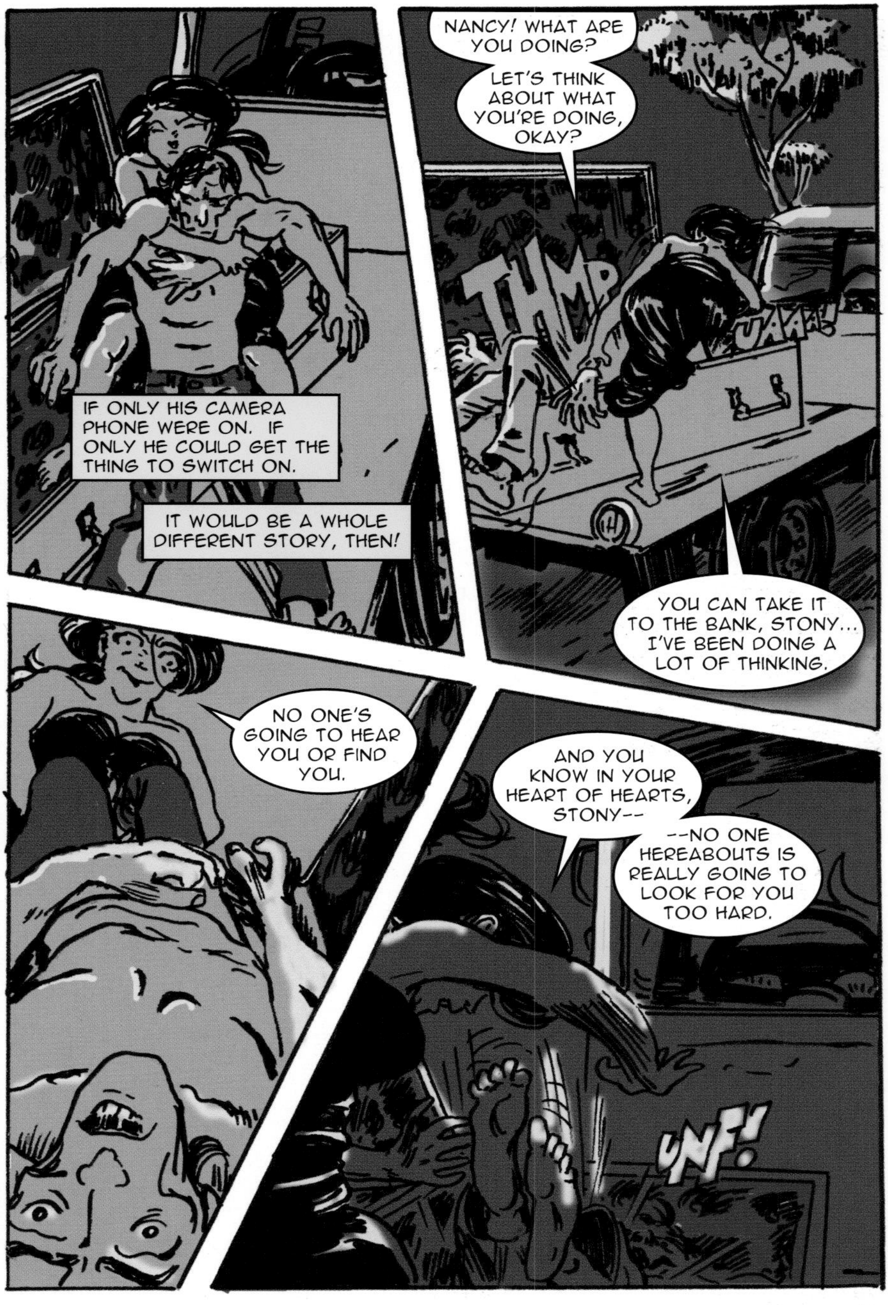

IF ONLY HIS CAMERA PHONE WERE ON. IF ONLY HE COULD GET THE THING TO SWITCH ON.
IT WOULD BE A WHOLE DIFFERENT STORY, THEN!
NANCY! WHAT ARE YOU DOING?
LET'S THINK ABOUT WHAT YOU'RE DOING, OKAY?
THMP
YOU CAN TAKE IT TO THE BANK, STONY... I'VE BEEN DOING A LOT OF THINKING.
NO ONE'S GOING TO HEAR YOU OR FIND YOU.
AND YOU KNOW IN YOUR HEART OF HEARTS, STONY--
--NO ONE HEREABOUTS IS REALLY GOING TO LOOK FOR YOU TOO HARD.
UNF!

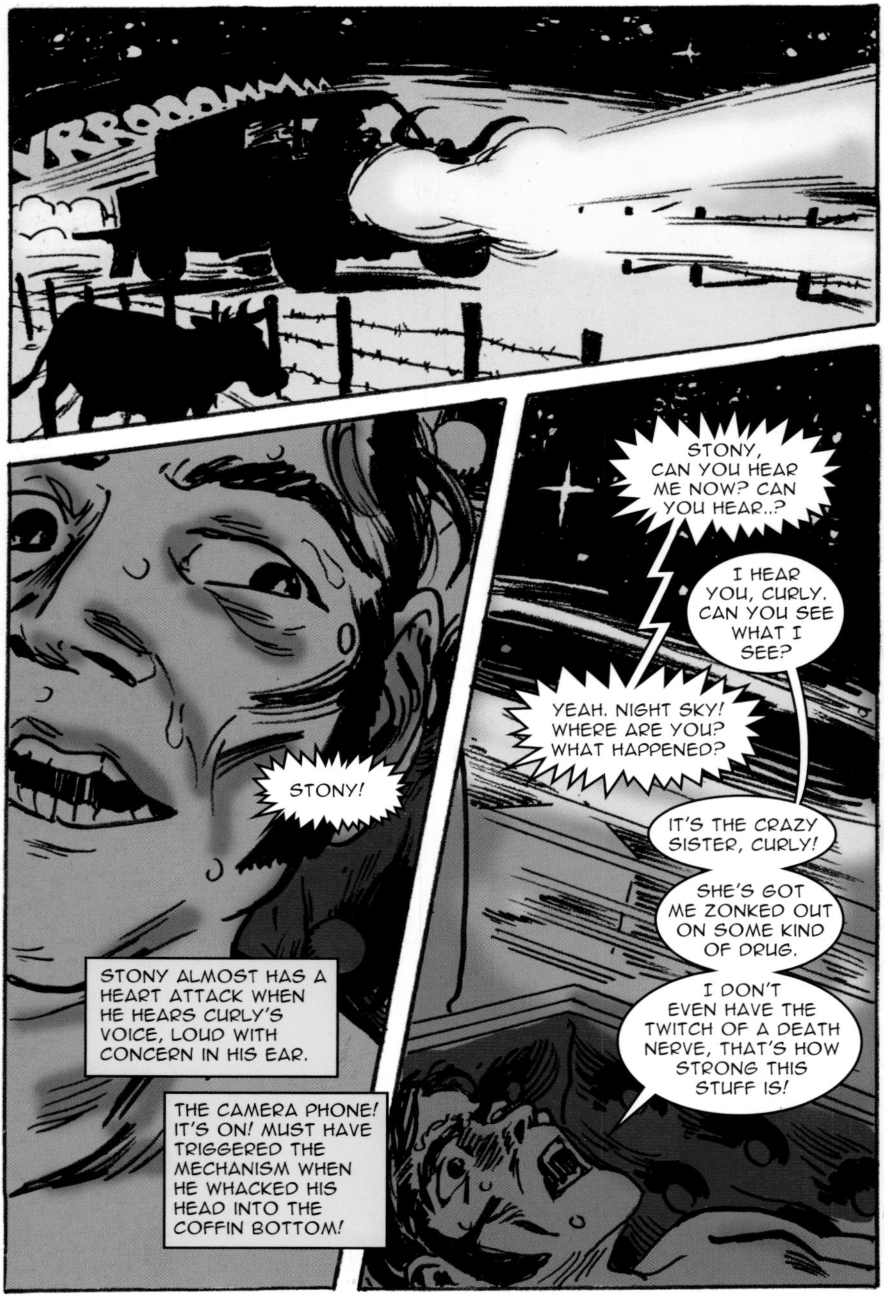
VRROOOMMM
STONY!
STONY ALMOST HAS A HEART ATTACK WHEN HE HEARS CURLY'S VOICE, LOUD WITH CONCERN IN HIS EAR.
THE CAMERA PHONE! IT'S ON! MUST HAVE TRIGGERED THE MECHANISM WHEN HE WHACKED HIS HEAD INTO THE COFFIN BOTTOM!
STONY, CAN YOU HEAR ME NOW? CAN YOU HEAR..?
I HEAR YOU, CURLY. CAN YOU SEE WHAT I SEE?
YEAH. NIGHT SKY! WHERE ARE YOU? WHAT HAPPENED?
IT'S THE CRAZY SISTER, CURLY!
SHE'S GOT ME ZONKED OUT ON SOME KIND OF DRUG.
I DON'T EVEN HAVE THE TWITCH OF A DEATH NERVE, THAT'S HOW STRONG THIS STUFF IS!

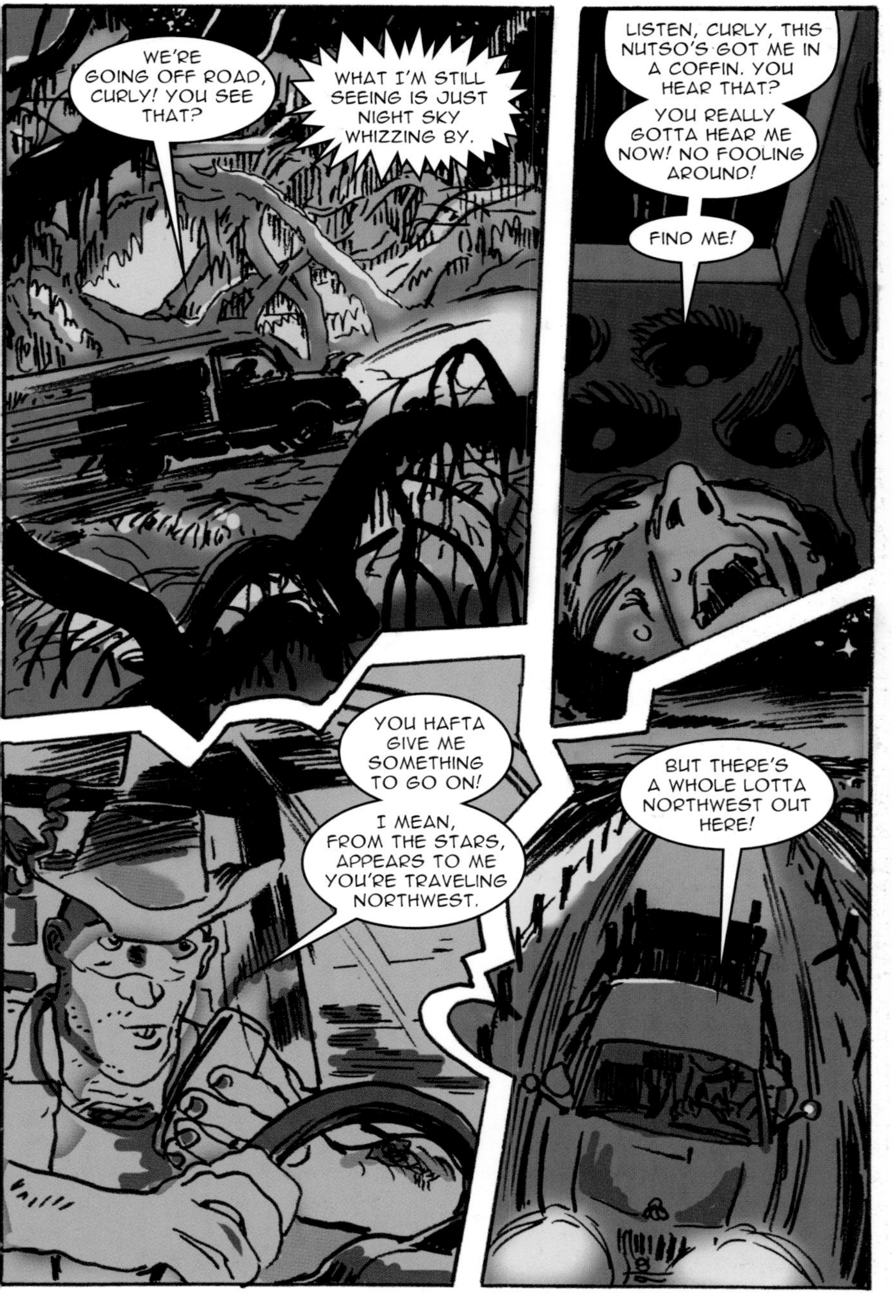
WE'RE GOING OFF ROAD, CURLY! YOU SEE THAT?
WHAT I'M STILL SEEING IS JUST NIGHT SKY WHIZZING BY.
LISTEN, CURLY, THIS NUTSO'S GOT ME IN A COFFIN. YOU HEAR THAT?
YOU REALLY GOTTA HEAR ME NOW! NO FOOLING AROUND!
FIND ME!
YOU HAFTA GIVE ME SOMETHING TO GO ON!
I MEAN, FROM THE STARS, APPEARS TO ME YOU'RE TRAVELING NORTHWEST.
BUT THERE'S A WHOLE LOTTA NORTHWEST OUT HERE!

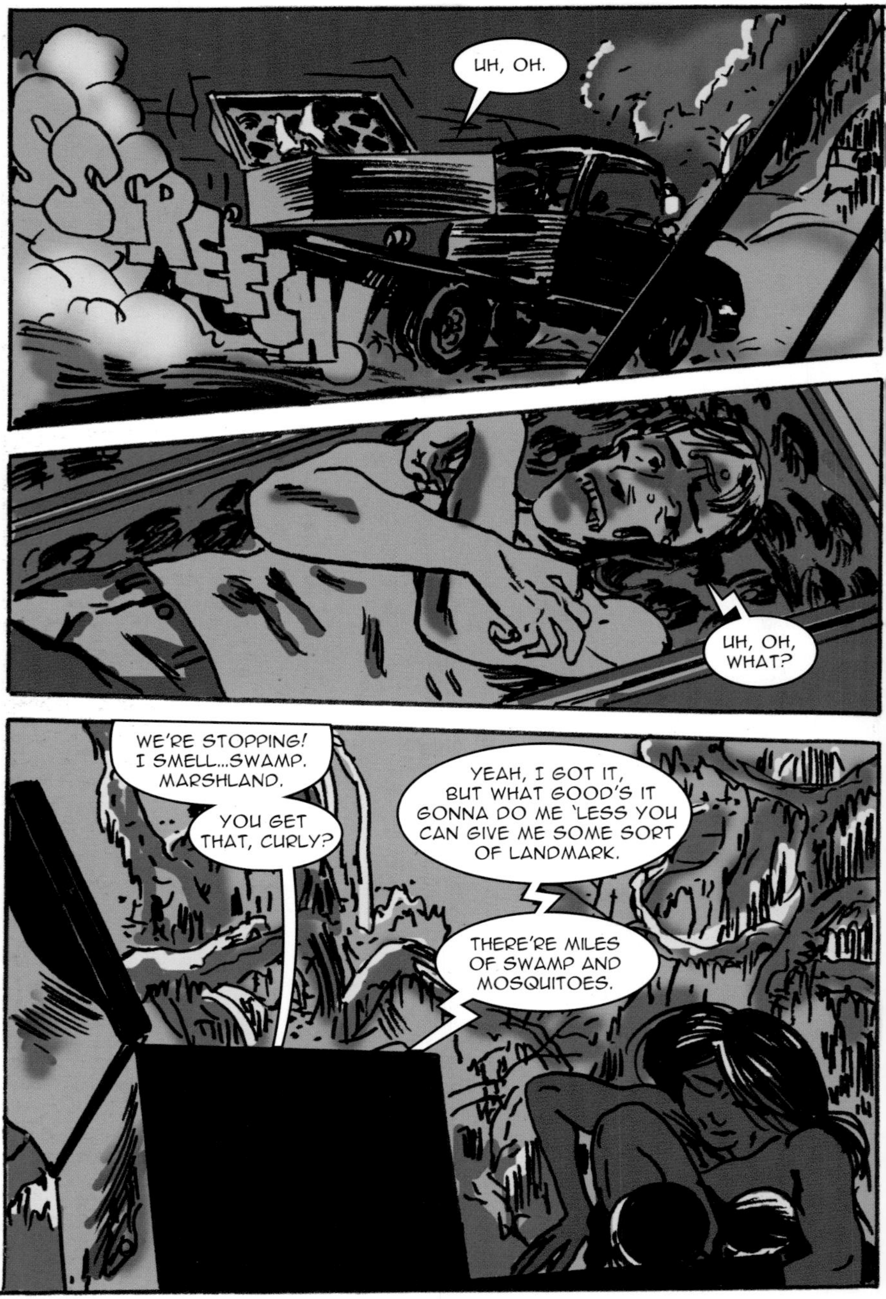
UH, OH.
SCREECH
UH, OH, WHAT?
WE'RE STOPPING! I SMELL...SWAMP. MARSHLAND.
YOU GET THAT, CURLY?
YEAH, I GOT IT, BUT WHAT GOOD'S IT GONNA DO ME 'LESS YOU CAN GIVE ME SOME SORT OF LANDMARK.
THERE'RE MILES OF SWAMP AND MOSQUITOES.

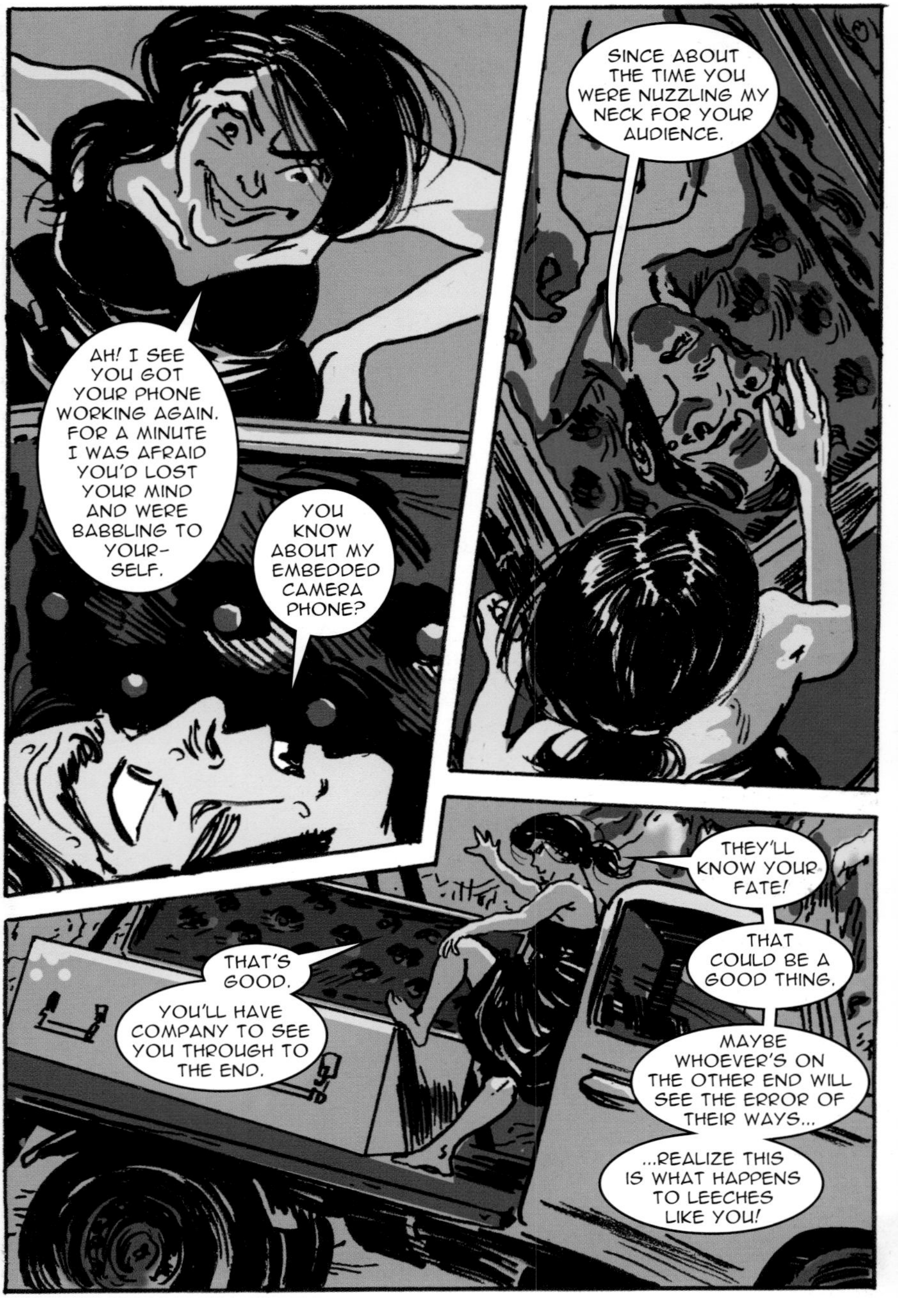
AH! I SEE YOU GOT YOUR PHONE WORKING AGAIN. FOR A MINUTE I WAS AFRAID YOU'D LOST YOUR MIND AND WERE BABBLING TO YOUR-SELF.
YOU KNOW ABOUT MY EMBEDDED CAMERA PHONE?
SINCE ABOUT THE TIME YOU WERE NUZZLING MY NECK FOR YOUR AUDIENCE.
THEY'LL KNOW YOUR FATE!
THAT COULD BE A GOOD THING.
THAT'S GOOD.
YOU'LL HAVE COMPANY TO SEE YOU THROUGH TO THE END.
MAYBE WHOEVER'S ON THE OTHER END WILL SEE THE ERROR OF THEIR WAYS...
...REALIZE THIS IS WHAT HAPPENS TO LEECHES LIKE YOU!

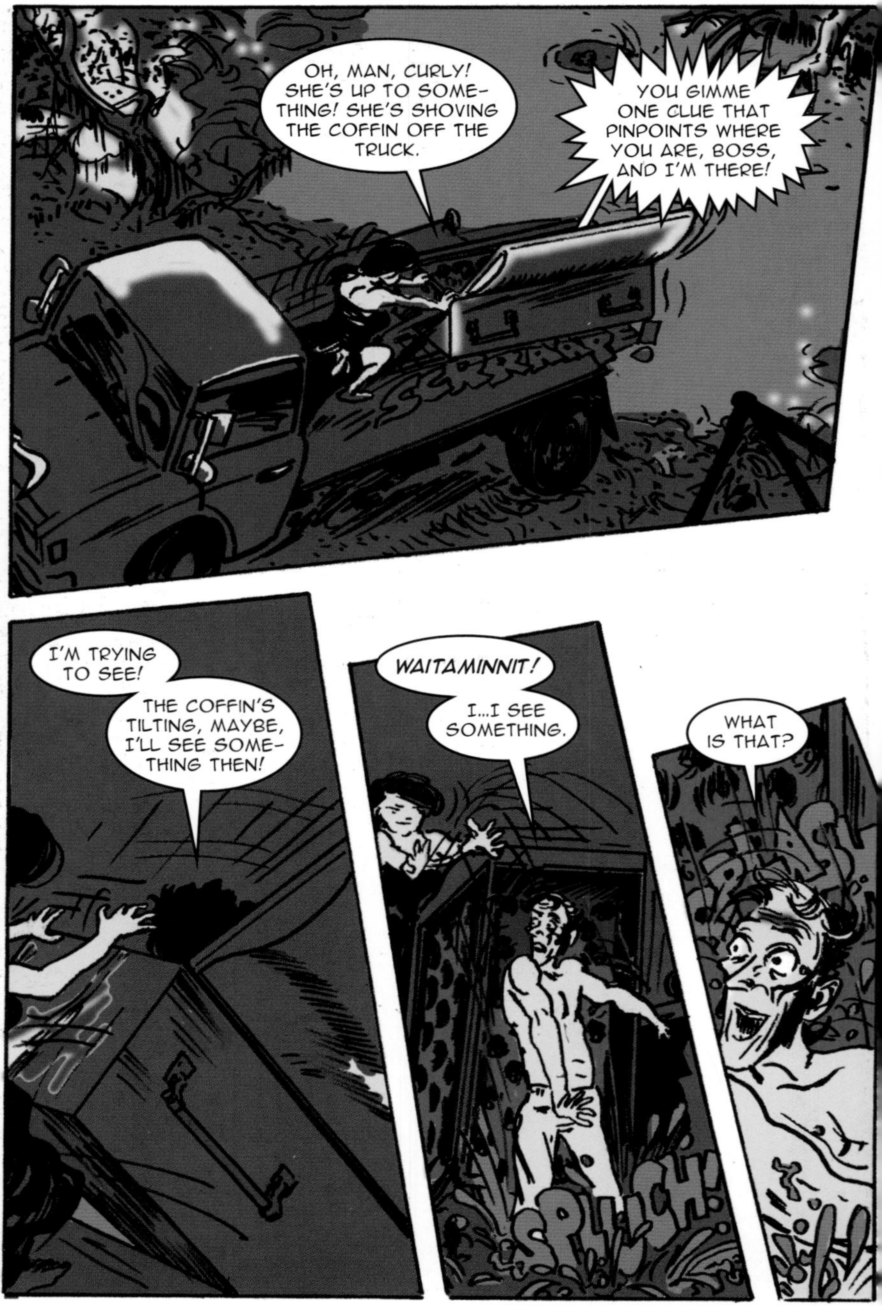
OH, MAN, CURLY! SHE'S UP TO SOME-THING! SHE'S SHOVING THE COFFIN OFF THE TRUCK.
YOU GIMME ONE CLUE THAT PINPOINTS WHERE YOU ARE, BOSS, AND I'M THERE!
SCRRAAPE!
I'M TRYING TO SEE!
THE COFFIN'S TILTING, MAYBE, I'LL SEE SOME-THING THEN!
WAITAMINNIT!
I...I SEE SOMETHING.
SPLUCH!
WHAT IS THAT?

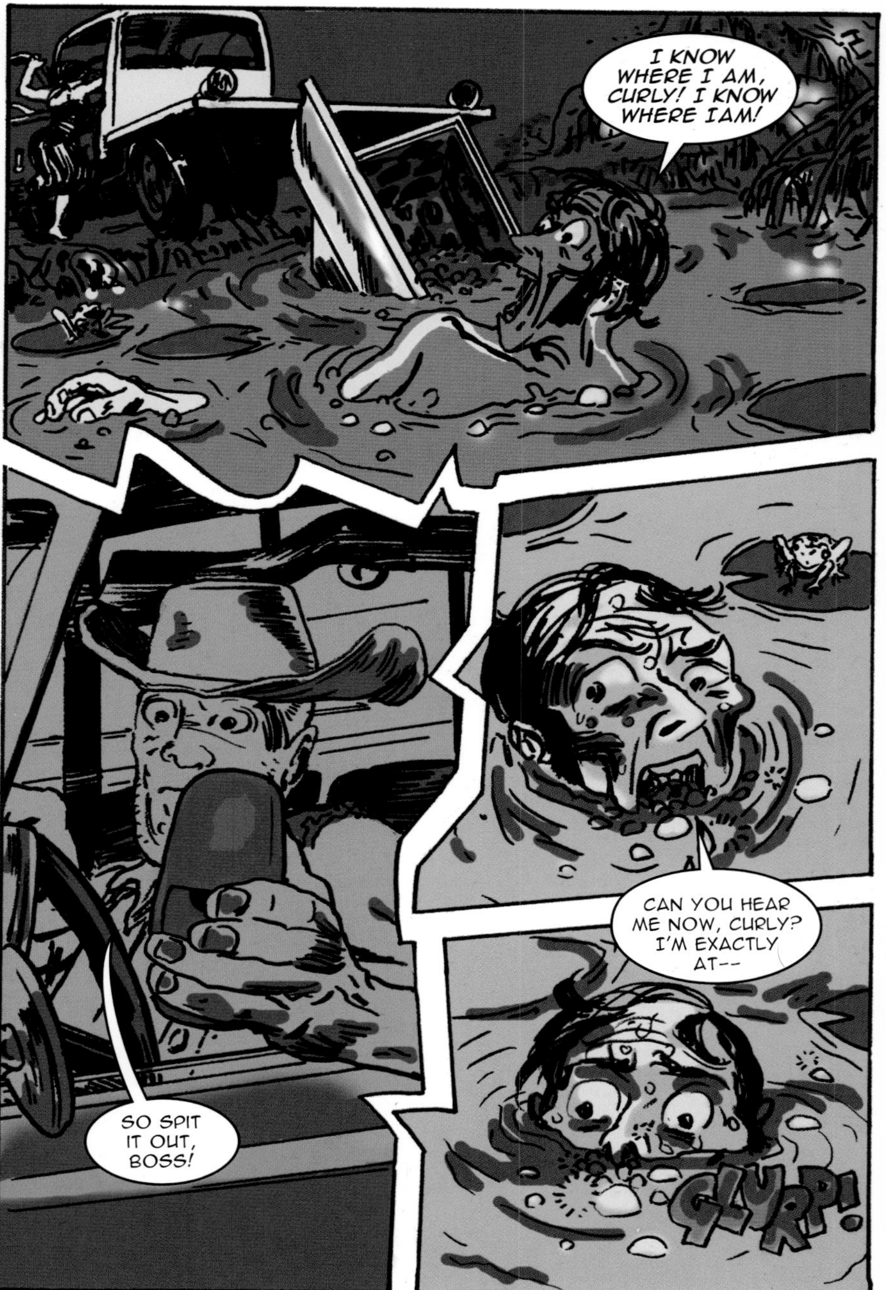
I KNOW WHERE I AM, CURLY! I KNOW WHERE IAM!
SO SPIT IT OUT, BOSS!
CAN YOU HEAR ME NOW, CURLY? I'M EXACTLY AT--
GLURP!

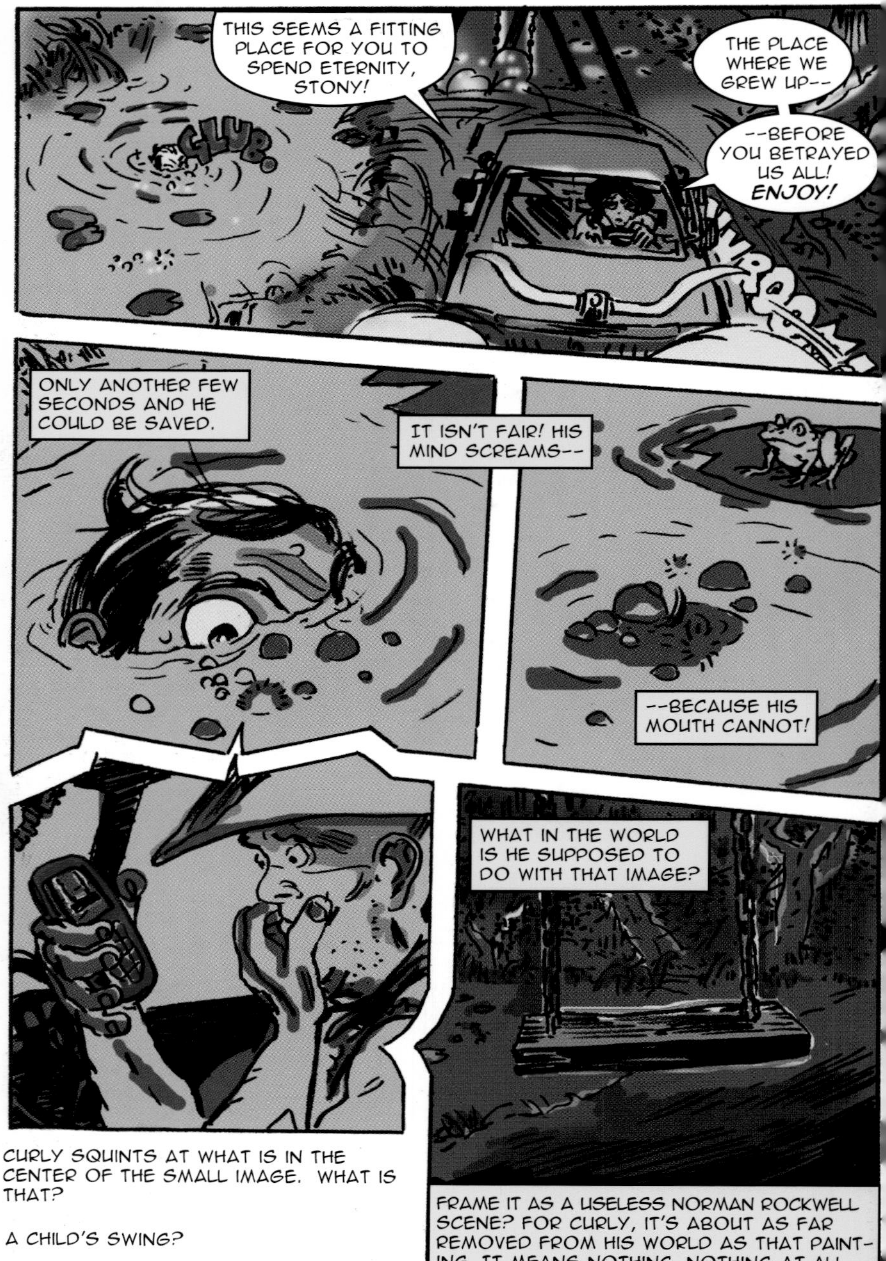
THIS SEEMS A FITTING PLACE FOR YOU TO SPEND ETERNITY, STONY!
THE PLACE WHERE WE GREW UP--
--BEFORE YOU BETRAYED US ALL! *ENJOY!*
GLUB
VROOM
ONLY ANOTHER FEW SECONDS AND HE COULD BE SAVED.
IT ISN'T FAIR! HIS MIND SCREAMS--
--BECAUSE HIS MOUTH CANNOT!
WHAT IN THE WORLD IS HE SUPPOSED TO DO WITH THAT IMAGE?
CURLY SQUINTS AT WHAT IS IN THE CENTER OF THE SMALL IMAGE. WHAT IS THAT?
A CHILD'S SWING?
FRAME IT AS A USELESS NORMAN ROCKWELL SCENE? FOR CURLY, IT'S ABOUT AS FAR REMOVED FROM HIS WORLD AS THAT PAINTING. IT MEANS NOTHING. NOTHING AT ALL.

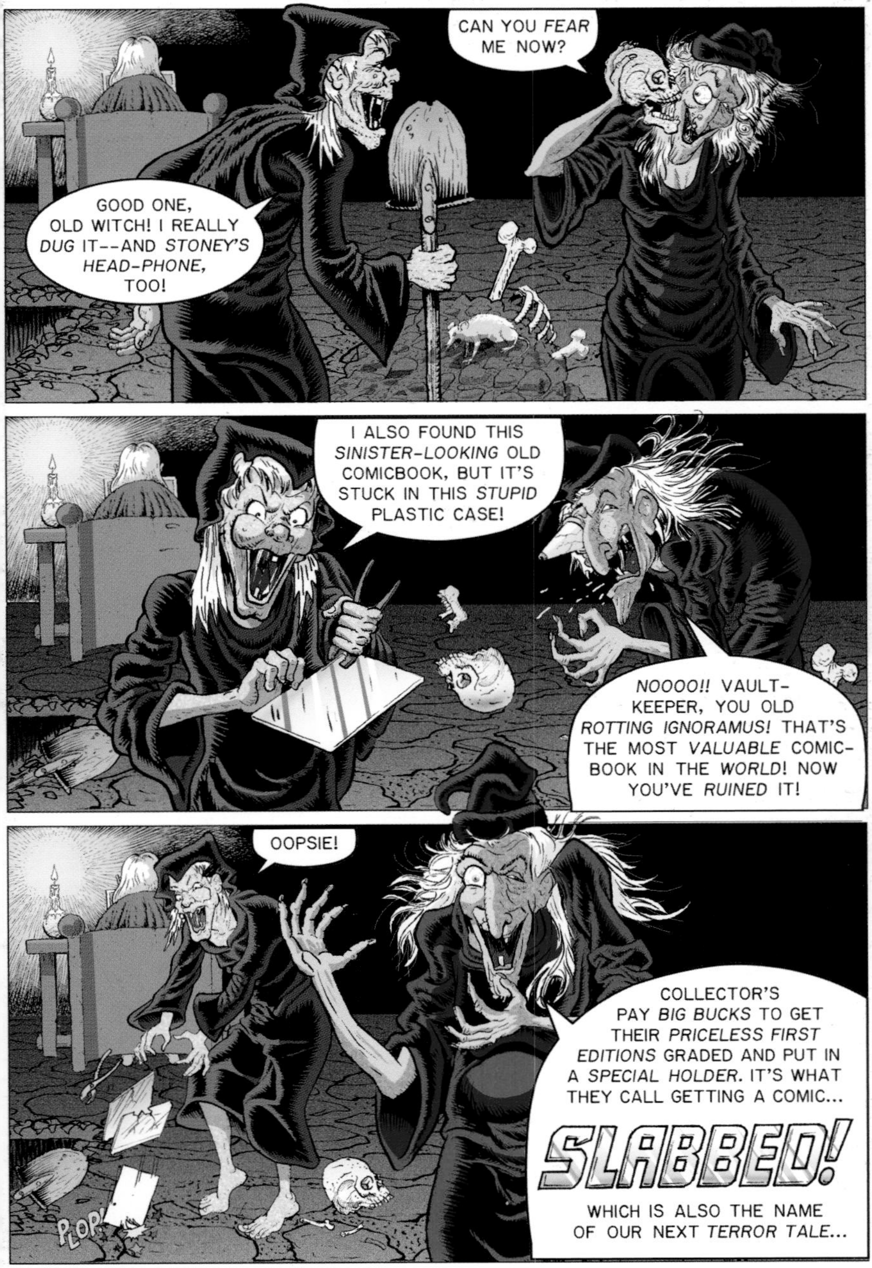
CAN YOU *FEAR* ME NOW?
GOOD ONE, OLD WITCH! I REALLY *DUG* IT--AND *STONEY'S HEAD-PHONE,* TOO!
I ALSO FOUND THIS *SINISTER-LOOKING* OLD COMICBOOK, BUT IT'S STUCK IN THIS *STUPID* PLASTIC CASE!
NOOOO!! VAULT-KEEPER, YOU OLD *ROTTING IGNORAMUS!* THAT'S THE MOST *VALUABLE* COMIC-BOOK IN THE *WORLD!* NOW YOU'VE *RUINED* IT!
OOPSIE!
COLLECTOR'S PAY *BIG BUCKS* TO GET THEIR *PRICELESS FIRST EDITIONS* GRADED AND PUT IN A *SPECIAL HOLDER.* IT'S WHAT THEY CALL GETTING A COMIC...
SLABBED!
WHICH IS ALSO THE NAME OF OUR NEXT *TERROR TALE...*
PLOP!

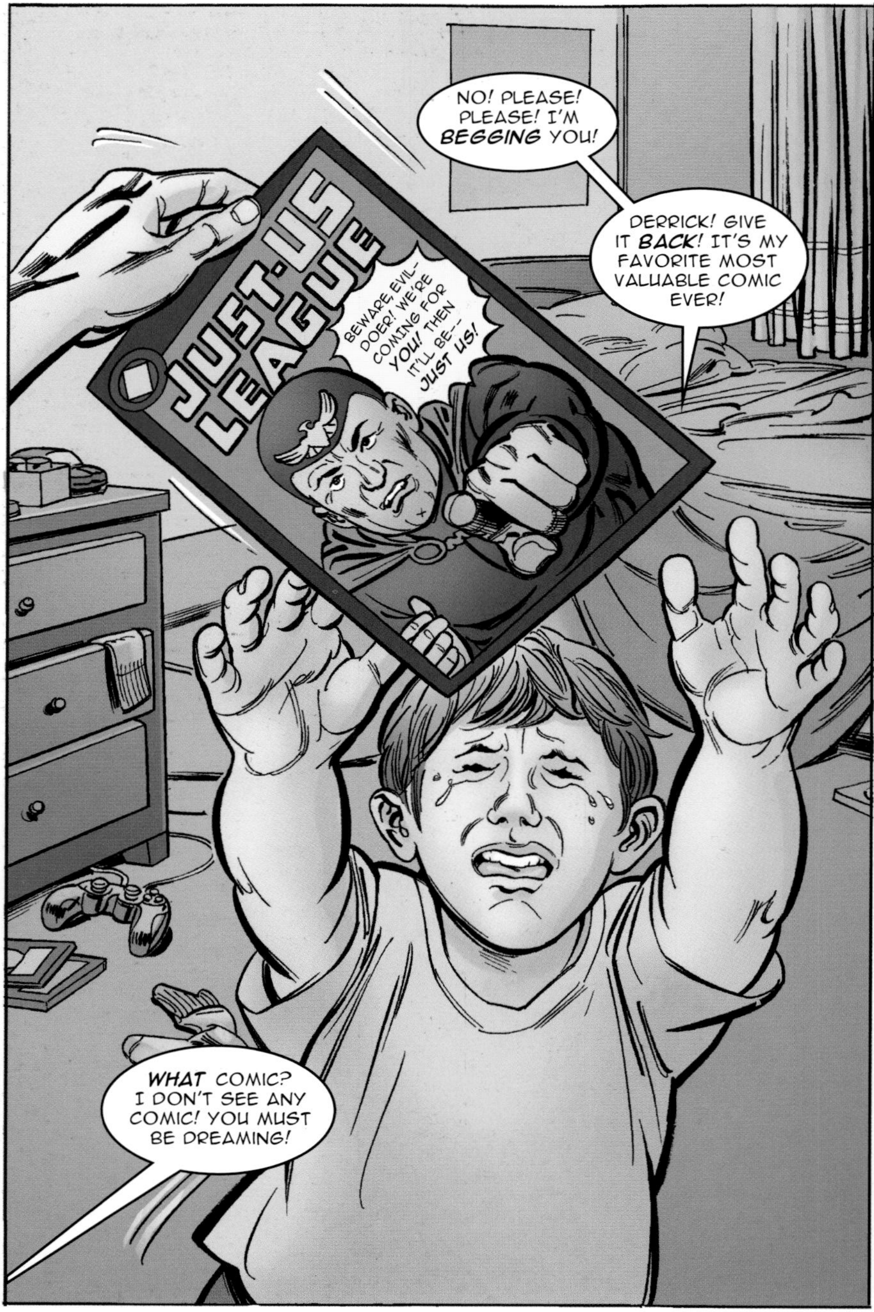
NO! PLEASE! PLEASE! I'M *BEGGING* YOU!
DERRICK! GIVE IT *BACK!* IT'S MY FAVORITE MOST VALUABLE COMIC EVER!
JUST-US LEAGUE
BEWARE, EVIL-DOER! WE'RE COMING FOR *YOU!* THEN IT'LL BE-- *JUST US!*
WHAT COMIC? I DON'T SEE ANY COMIC! YOU MUST BE DREAMING!

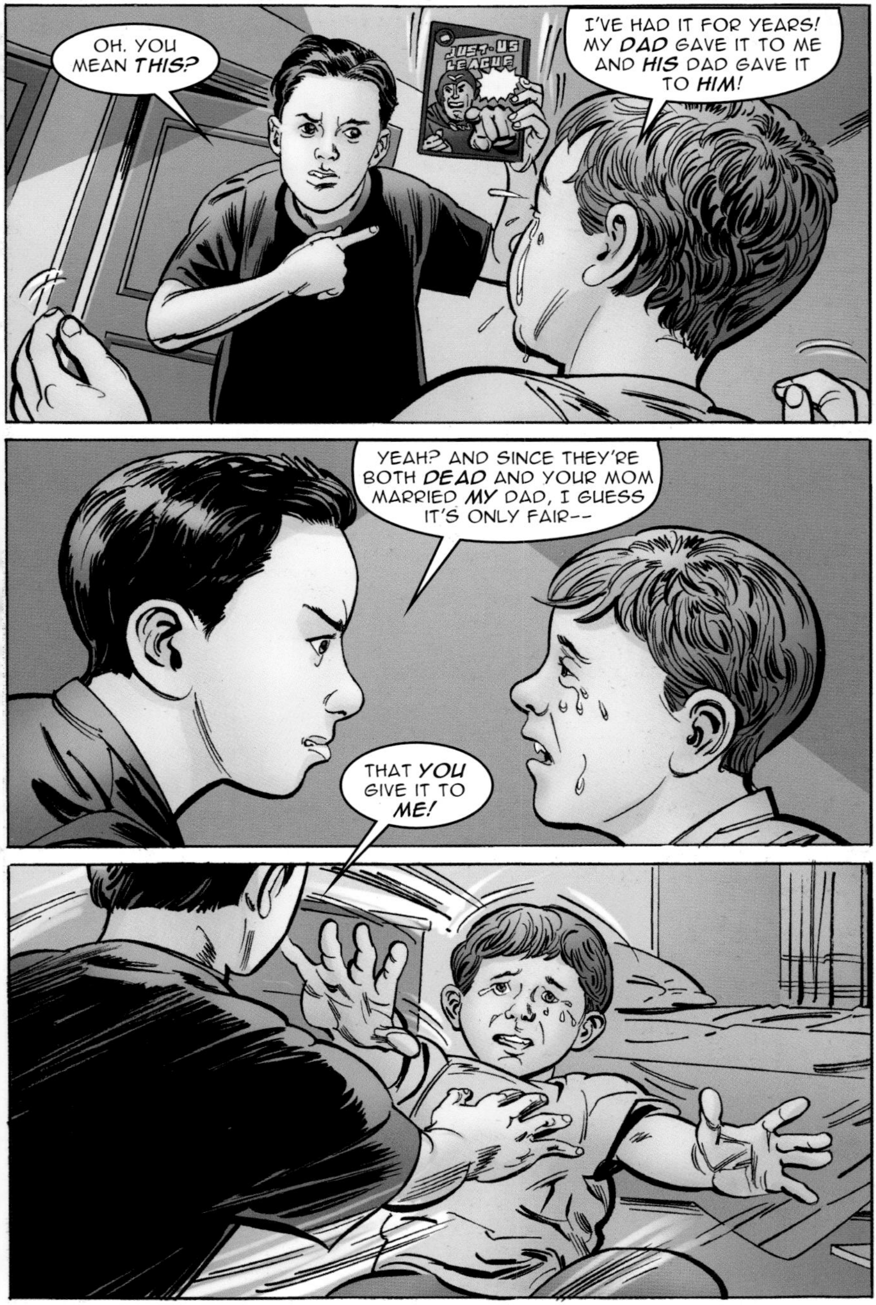
OH. YOU MEAN THIS?
JUST-US LEAGUE
I'VE HAD IT FOR YEARS! MY DAD GAVE IT TO ME AND HIS DAD GAVE IT TO HIM!
YEAH? AND SINCE THEY'RE BOTH DEAD AND YOUR MOM MARRIED MY DAD, I GUESS IT'S ONLY FAIR--
THAT YOU GIVE IT TO ME!

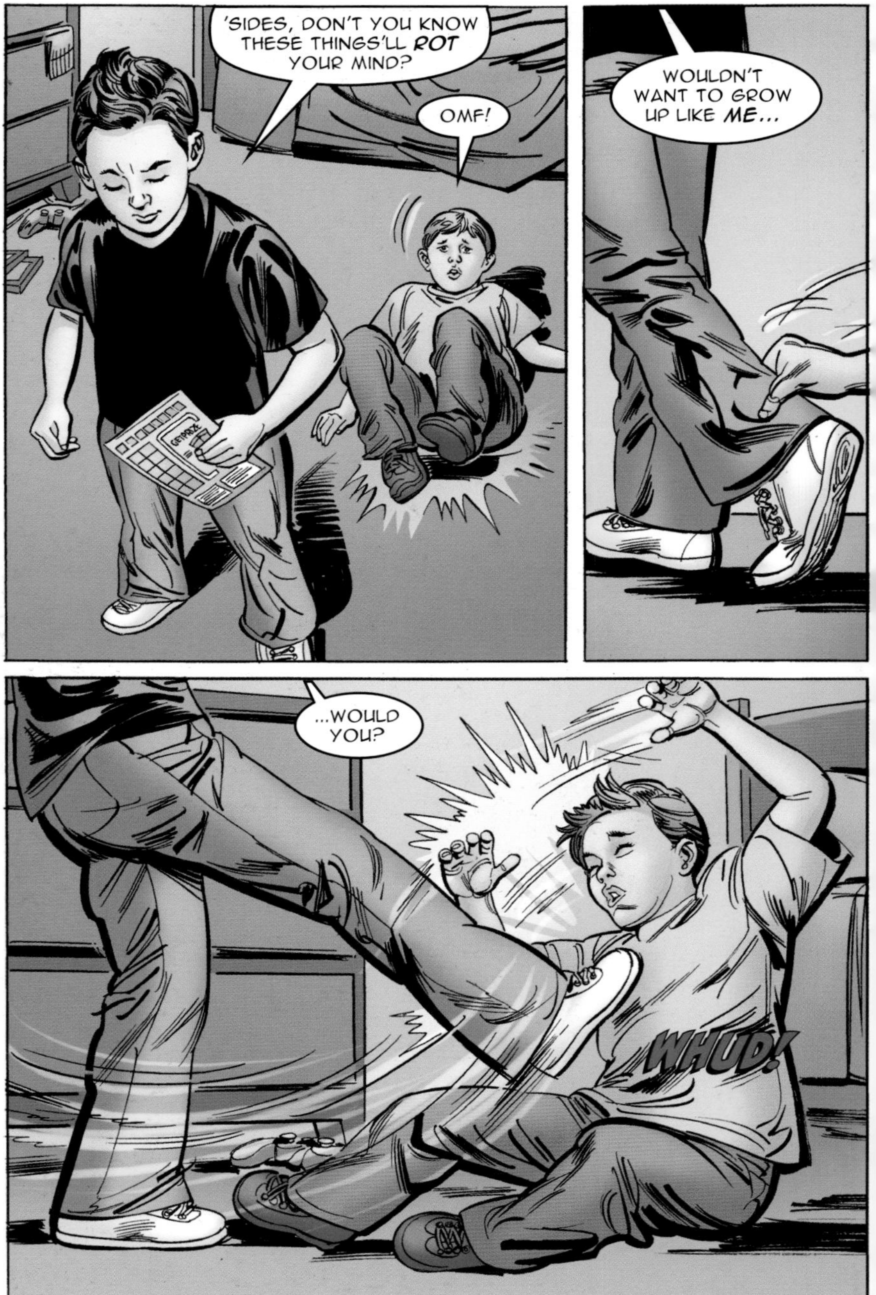
'SIDES, DON'T YOU KNOW THESE THINGS'LL ROT YOUR MIND?
OMF!
GETPRIZE
WOULDN'T WANT TO GROW UP LIKE ME...
...WOULD YOU?
WHUD!

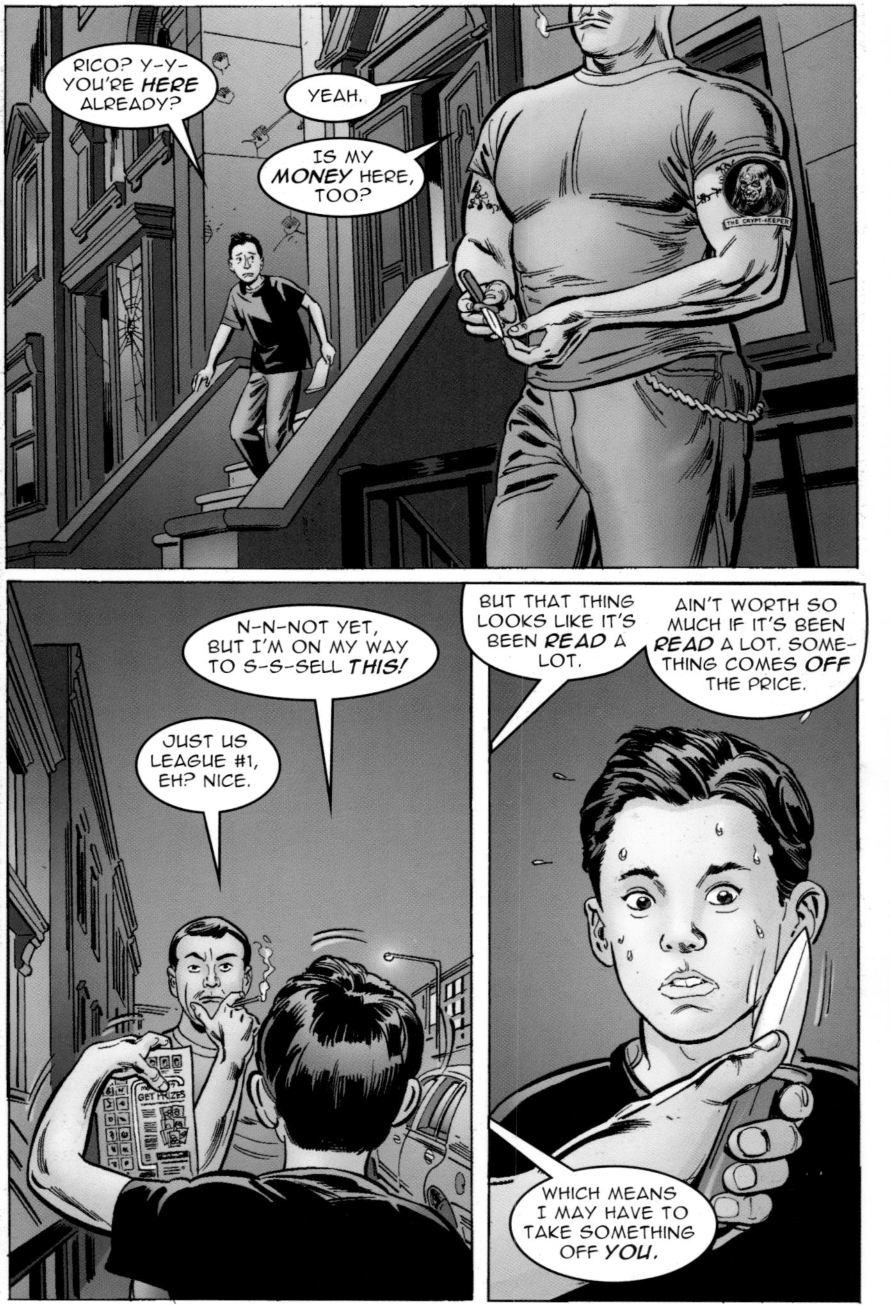
RICO? Y-Y-YOU'RE HERE ALREADY?
YEAH.
IS MY MONEY HERE, TOO?
THE CRYPT-KEEPER
N-N-NOT YET, BUT I'M ON MY WAY TO S-S-SELL THIS!
JUST US LEAGUE #1, EH? NICE.
GET PRIZES
BUT THAT THING LOOKS LIKE IT'S BEEN READ A LOT.
AIN'T WORTH SO MUCH IF IT'S BEEN READ A LOT. SOMETHING COMES OFF THE PRICE.
WHICH MEANS I MAY HAVE TO TAKE SOMETHING OFF YOU.

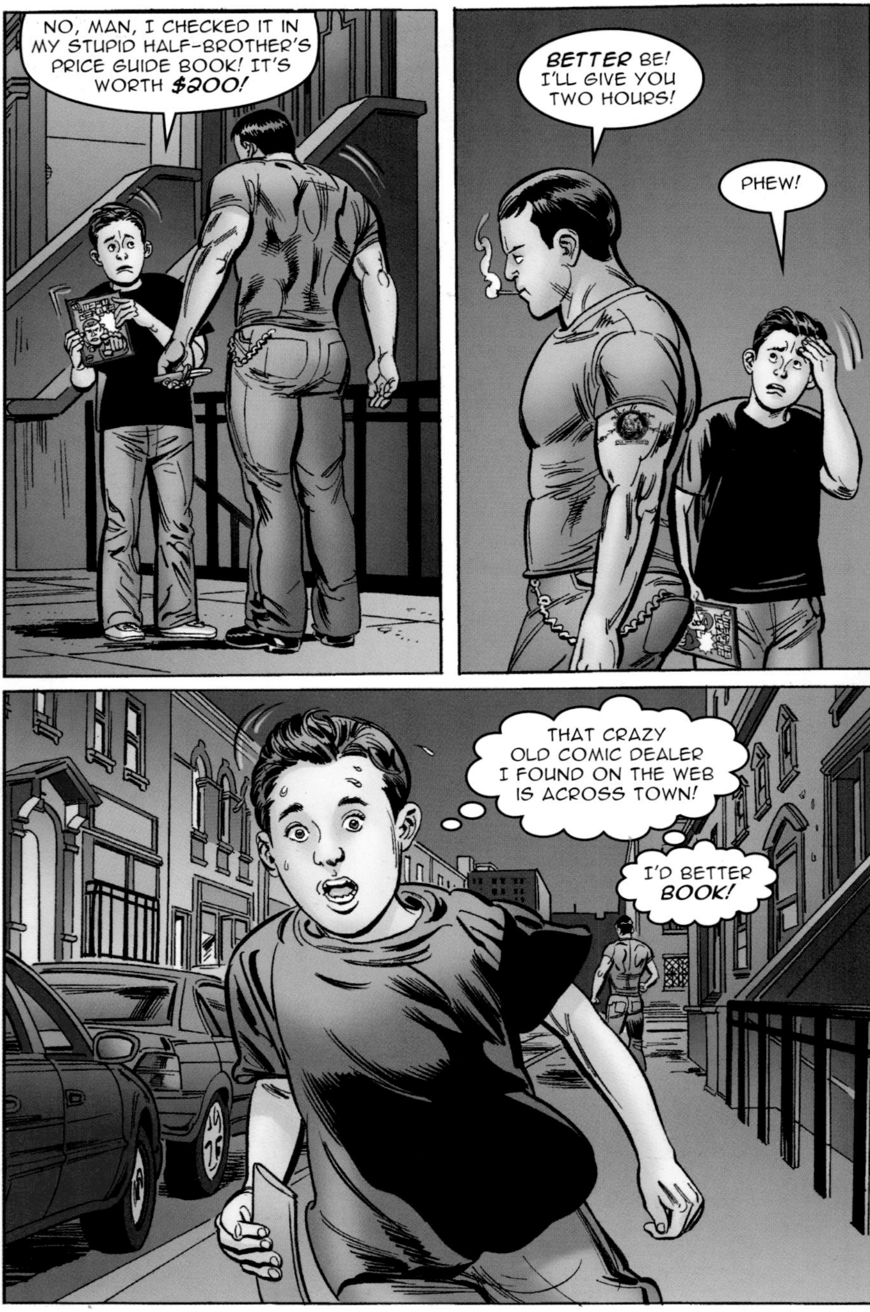
NO, MAN, I CHECKED IT IN MY STUPID HALF-BROTHER'S PRICE GUIDE BOOK! IT'S WORTH $200!
BETTER BE! I'LL GIVE YOU TWO HOURS!
PHEW!
THAT CRAZY OLD COMIC DEALER I FOUND ON THE WEB IS ACROSS TOWN!
I'D BETTER BOOK!

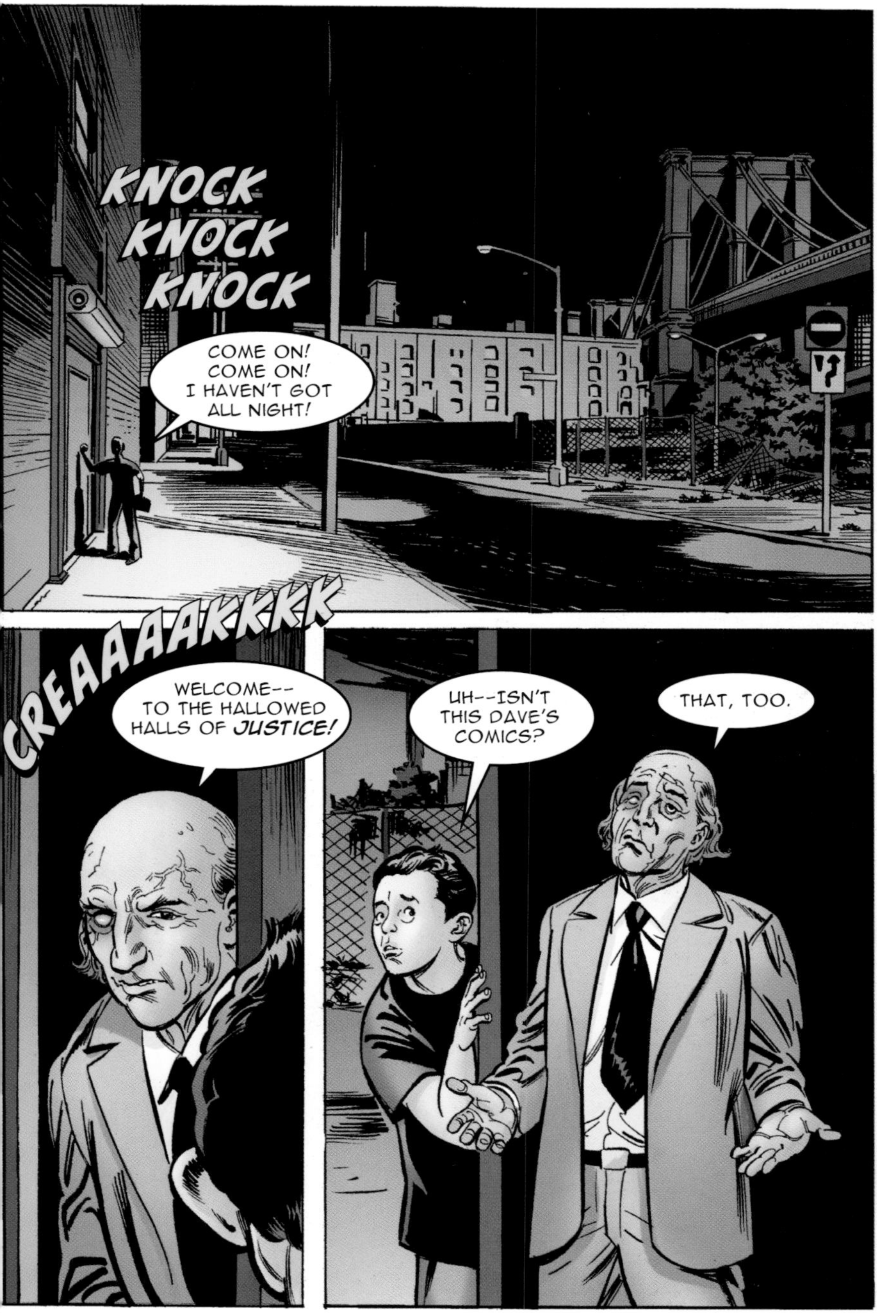
KNOCK
KNOCK
KNOCK
COME ON! COME ON! I HAVEN'T GOT ALL NIGHT!
CREAAAAKKKK
WELCOME-- TO THE HALLOWED HALLS OF JUSTICE!
UH--ISN'T THIS DAVE'S COMICS?
THAT, TOO.

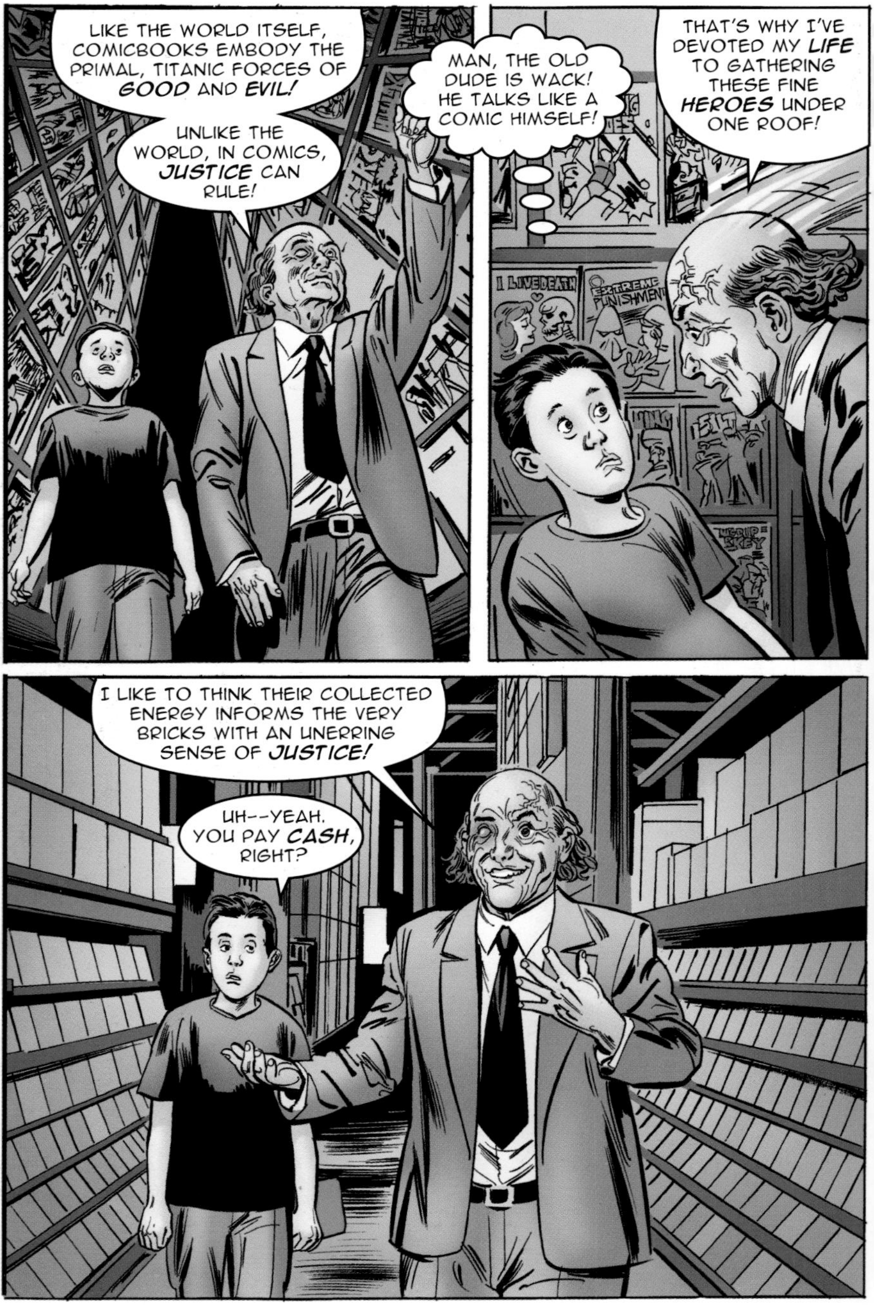
LIKE THE WORLD ITSELF, COMICBOOKS EMBODY THE PRIMAL, TITANIC FORCES OF **GOOD** AND **EVIL!**
UNLIKE THE WORLD, IN COMICS, **JUSTICE** CAN RULE!
MAN, THE OLD DUDE IS WACK! HE TALKS LIKE A COMIC HIMSELF!
THAT'S WHY I'VE DEVOTED MY **LIFE** TO GATHERING THESE FINE **HEROES** UNDER ONE ROOF!
I LIVE DEATH
EXTREME PUNISHMENT
I LIKE TO THINK THEIR COLLECTED ENERGY INFORMS THE VERY BRICKS WITH AN UNERRING SENSE OF **JUSTICE!**
UH--YEAH. YOU PAY **CASH**, RIGHT?

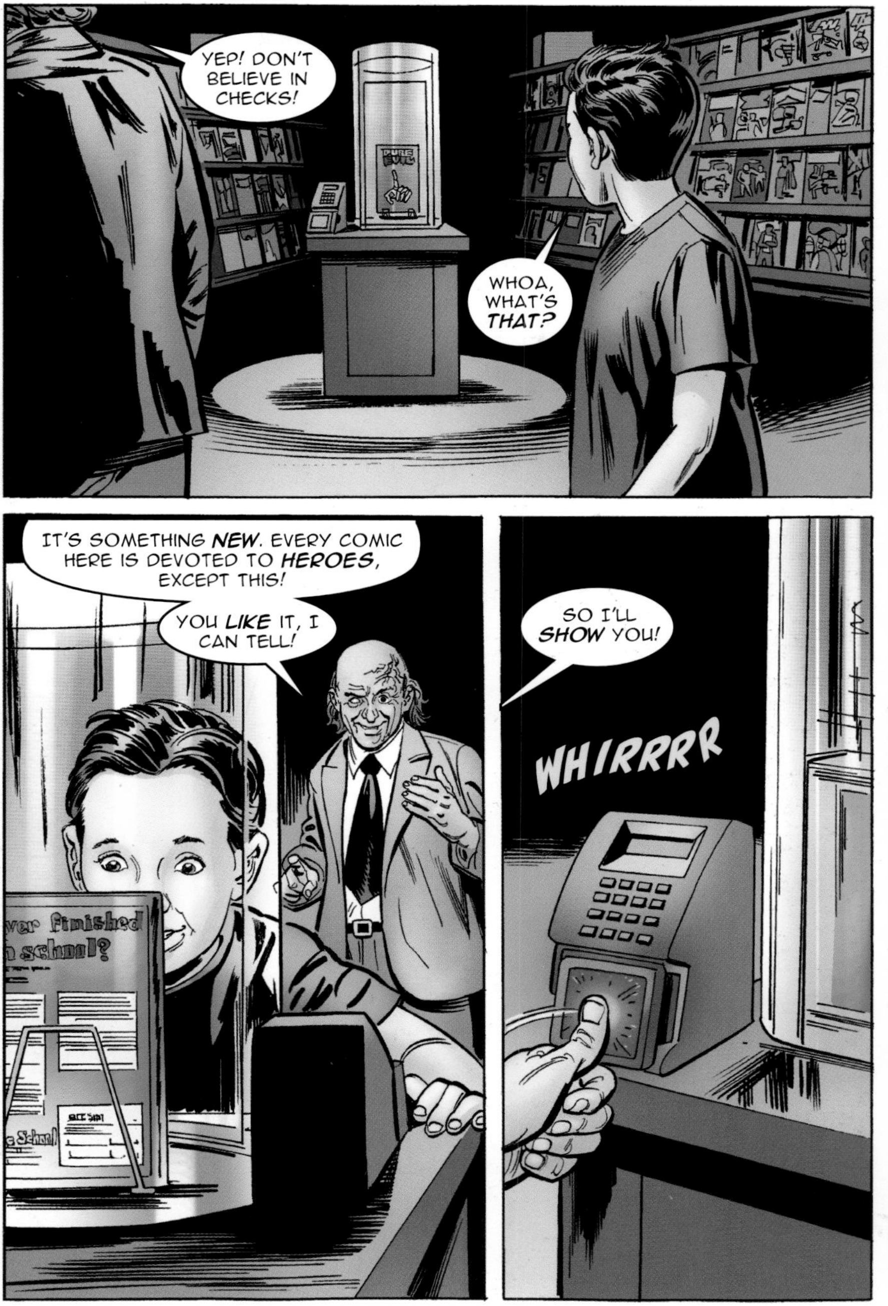
YEP! DON'T BELIEVE IN CHECKS!
WHOA, WHAT'S THAT?
IT'S SOMETHING NEW. EVERY COMIC HERE IS DEVOTED TO HEROES, EXCEPT THIS!
YOU LIKE IT, I CAN TELL!
SO I'LL SHOW YOU!
WHIRRRR

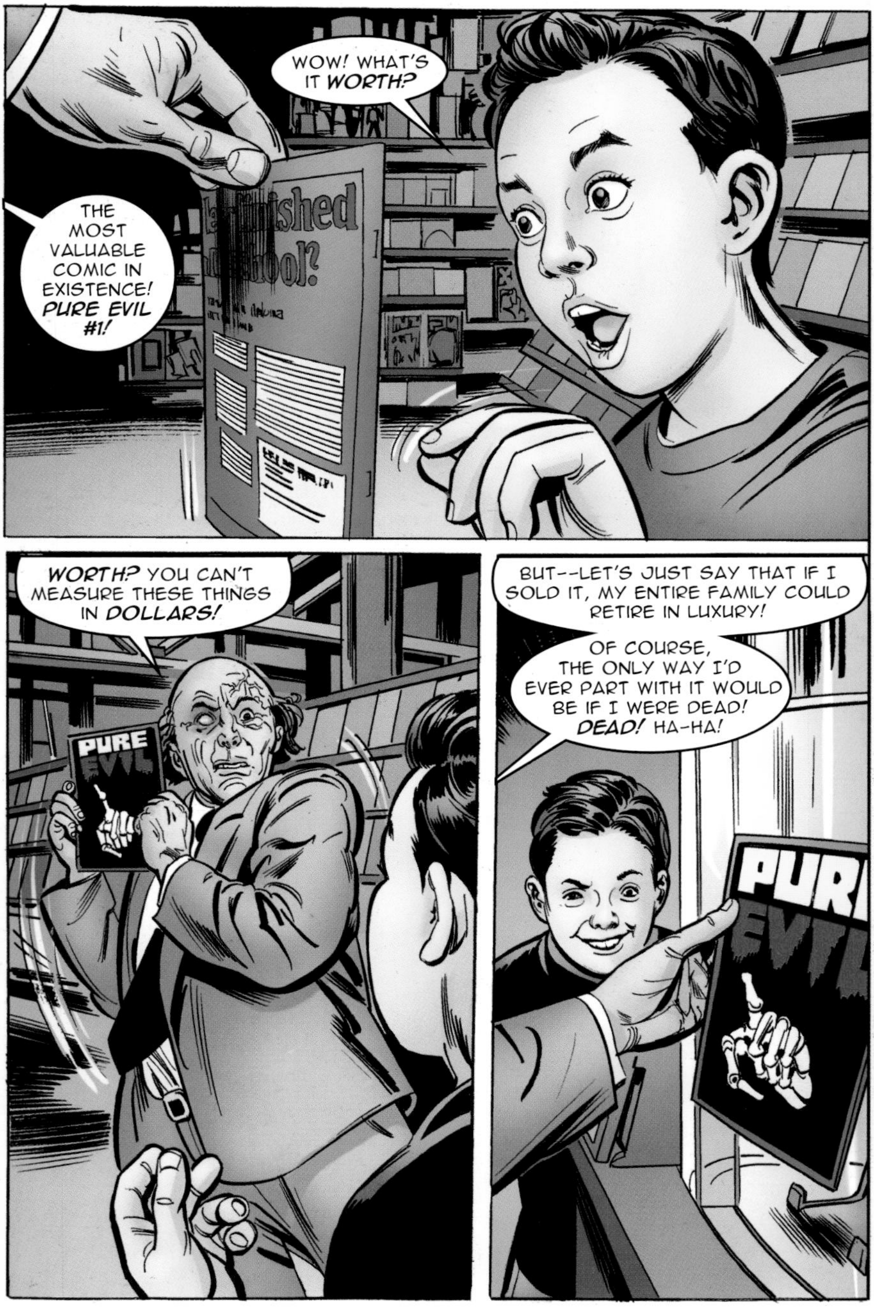
WOW! WHAT'S IT WORTH?
THE MOST VALUABLE COMIC IN EXISTENCE! PURE EVIL #1!
WORTH? YOU CAN'T MEASURE THESE THINGS IN DOLLARS!
PURE EVIL
BUT--LET'S JUST SAY THAT IF I SOLD IT, MY ENTIRE FAMILY COULD RETIRE IN LUXURY!
OF COURSE, THE ONLY WAY I'D EVER PART WITH IT WOULD BE IF I WERE DEAD! DEAD! HA-HA!

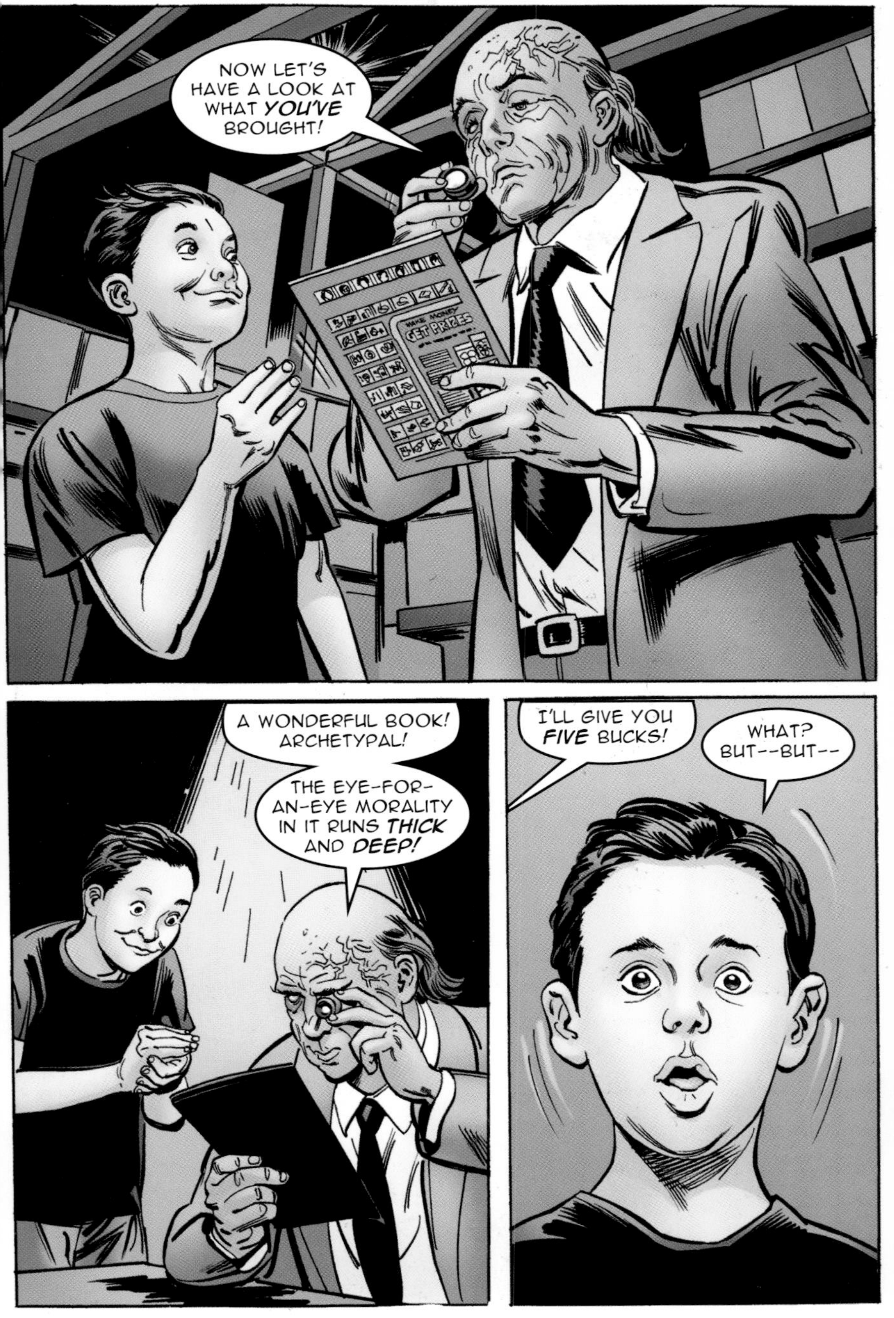
NOW LET'S HAVE A LOOK AT WHAT *YOU'VE* BROUGHT!
MAKE MONEY
GET PRIZES
A WONDERFUL BOOK! ARCHETYPAL!
THE EYE-FOR-AN-EYE MORALITY IN IT RUNS *THICK* AND *DEEP!*
I'LL GIVE YOU *FIVE* BUCKS!
WHAT? BUT--BUT--

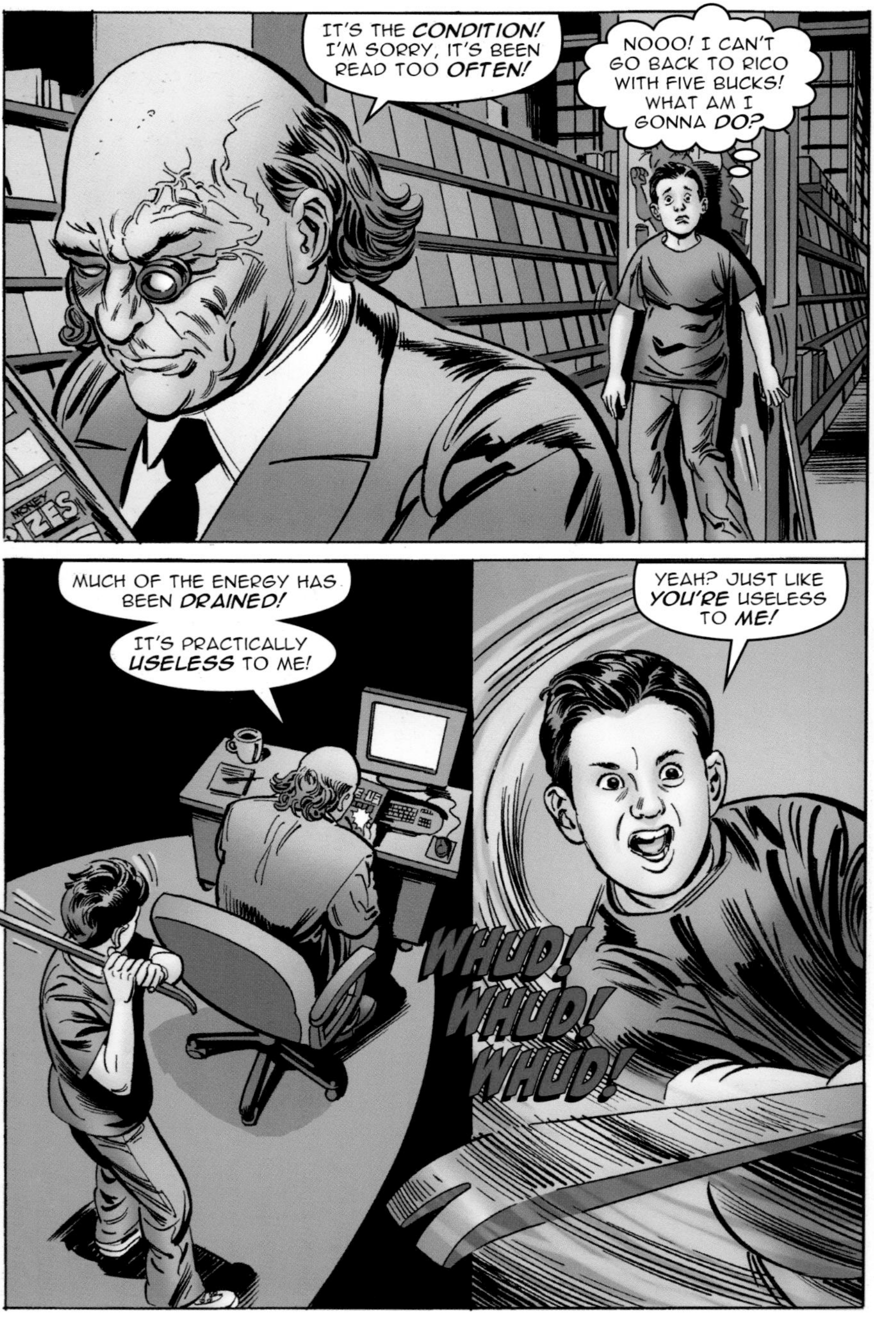
IT'S THE CONDITION! I'M SORRY, IT'S BEEN READ TOO OFTEN!
NOOO! I CAN'T GO BACK TO RICO WITH FIVE BUCKS! WHAT AM I GONNA DO?
MUCH OF THE ENERGY HAS BEEN DRAINED!
IT'S PRACTICALLY USELESS TO ME!
YEAH? JUST LIKE YOU'RE USELESS TO ME!
WHUD! WHUD! WHUD!

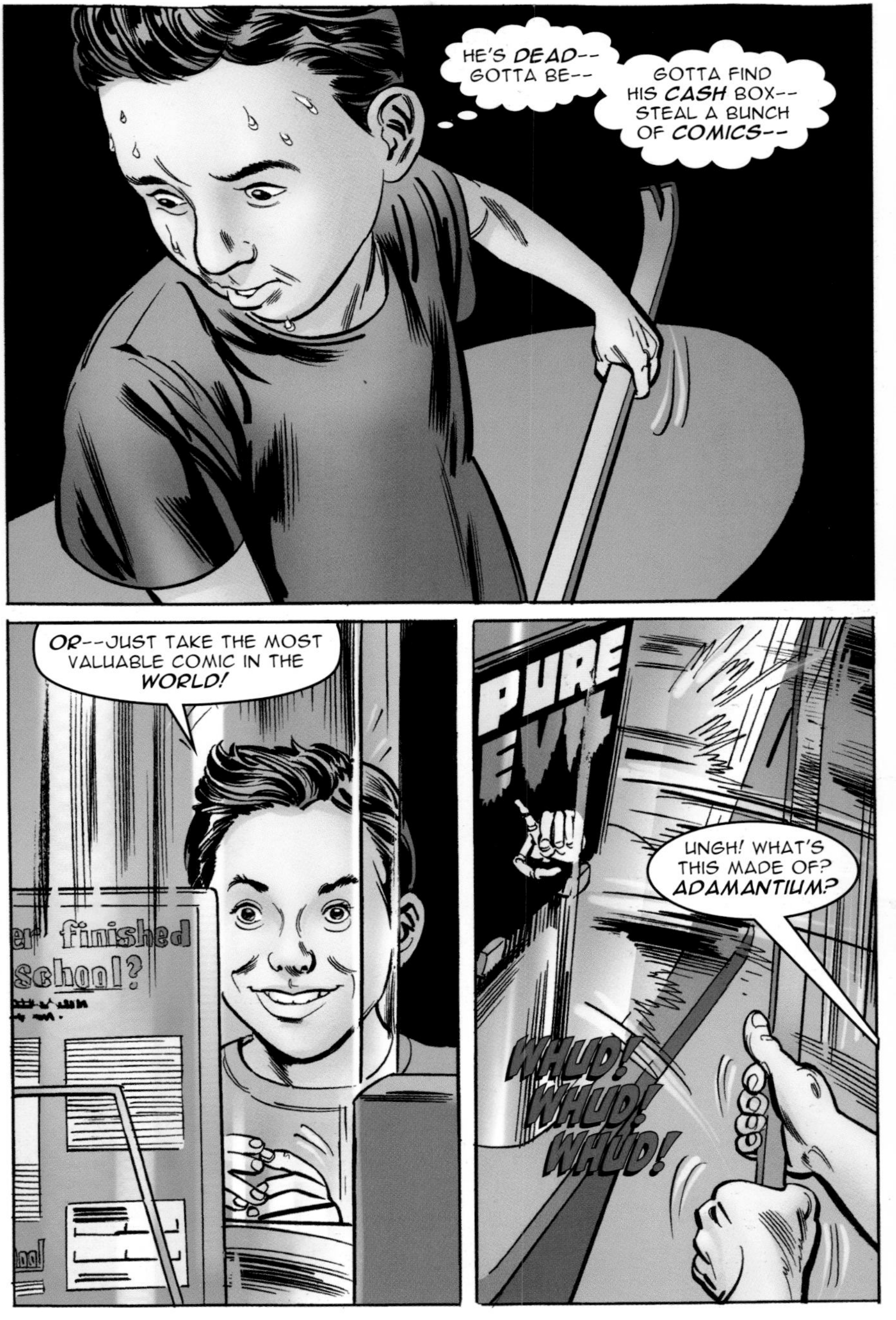
HE'S DEAD-- GOTTA BE--
GOTTA FIND HIS CASH BOX-- STEAL A BUNCH OF COMICS--
OR--JUST TAKE THE MOST VALUABLE COMIC IN THE WORLD!
finished
school?
PURE
UNGH! WHAT'S THIS MADE OF? ADAMANTIUM?
WHUD! WHUD! WHUD!

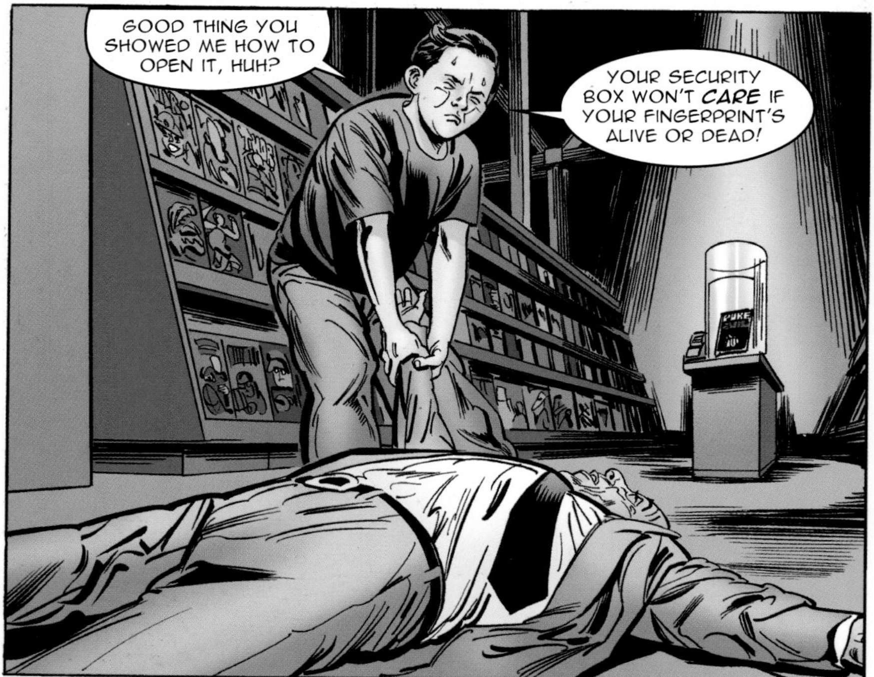
GOOD THING YOU SHOWED ME HOW TO OPEN IT, HUH?
YOUR SECURITY BOX WON'T **CARE** IF YOUR FINGERPRINT'S ALIVE OR DEAD!

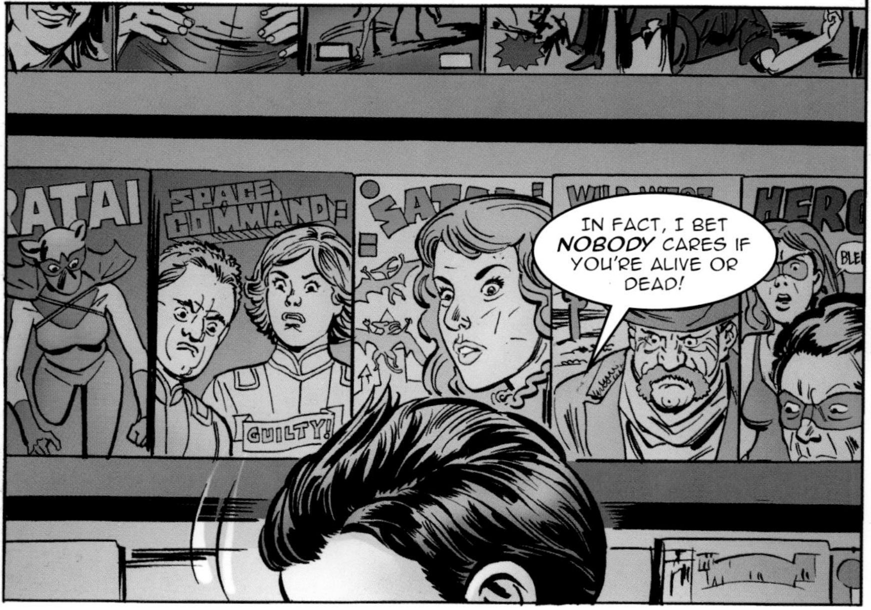
SPACE COMMAND
GUILTY!
IN FACT, I BET **NOBODY** CARES IF YOU'RE ALIVE OR DEAD!

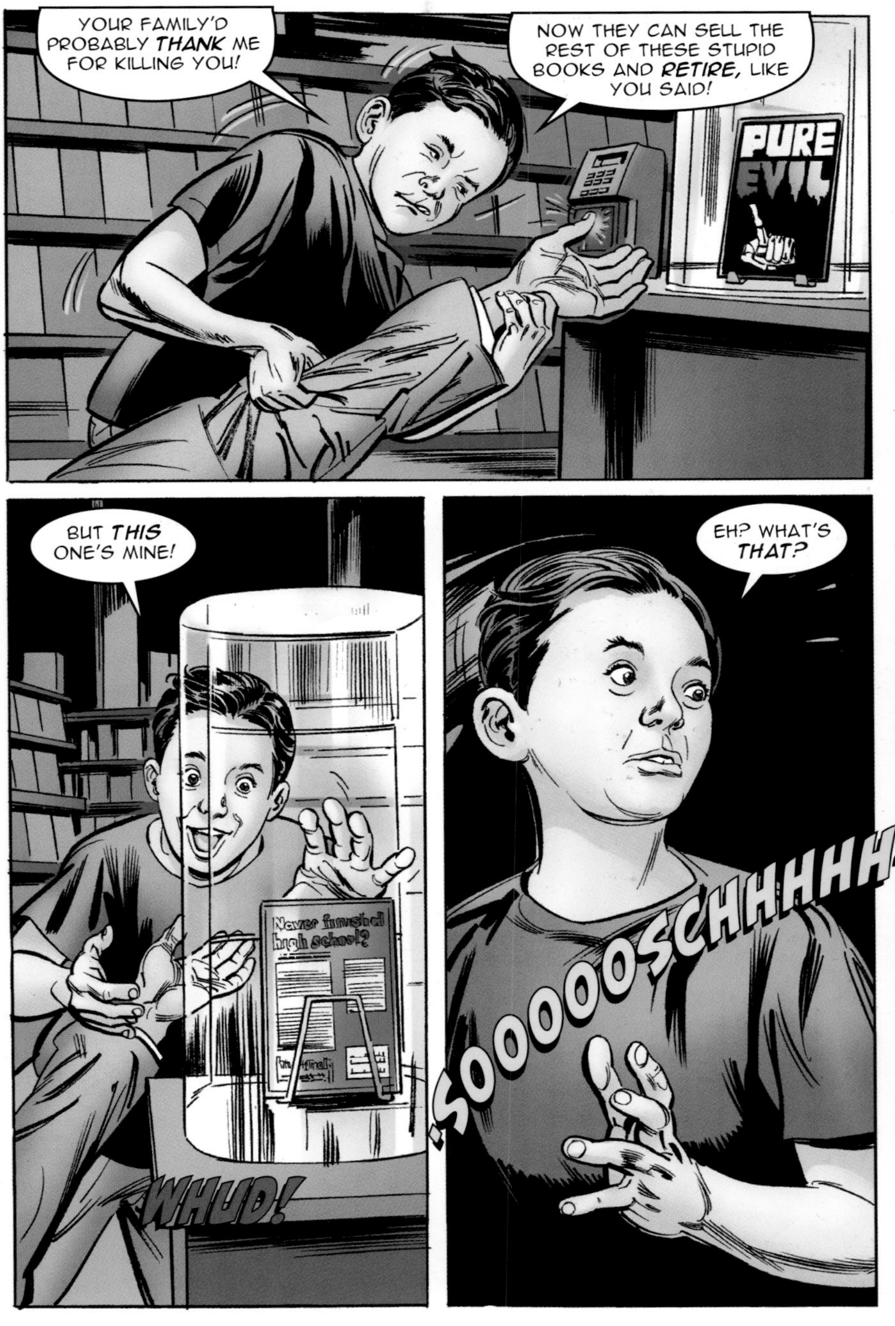
YOUR FAMILY'D PROBABLY THANK ME FOR KILLING YOU!
NOW THEY CAN SELL THE REST OF THESE STUPID BOOKS AND RETIRE, LIKE YOU SAID!
PURE EVIL
BUT THIS ONE'S MINE!
Never finished high school?
WHUD!
EH? WHAT'S THAT?
SOOOOOSCHHHHHH

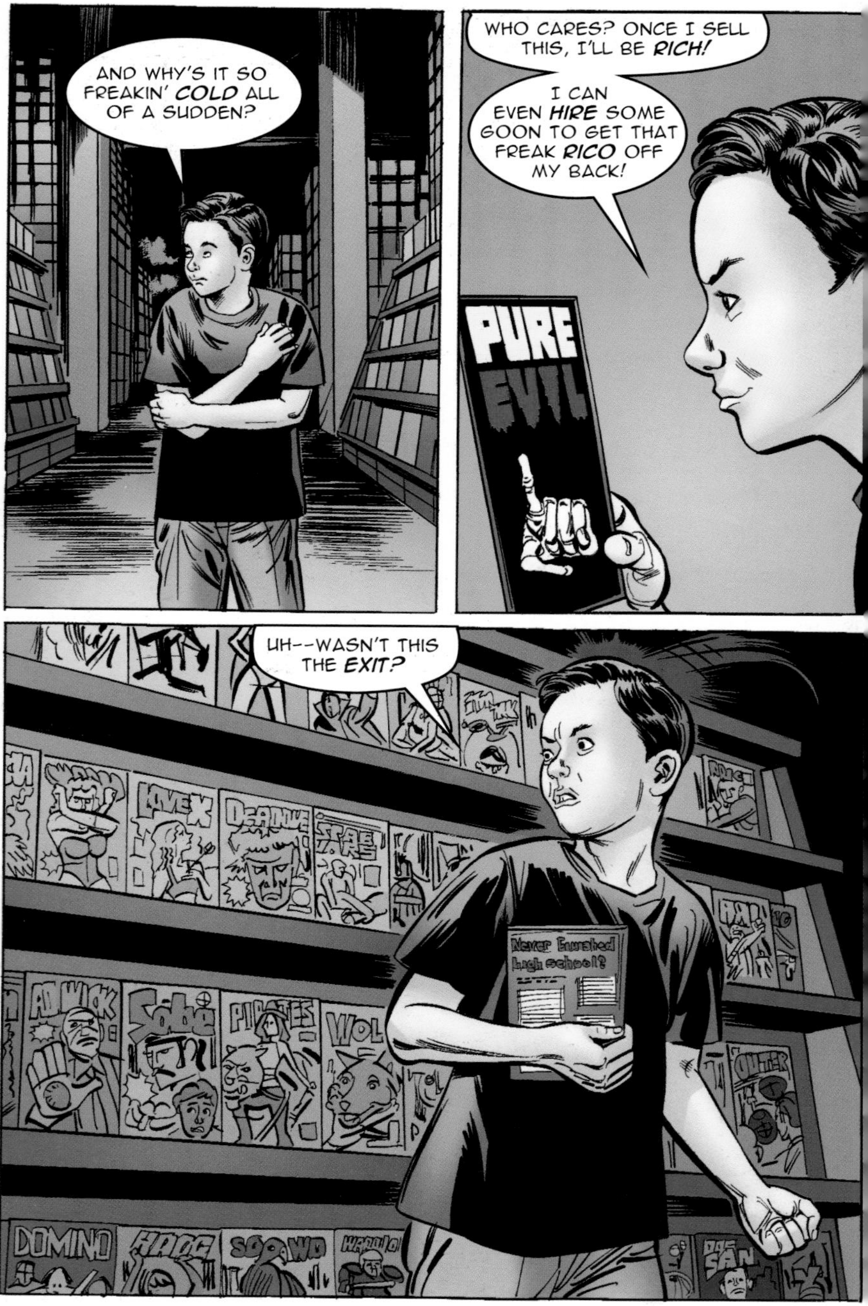
AND WHY'S IT SO FREAKIN' *COLD* ALL OF A SUDDEN?
WHO CARES? ONCE I SELL THIS, I'LL BE *RICH!*
I CAN EVEN *HIRE* SOME GOON TO GET THAT FREAK *RICO* OFF MY BACK!
PURE EVIL
UH--WASN'T THIS THE *EXIT?*

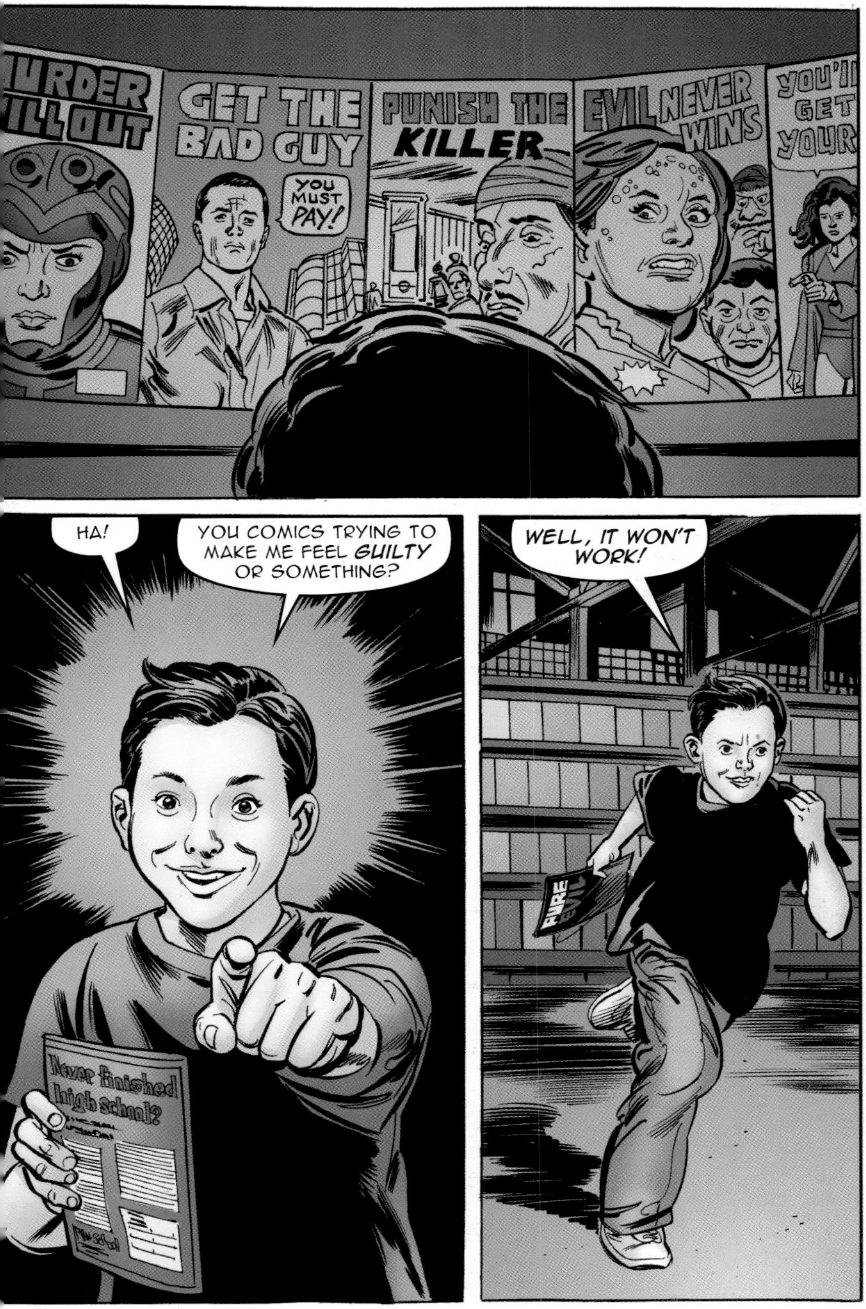
GET THE BAD GUY
YOU MUST PAY!
PUNISH THE KILLER
EVIL NEVER WINS
HA!
YOU COMICS TRYING TO MAKE ME FEEL GUILTY OR SOMETHING?
Never finished high school?
WELL, IT WON'T WORK!

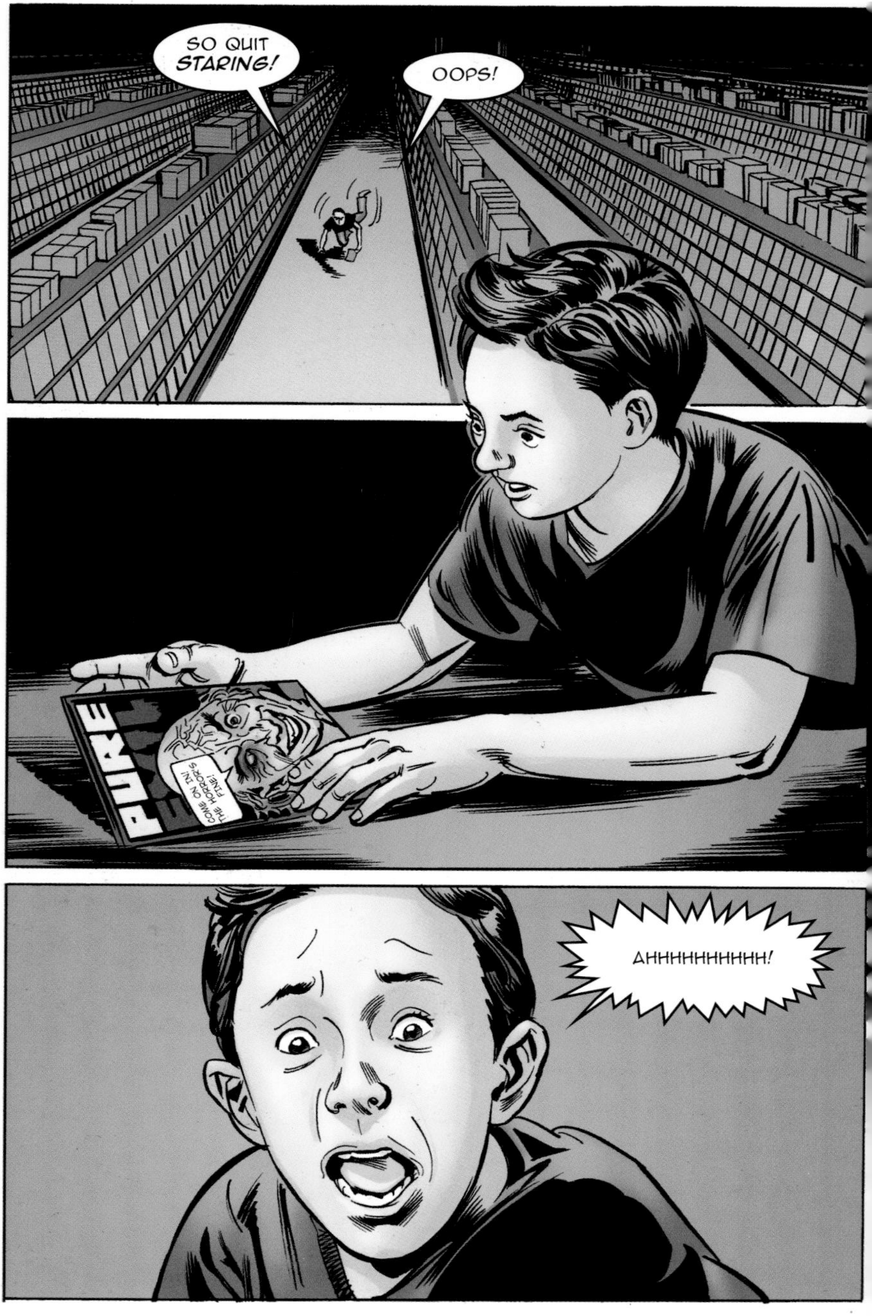
SO QUIT STARING!
OOPS!
PURE
COME ON IN! THE HORROR'S FINE!
AHHHHHHHHHH!

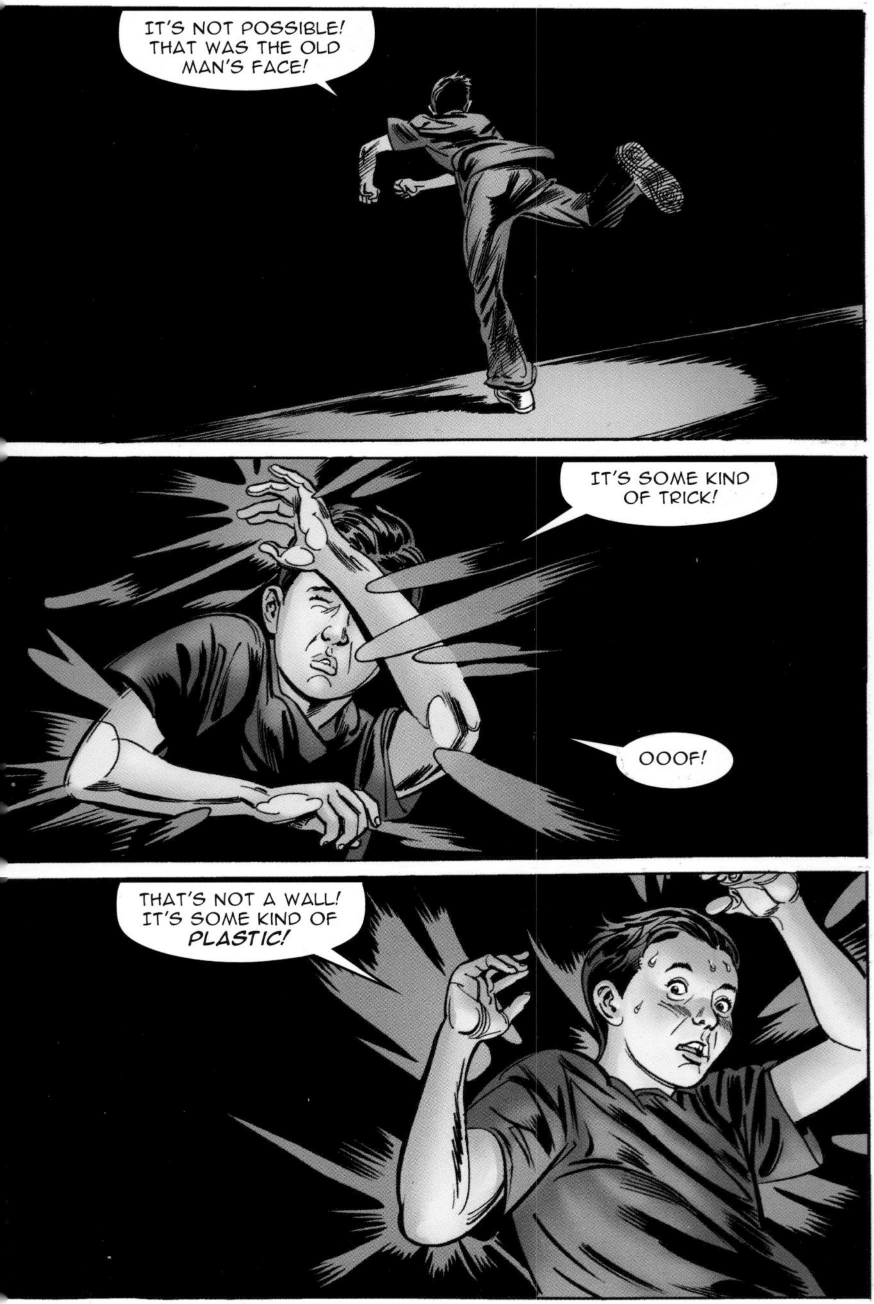
IT'S NOT POSSIBLE! THAT WAS THE OLD MAN'S FACE!
IT'S SOME KIND OF TRICK!
OOOF!
THAT'S NOT A WALL! IT'S SOME KIND OF *PLASTIC!*

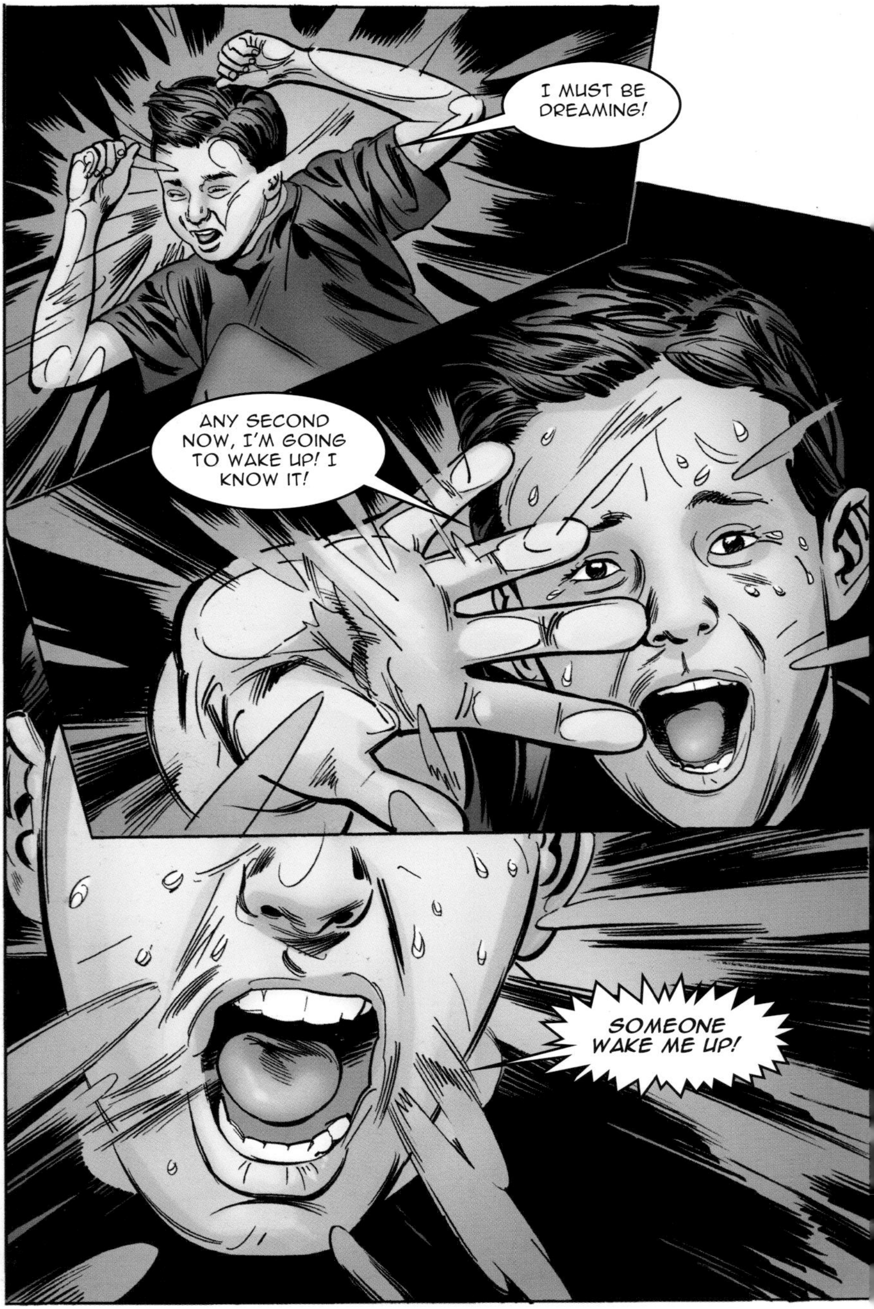
I MUST BE DREAMING!
ANY SECOND NOW, I'M GOING TO WAKE UP! I KNOW IT!
SOMEONE WAKE ME UP!

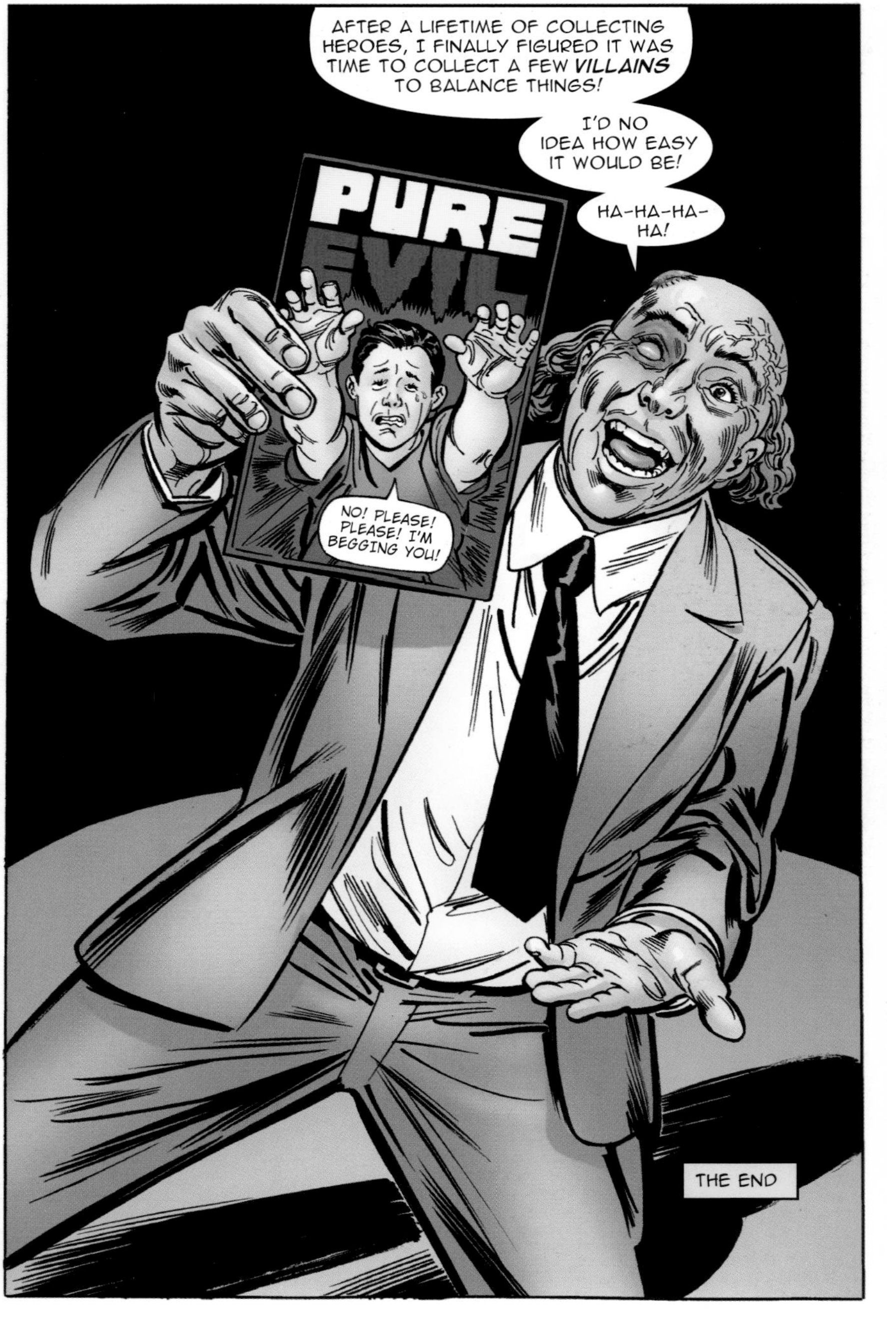
AFTER A LIFETIME OF COLLECTING HEROES, I FINALLY FIGURED IT WAS TIME TO COLLECT A FEW *VILLAINS* TO BALANCE THINGS!
I'D NO IDEA HOW EASY IT WOULD BE!
HA-HA-HA-HA!
PURE EVIL
NO! PLEASE! PLEASE! I'M BEGGING YOU!
THE END

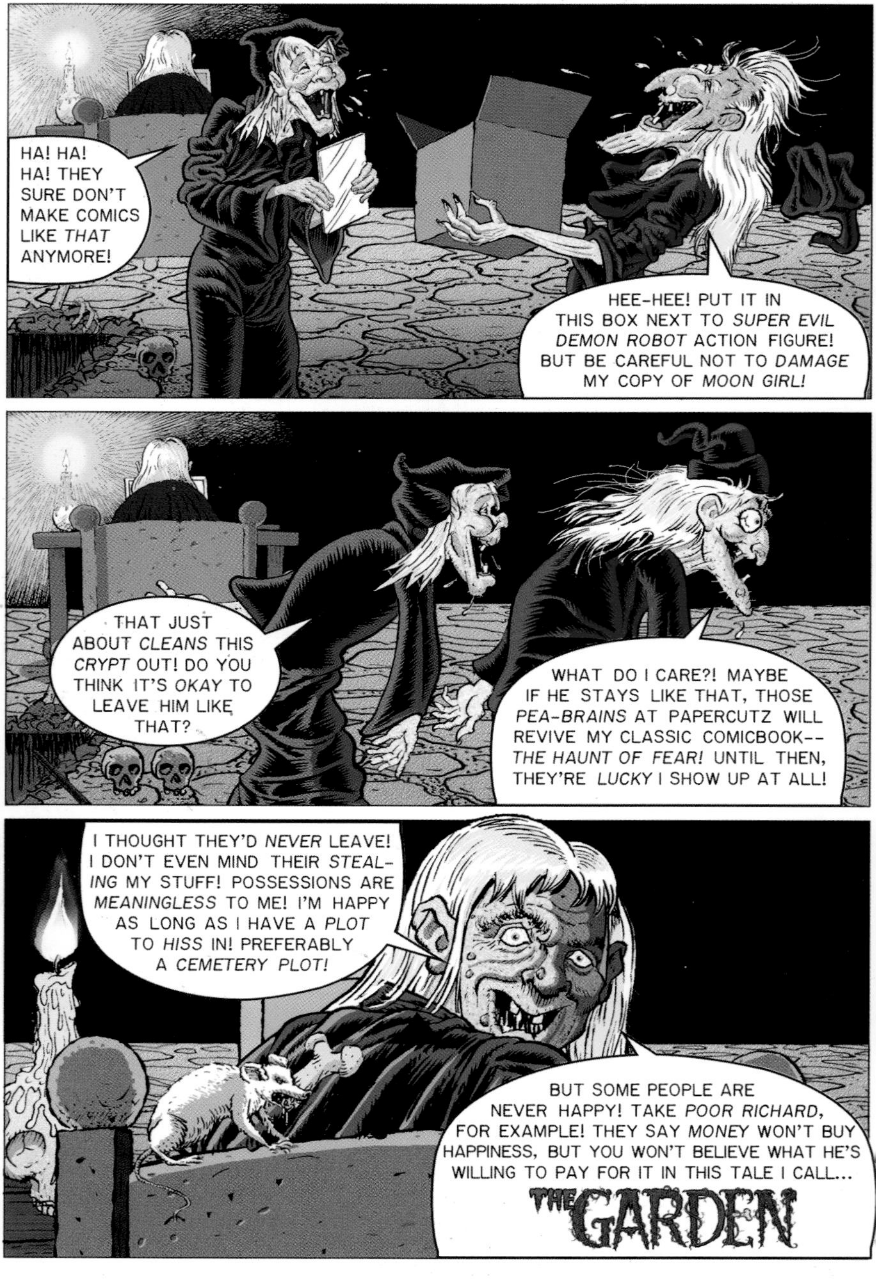
HA! HA! HA! THEY SURE DON'T MAKE COMICS LIKE *THAT* ANYMORE!
HEE-HEE! PUT IT IN THIS BOX NEXT TO *SUPER EVIL DEMON ROBOT* ACTION FIGURE! BUT BE CAREFUL NOT TO *DAMAGE* MY COPY OF *MOON GIRL!*
THAT JUST ABOUT *CLEANS* THIS *CRYPT* OUT! DO YOU THINK IT'S *OKAY* TO LEAVE HIM LIKE THAT?
WHAT DO I CARE?! MAYBE IF HE STAYS LIKE THAT, THOSE *PEA-BRAINS* AT PAPERCUTZ WILL REVIVE MY CLASSIC COMICBOOK-- *THE HAUNT OF FEAR!* UNTIL THEN, THEY'RE *LUCKY* I SHOW UP AT ALL!
I THOUGHT THEY'D *NEVER* LEAVE! I DON'T EVEN MIND THEIR *STEALING* MY STUFF! POSSESSIONS ARE *MEANINGLESS* TO ME! I'M HAPPY AS LONG AS I HAVE A *PLOT* TO *HISS* IN! PREFERABLY A *CEMETERY PLOT!*
BUT SOME PEOPLE ARE NEVER HAPPY! TAKE *POOR RICHARD*, FOR EXAMPLE! THEY SAY *MONEY* WON'T BUY HAPPINESS, BUT YOU WON'T BELIEVE WHAT HE'S WILLING TO PAY FOR IT IN THIS TALE I CALL...
THE GARDEN

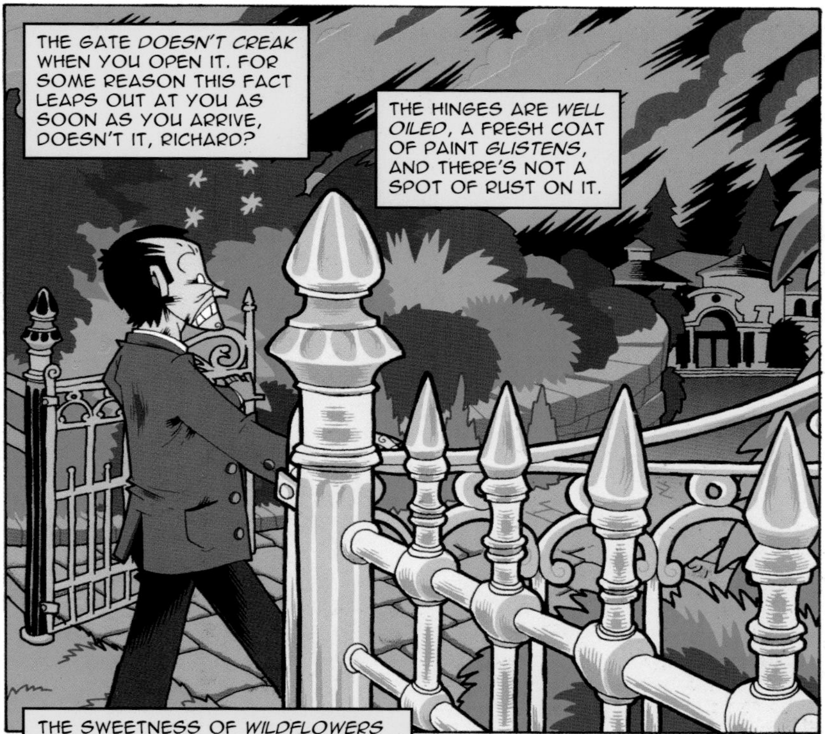
THE GATE *DOESN'T CREAK* WHEN YOU OPEN IT. FOR SOME REASON THIS FACT LEAPS OUT AT YOU AS SOON AS YOU ARRIVE, DOESN'T IT, RICHARD?
THE HINGES ARE *WELL OILED*, A FRESH COAT OF PAINT *GLISTENS*, AND THERE'S NOT A SPOT OF RUST ON IT.

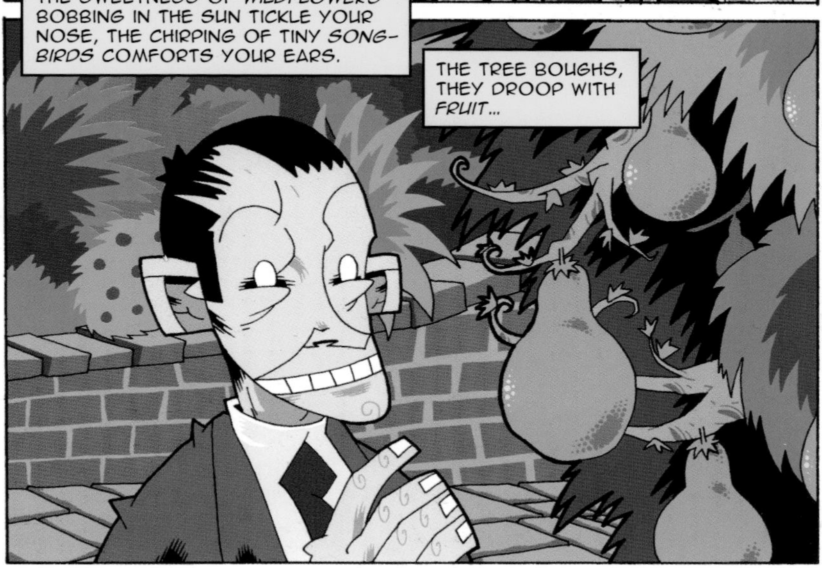
THE SWEETNESS OF *WILDFLOWERS* BOBBING IN THE SUN TICKLE YOUR NOSE, THE CHIRPING OF TINY *SONG-BIRDS* COMFORTS YOUR EARS.
THE TREE BOUGHS, THEY DROOP WITH *FRUIT*...

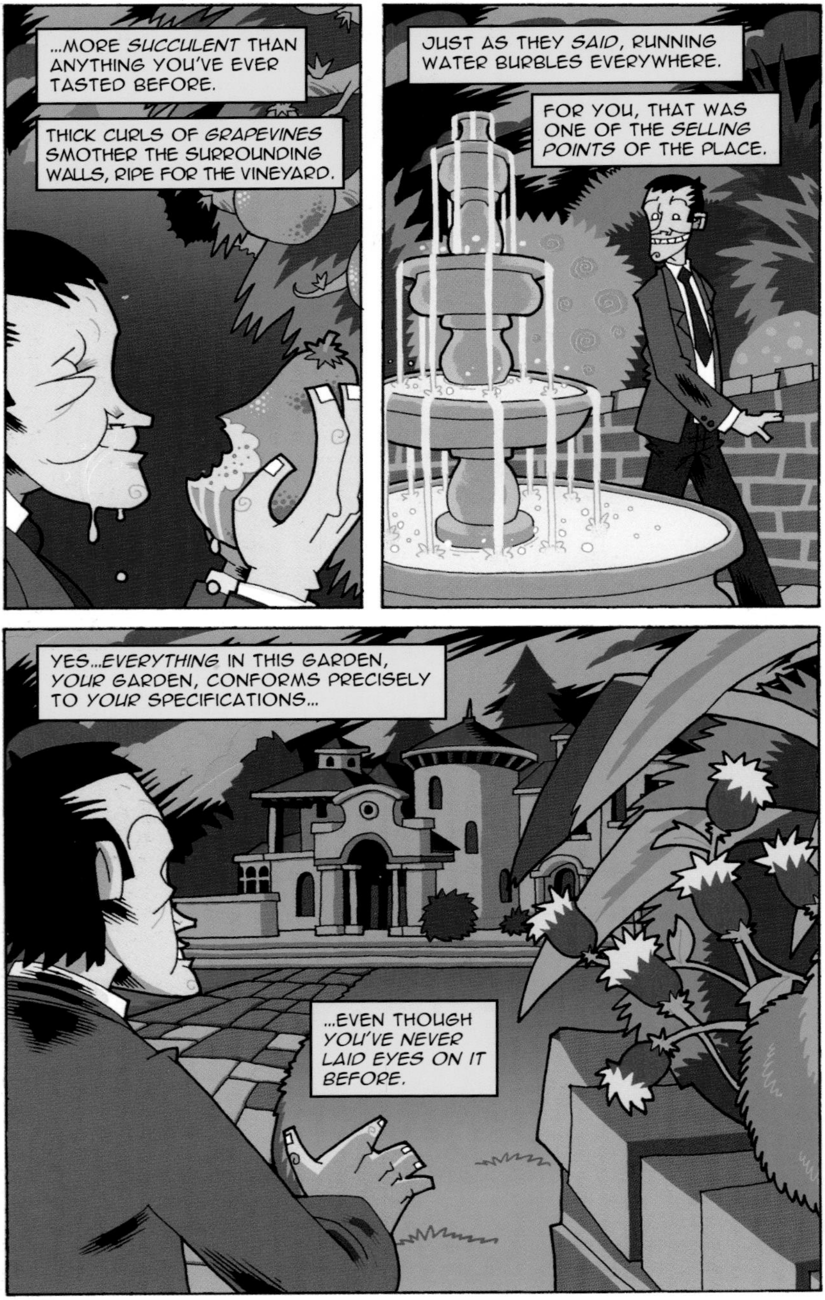
...MORE SUCCULENT THAN ANYTHING YOU'VE EVER TASTED BEFORE.
THICK CURLS OF GRAPEVINES SMOTHER THE SURROUNDING WALLS, RIPE FOR THE VINEYARD.
JUST AS THEY SAID, RUNNING WATER BURBLES EVERYWHERE.
FOR YOU, THAT WAS ONE OF THE SELLING POINTS OF THE PLACE.
YES...EVERYTHING IN THIS GARDEN, YOUR GARDEN, CONFORMS PRECISELY TO YOUR SPECIFICATIONS...
...EVEN THOUGH YOU'VE NEVER LAID EYES ON IT BEFORE.

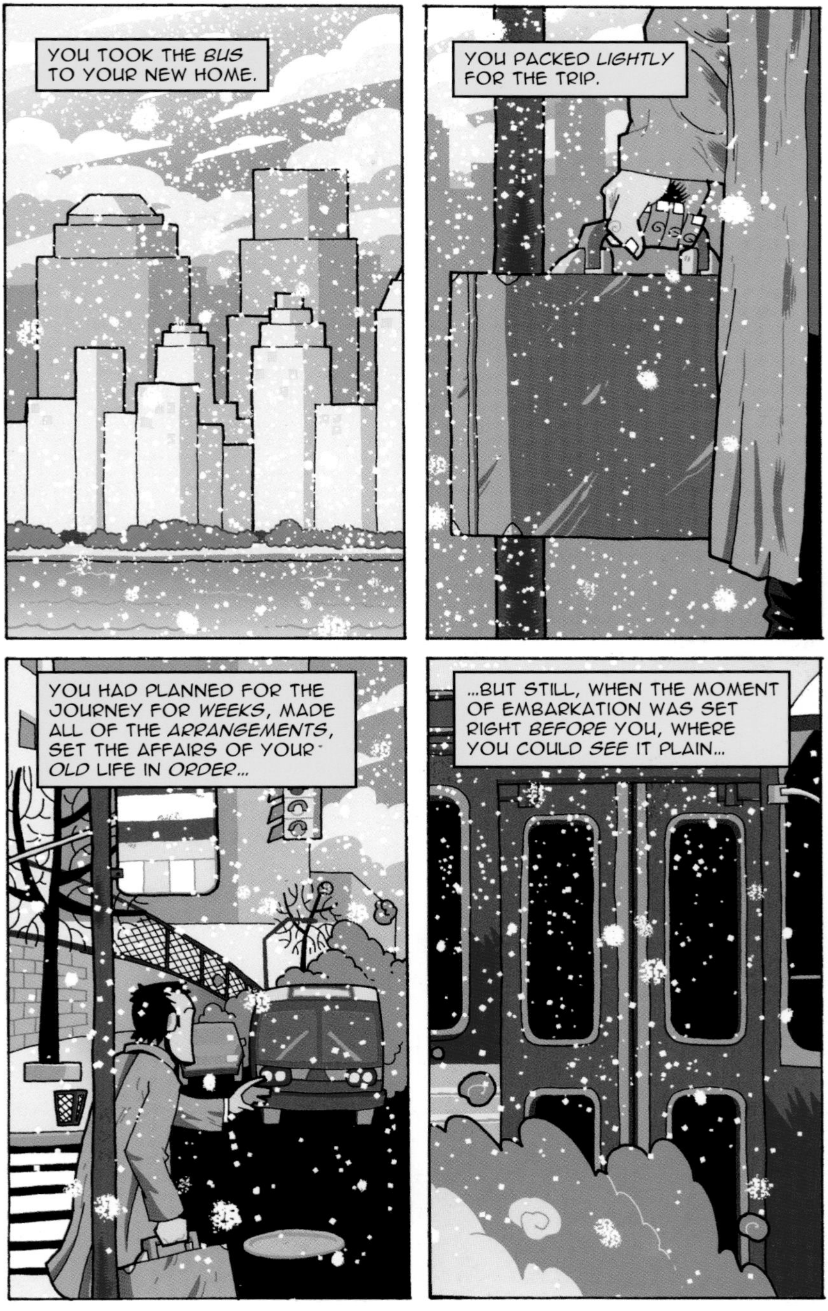
YOU TOOK THE BUS TO YOUR NEW HOME.
YOU PACKED LIGHTLY FOR THE TRIP.
YOU HAD PLANNED FOR THE JOURNEY FOR WEEKS, MADE ALL OF THE ARRANGEMENTS, SET THE AFFAIRS OF YOUR OLD LIFE IN ORDER...
...BUT STILL, WHEN THE MOMENT OF EMBARKATION WAS SET RIGHT BEFORE YOU, WHERE YOU COULD SEE IT PLAIN...

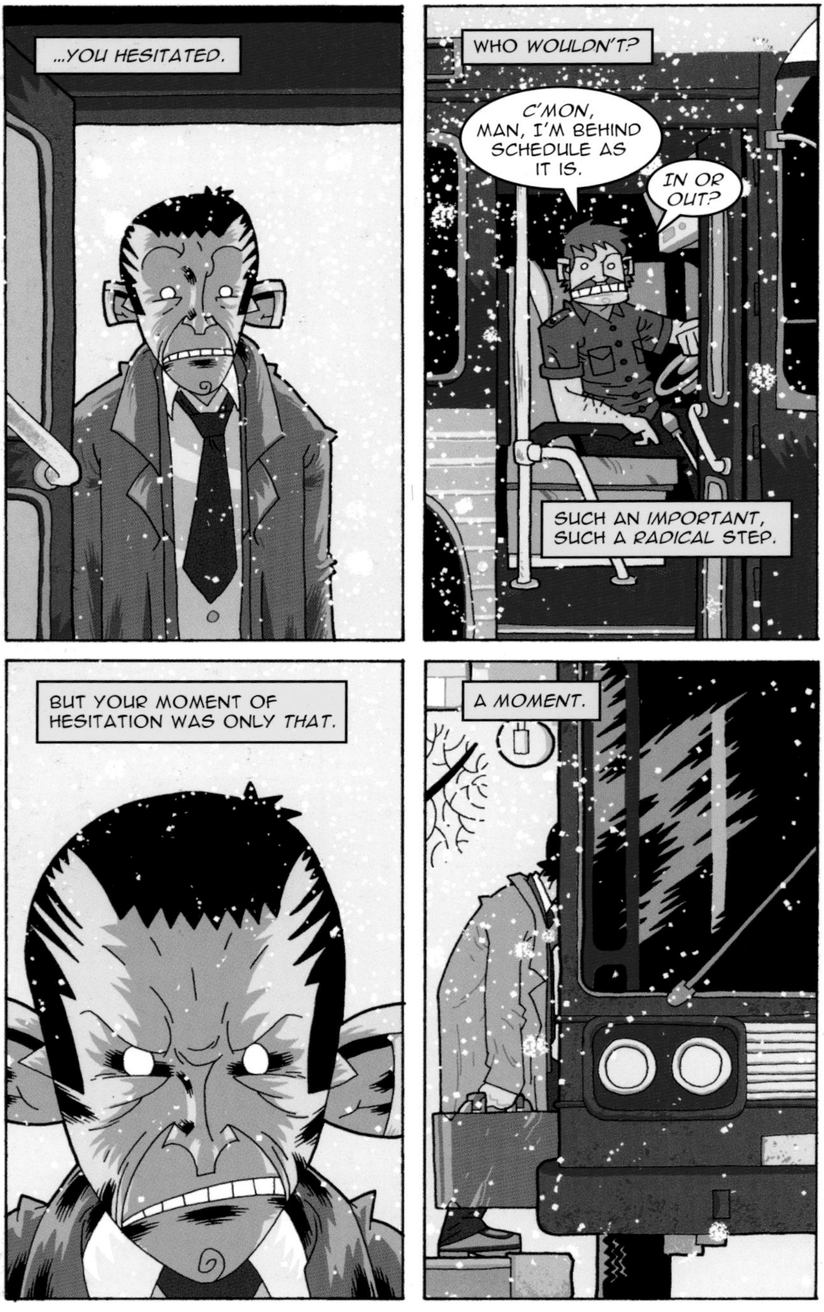
...YOU HESITATED.
WHO WOULDN'T?
C'MON, MAN, I'M BEHIND SCHEDULE AS IT IS.
IN OR OUT?
SUCH AN IMPORTANT, SUCH A RADICAL STEP.
BUT YOUR MOMENT OF HESITATION WAS ONLY THAT.
A MOMENT.

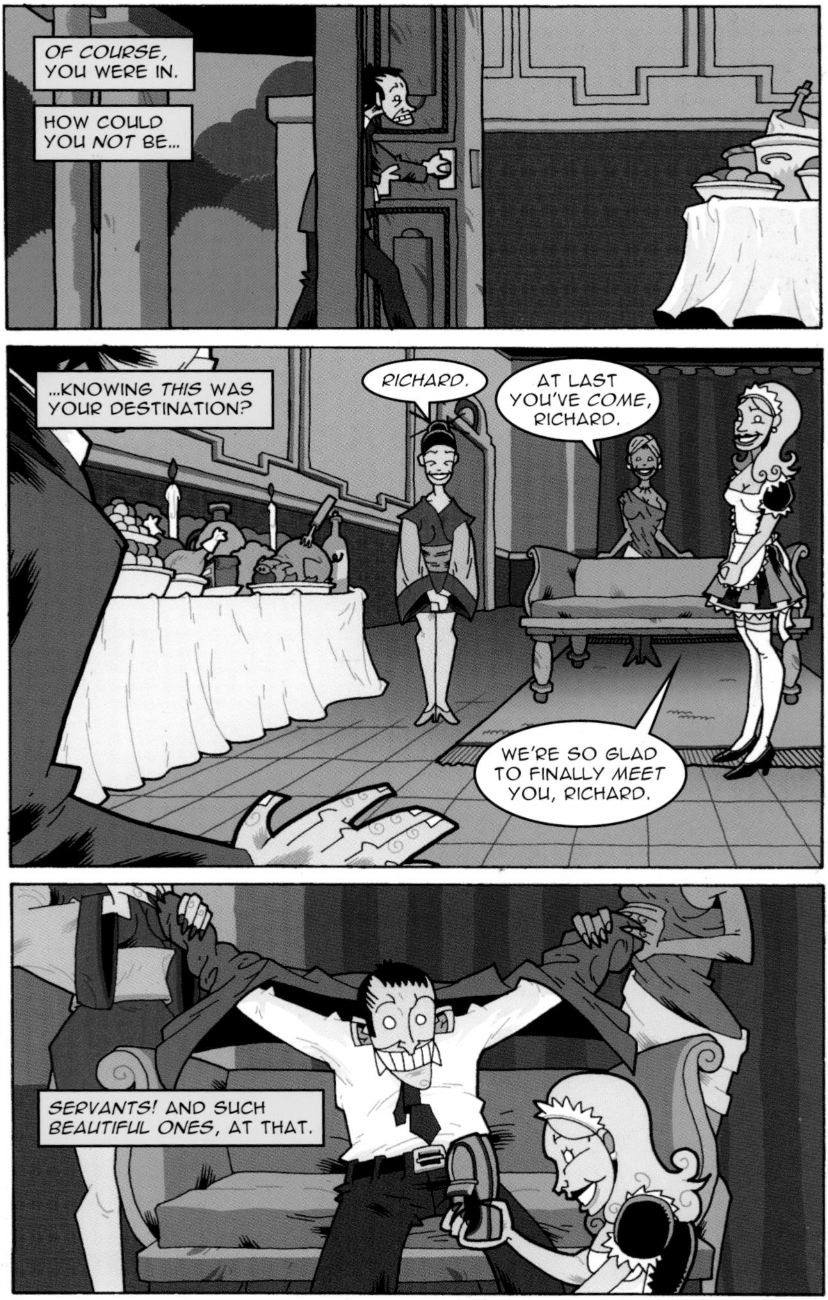
OF COURSE, YOU WERE IN.
HOW COULD YOU NOT BE...
...KNOWING THIS WAS YOUR DESTINATION?
RICHARD.
AT LAST YOU'VE COME, RICHARD.
WE'RE SO GLAD TO FINALLY MEET YOU, RICHARD.
SERVANTS! AND SUCH BEAUTIFUL ONES, AT THAT.

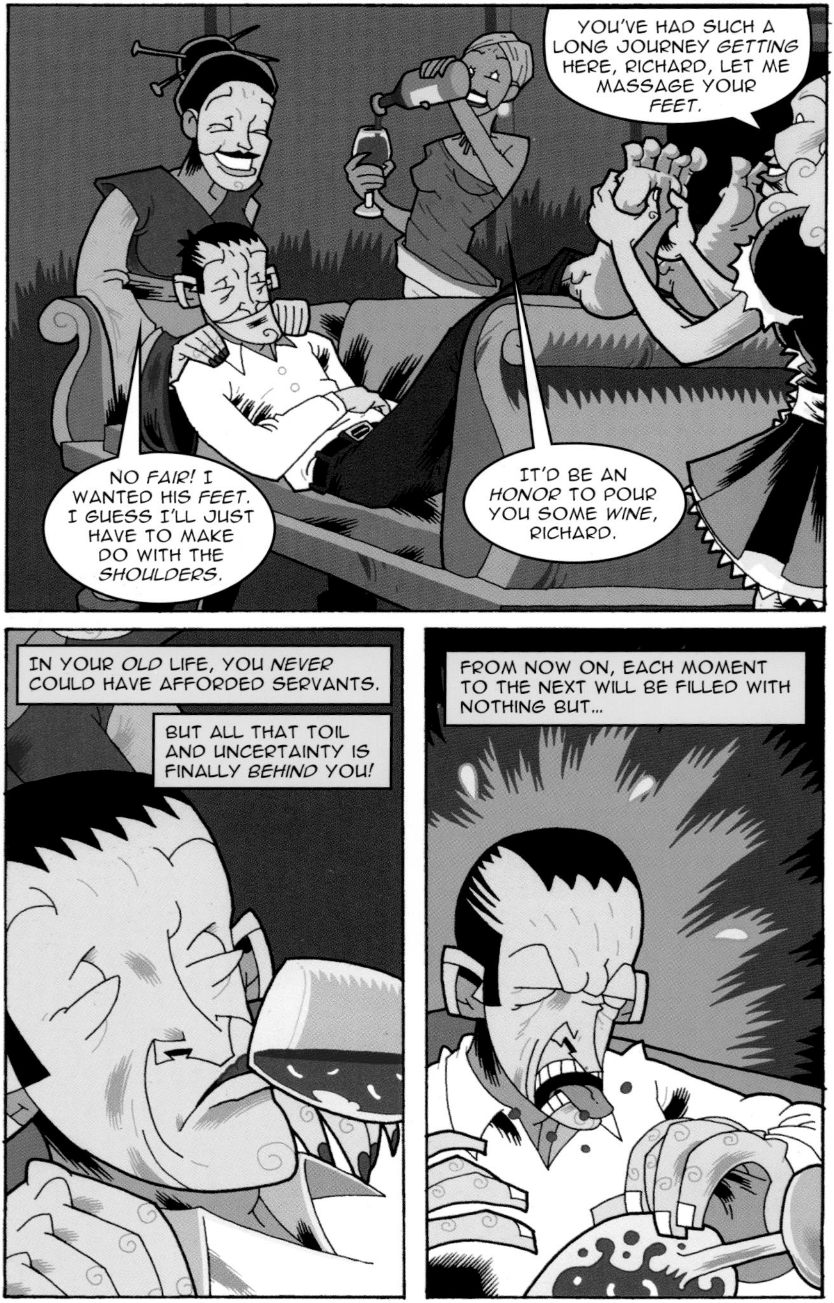
YOU'VE HAD SUCH A LONG JOURNEY *GETTING* HERE, RICHARD, LET ME MASSAGE YOUR *FEET*.
NO *FAIR*! I WANTED HIS *FEET*. I GUESS I'LL JUST HAVE TO MAKE DO WITH THE *SHOULDERS*.
IT'D BE AN *HONOR* TO POUR YOU SOME *WINE*, RICHARD.
IN YOUR *OLD* LIFE, YOU *NEVER* COULD HAVE AFFORDED SERVANTS.
BUT ALL THAT TOIL AND UNCERTAINTY IS FINALLY *BEHIND* YOU!
FROM NOW ON, EACH MOMENT TO THE NEXT WILL BE FILLED WITH NOTHING BUT...

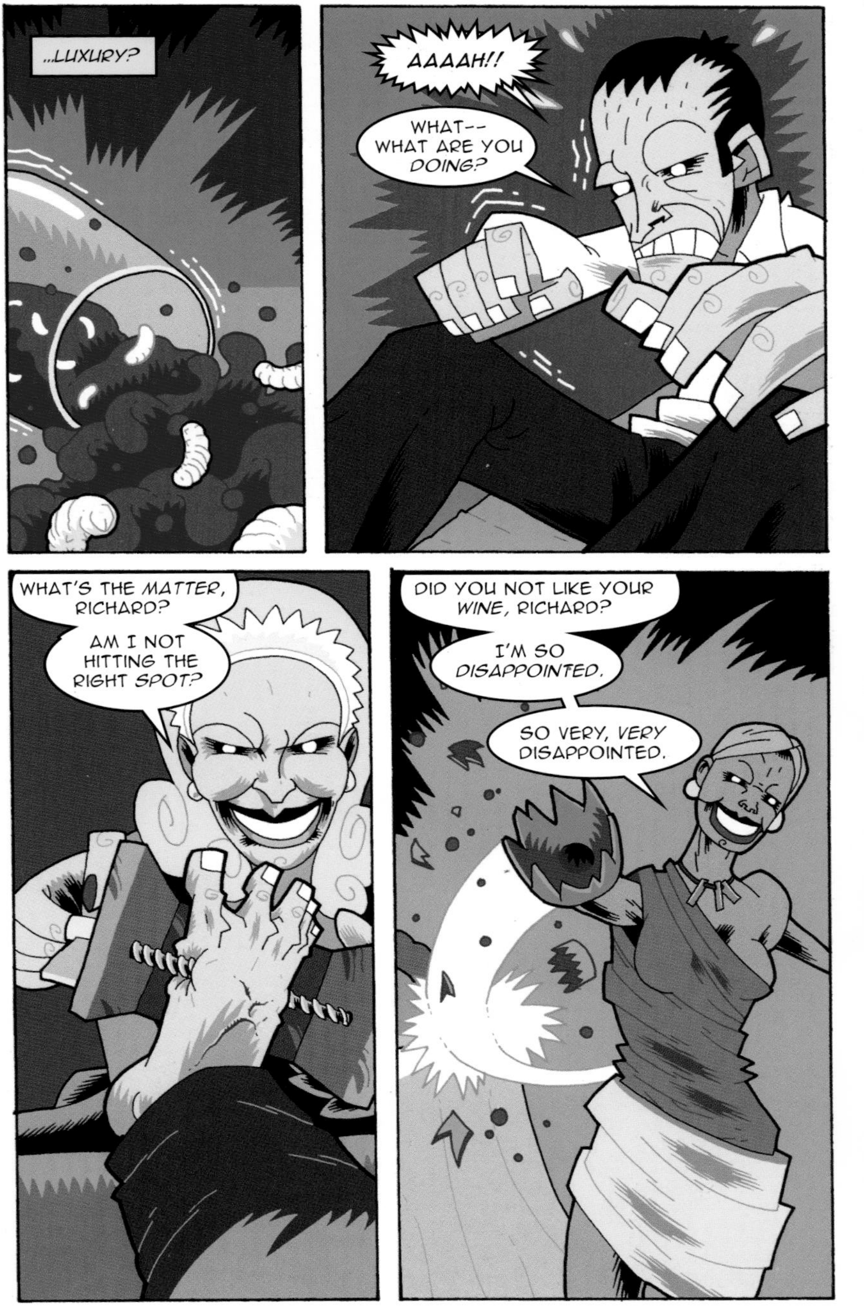

...LUXURY?
AAAAH!!
WHAT--
WHAT ARE YOU DOING?
WHAT'S THE MATTER, RICHARD?
AM I NOT HITTING THE RIGHT SPOT?
DID YOU NOT LIKE YOUR WINE, RICHARD?
I'M SO DISAPPOINTED.
SO VERY, VERY DISAPPOINTED.

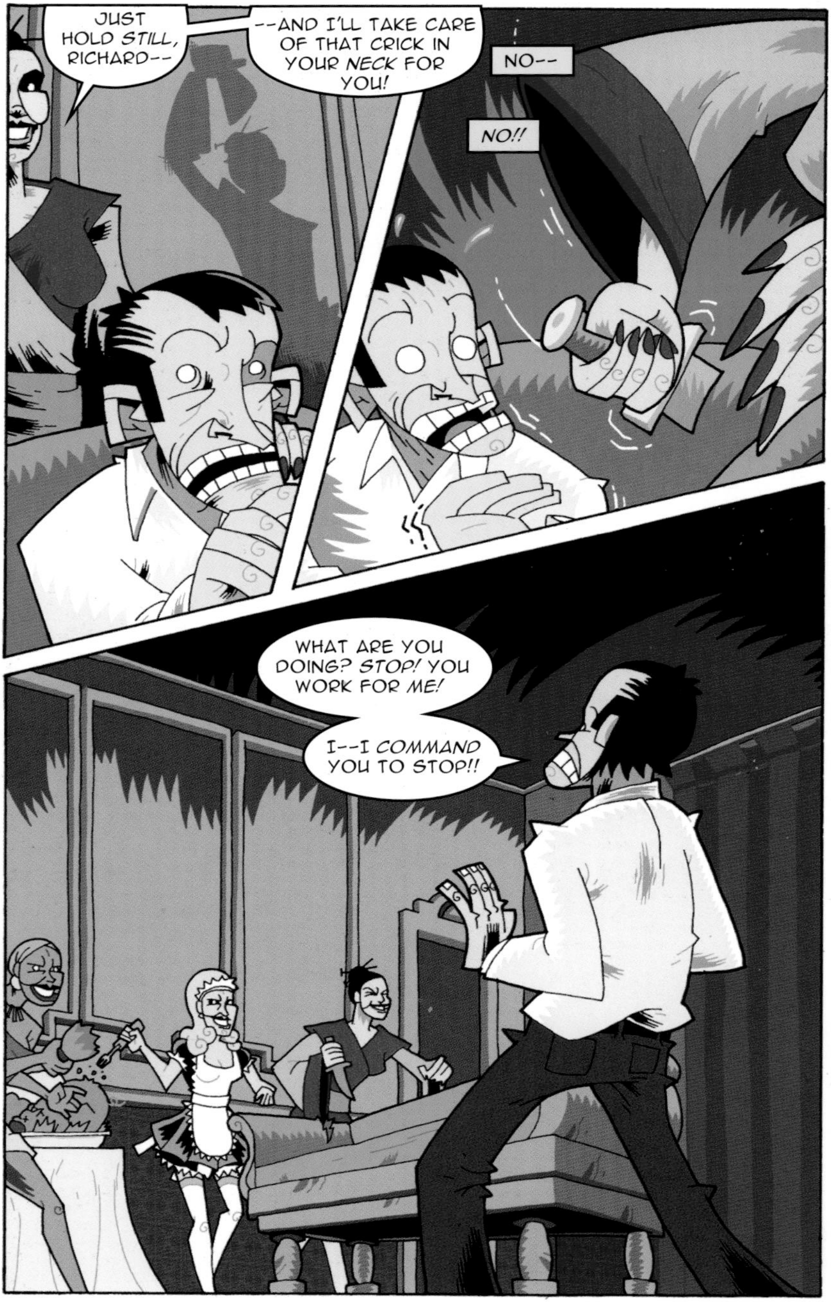
JUST HOLD STILL, RICHARD--
--AND I'LL TAKE CARE OF THAT CRICK IN YOUR NECK FOR YOU!
NO--
NO!!
WHAT ARE YOU DOING? STOP! YOU WORK FOR ME!
I--I COMMAND YOU TO STOP!!

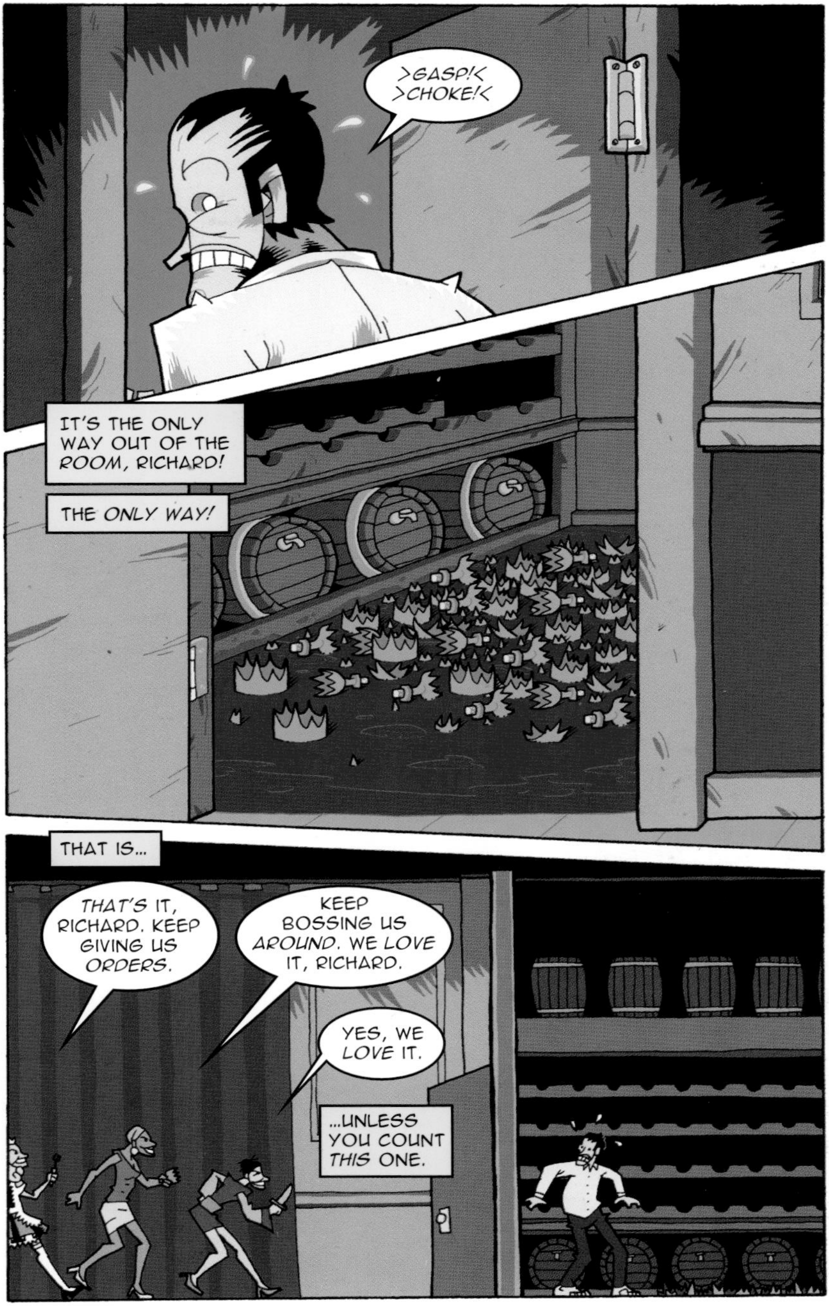
>GASP!< >CHOKE!<
IT'S THE ONLY WAY OUT OF THE ROOM, RICHARD!
THE ONLY WAY!
THAT IS...
THAT'S IT, RICHARD. KEEP GIVING US ORDERS.
KEEP BOSSING US AROUND. WE LOVE IT, RICHARD.
YES, WE LOVE IT.
...UNLESS YOU COUNT THIS ONE.

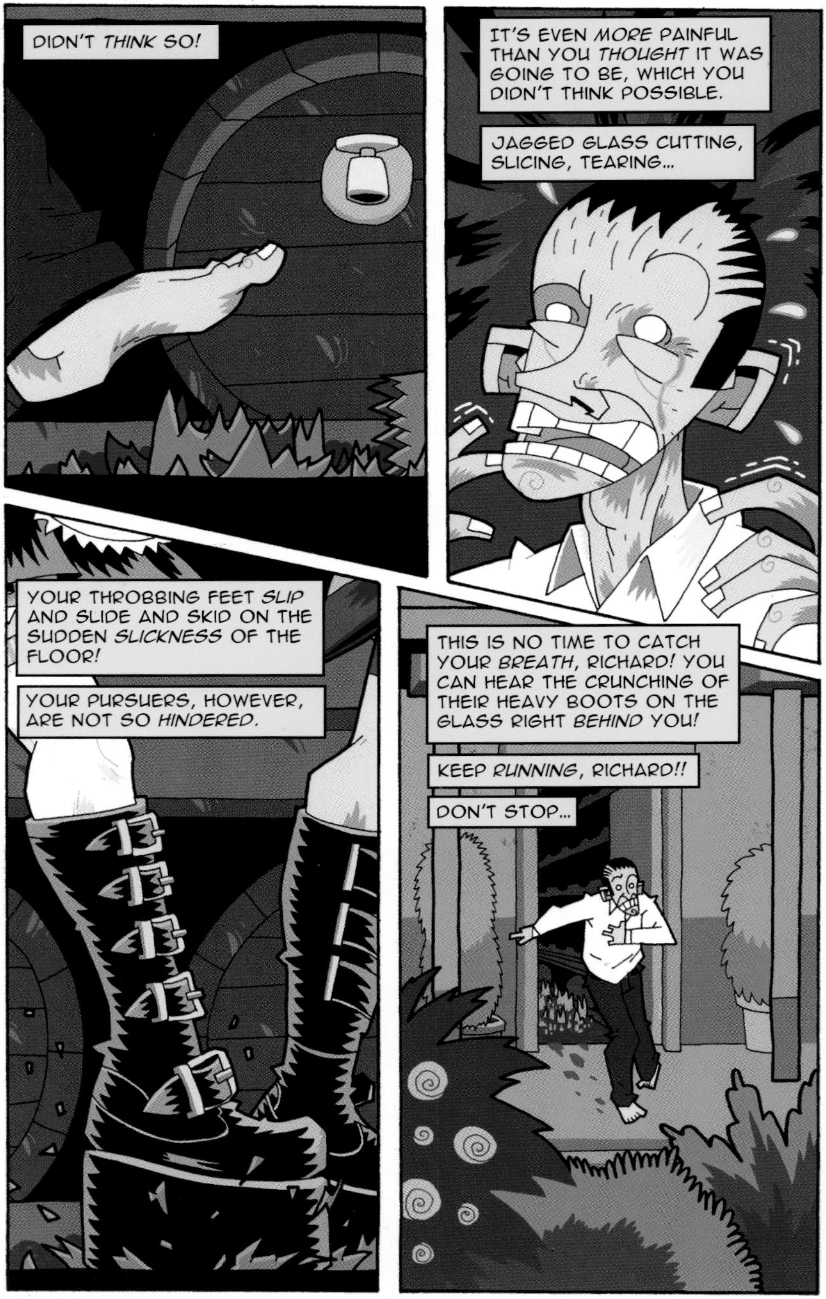
DIDN'T THINK SO!
IT'S EVEN MORE PAINFUL THAN YOU THOUGHT IT WAS GOING TO BE, WHICH YOU DIDN'T THINK POSSIBLE.
JAGGED GLASS CUTTING, SLICING, TEARING...
YOUR THROBBING FEET SLIP AND SLIDE AND SKID ON THE SUDDEN SLICKNESS OF THE FLOOR!
YOUR PURSUERS, HOWEVER, ARE NOT SO HINDERED.
THIS IS NO TIME TO CATCH YOUR BREATH, RICHARD! YOU CAN HEAR THE CRUNCHING OF THEIR HEAVY BOOTS ON THE GLASS RIGHT BEHIND YOU!
KEEP RUNNING, RICHARD!!
DON'T STOP...

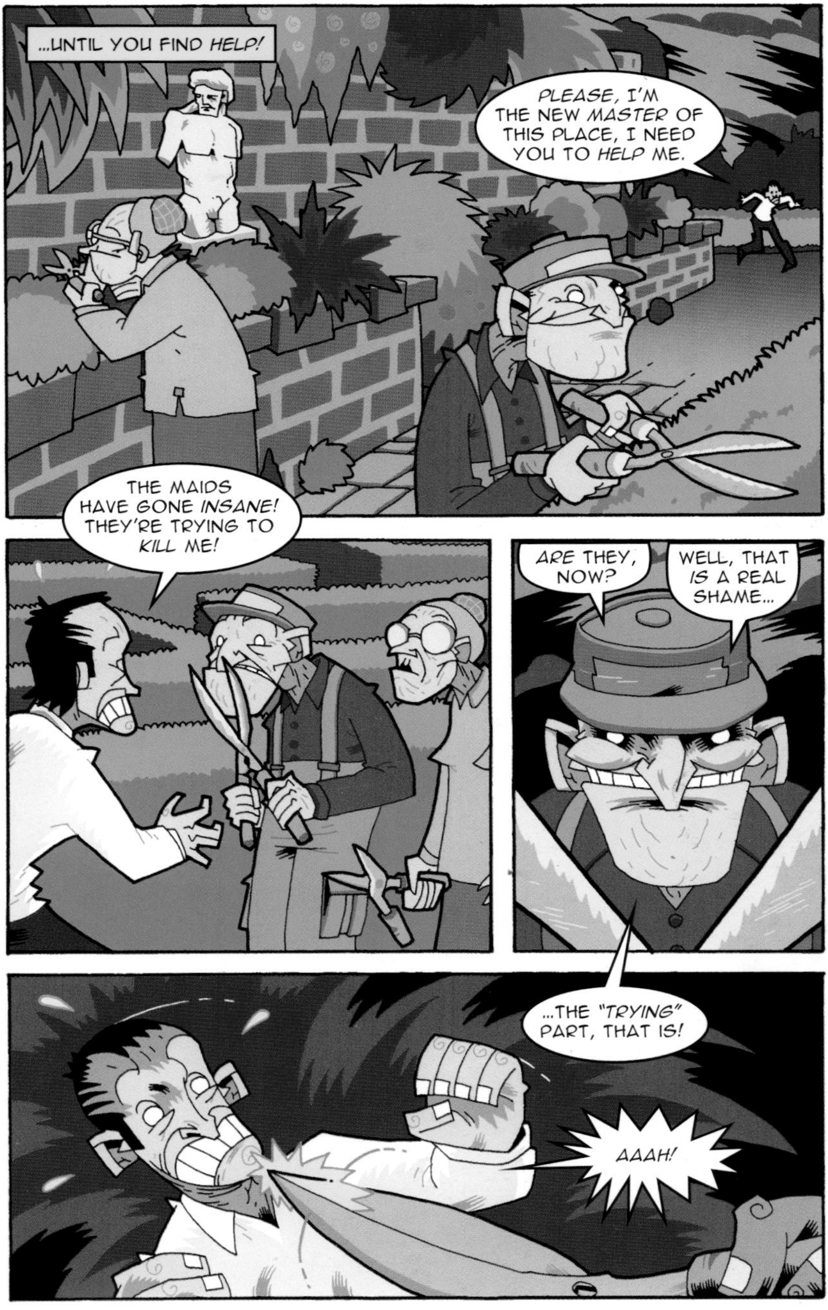
...UNTIL YOU FIND HELP!
PLEASE, I'M THE NEW MASTER OF THIS PLACE, I NEED YOU TO HELP ME.
THE MAIDS HAVE GONE INSANE! THEY'RE TRYING TO KILL ME!
ARE THEY, NOW?
WELL, THAT IS A REAL SHAME...
...THE "TRYING" PART, THAT IS!
AAAH!

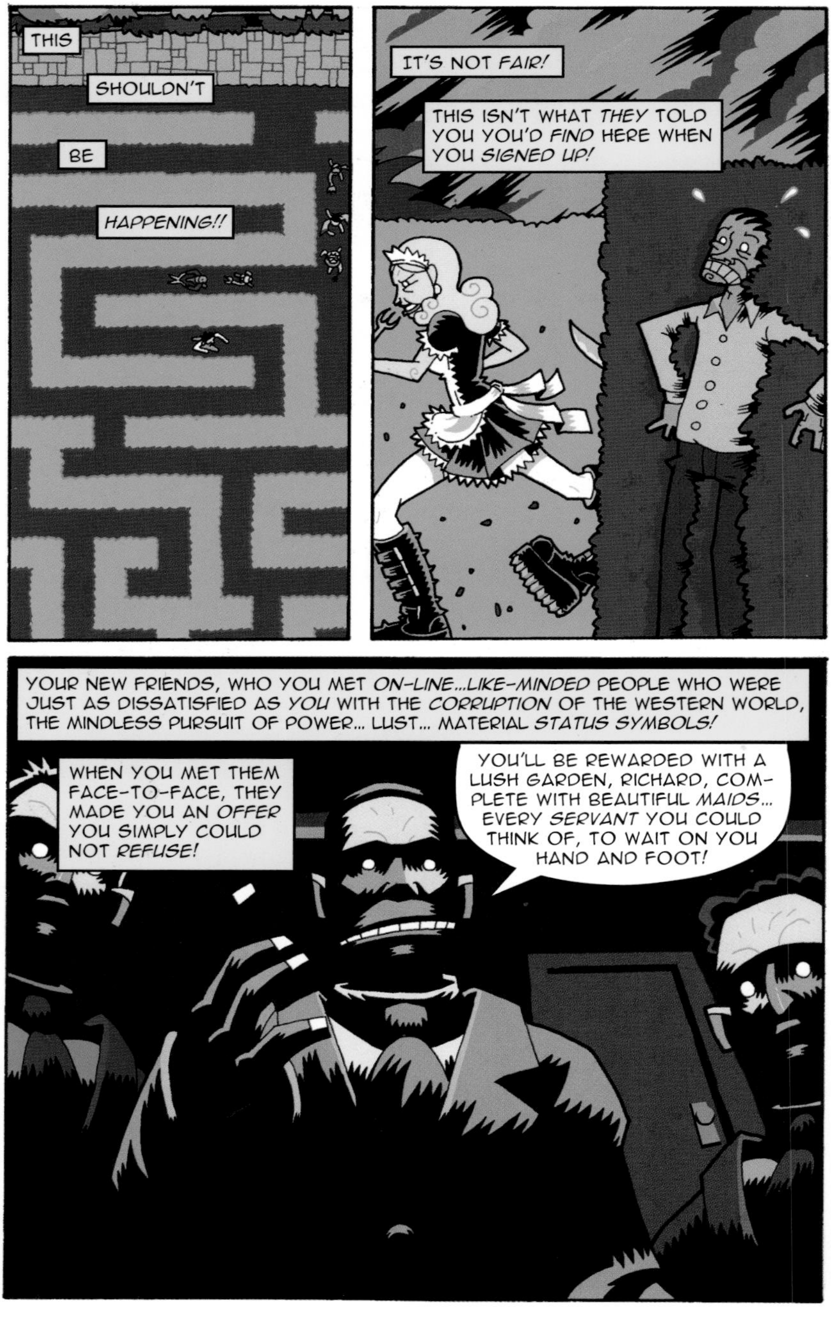
THIS
SHOULDN'T
BE
HAPPENING!!
IT'S NOT FAIR!
THIS ISN'T WHAT THEY TOLD YOU YOU'D FIND HERE WHEN YOU SIGNED UP!
YOUR NEW FRIENDS, WHO YOU MET ON-LINE...LIKE-MINDED PEOPLE WHO WERE JUST AS DISSATISFIED AS YOU WITH THE CORRUPTION OF THE WESTERN WORLD, THE MINDLESS PURSUIT OF POWER... LUST... MATERIAL STATUS SYMBOLS!
WHEN YOU MET THEM FACE-TO-FACE, THEY MADE YOU AN OFFER YOU SIMPLY COULD NOT REFUSE!
YOU'LL BE REWARDED WITH A LUSH GARDEN, RICHARD, COMPLETE WITH BEAUTIFUL MAIDS... EVERY SERVANT YOU COULD THINK OF, TO WAIT ON YOU HAND AND FOOT!

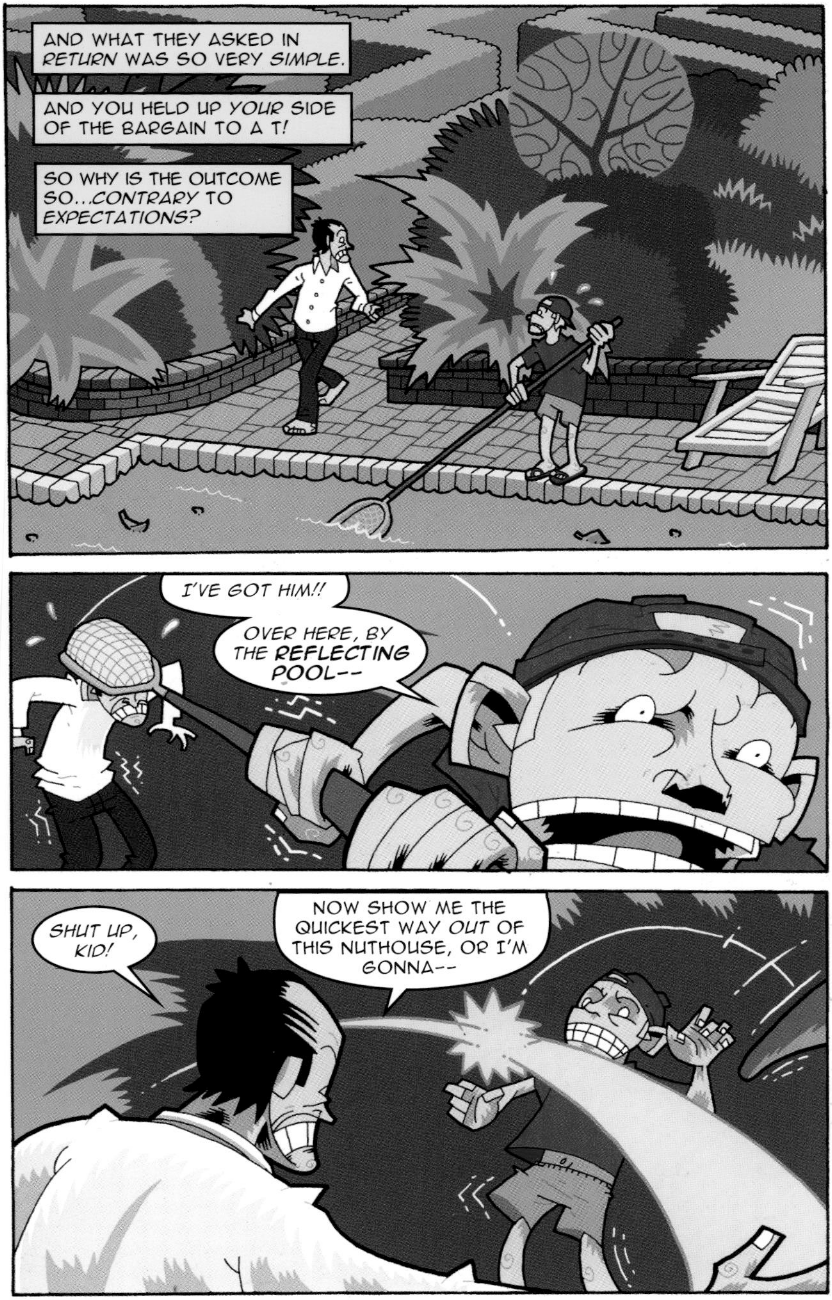
AND WHAT THEY ASKED IN RETURN WAS SO VERY SIMPLE.
AND YOU HELD UP YOUR SIDE OF THE BARGAIN TO A T!
SO WHY IS THE OUTCOME SO...CONTRARY TO EXPECTATIONS?
I'VE GOT HIM!!
OVER HERE, BY THE REFLECTING POOL--
SHUT UP, KID!
NOW SHOW ME THE QUICKEST WAY OUT OF THIS NUTHOUSE, OR I'M GONNA--

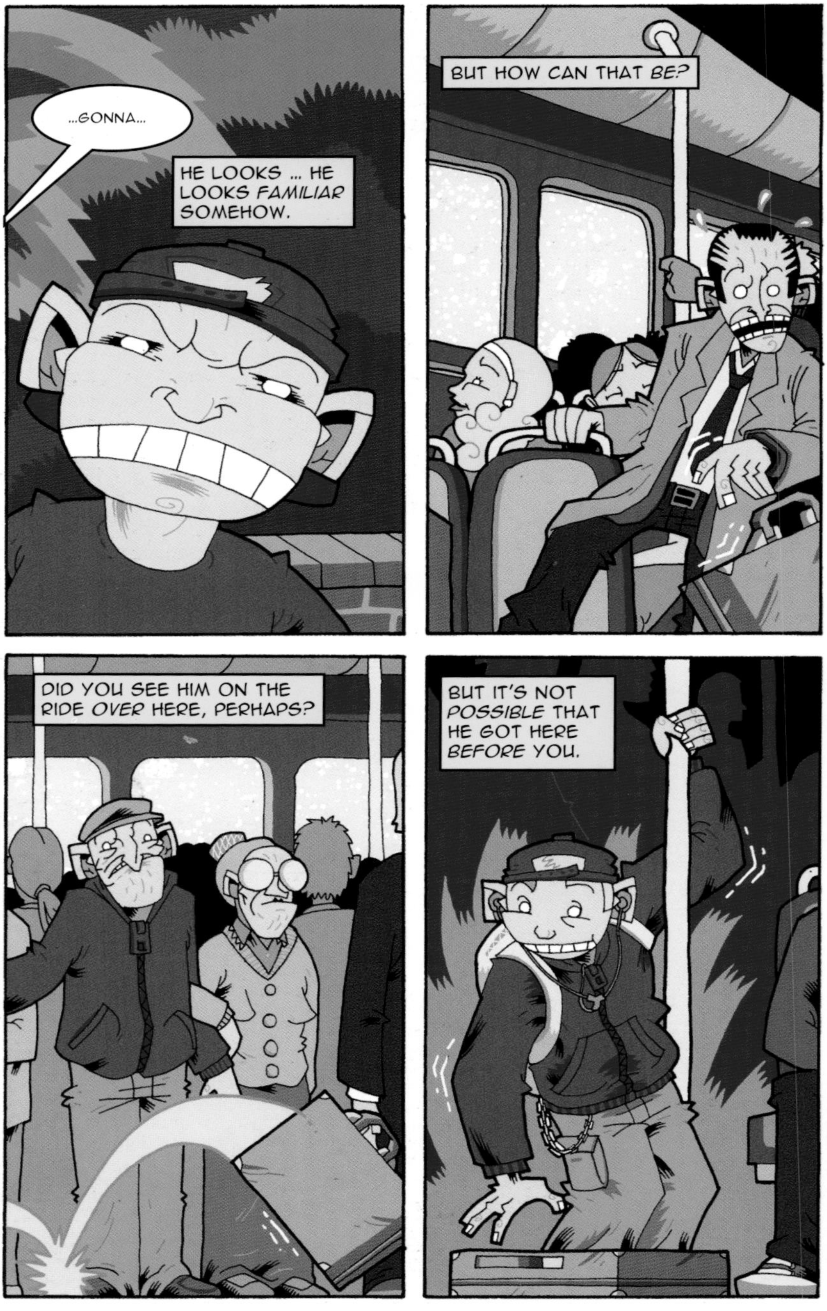
...GONNA...
HE LOOKS ... HE LOOKS *FAMILIAR* SOMEHOW.
BUT HOW CAN THAT *BE?*
DID YOU SEE HIM ON THE RIDE *OVER* HERE, PERHAPS?
BUT IT'S NOT *POSSIBLE* THAT HE GOT HERE *BEFORE* YOU.

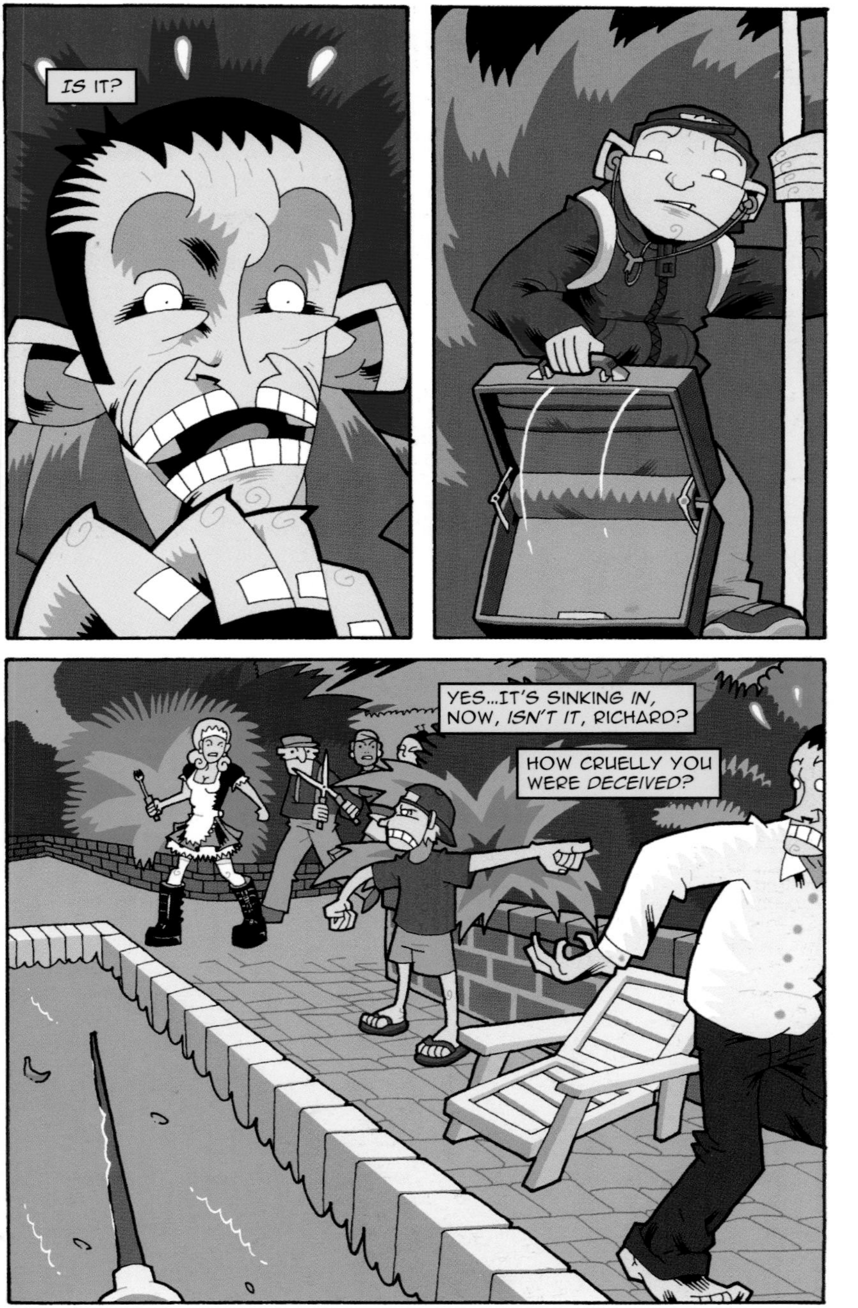
IS IT?
YES...IT'S SINKING *IN*, NOW, *ISN'T IT*, RICHARD?
HOW CRUELLY YOU WERE *DECEIVED*?

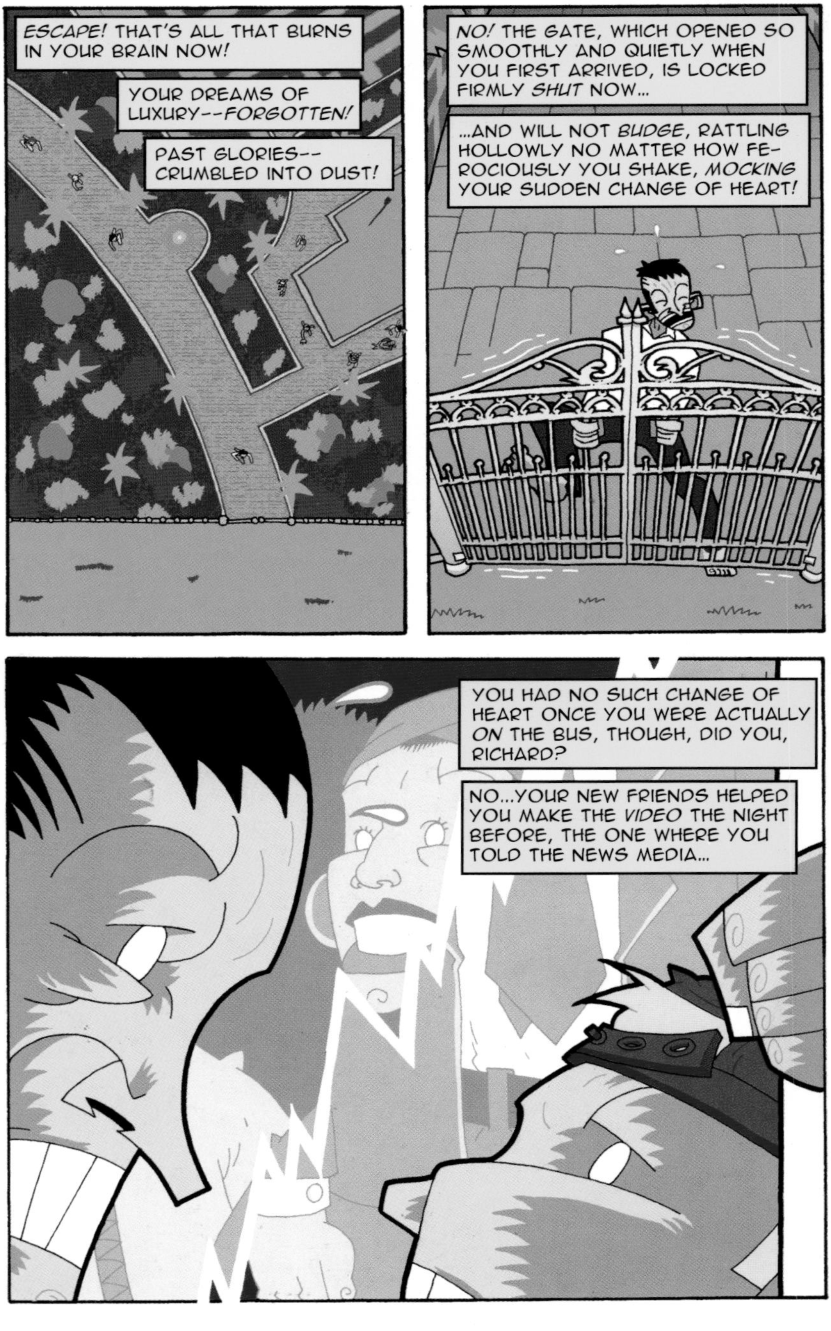
ESCAPE! THAT'S ALL THAT BURNS IN YOUR BRAIN NOW!
YOUR DREAMS OF LUXURY--FORGOTTEN!
PAST GLORIES--CRUMBLED INTO DUST!
NO! THE GATE, WHICH OPENED SO SMOOTHLY AND QUIETLY WHEN YOU FIRST ARRIVED, IS LOCKED FIRMLY SHUT NOW...
...AND WILL NOT BUDGE, RATTLING HOLLOWLY NO MATTER HOW FEROCIOUSLY YOU SHAKE, MOCKING YOUR SUDDEN CHANGE OF HEART!
YOU HAD NO SUCH CHANGE OF HEART ONCE YOU WERE ACTUALLY ON THE BUS, THOUGH, DID YOU, RICHARD?
NO...YOUR NEW FRIENDS HELPED YOU MAKE THE VIDEO THE NIGHT BEFORE, THE ONE WHERE YOU TOLD THE NEWS MEDIA...

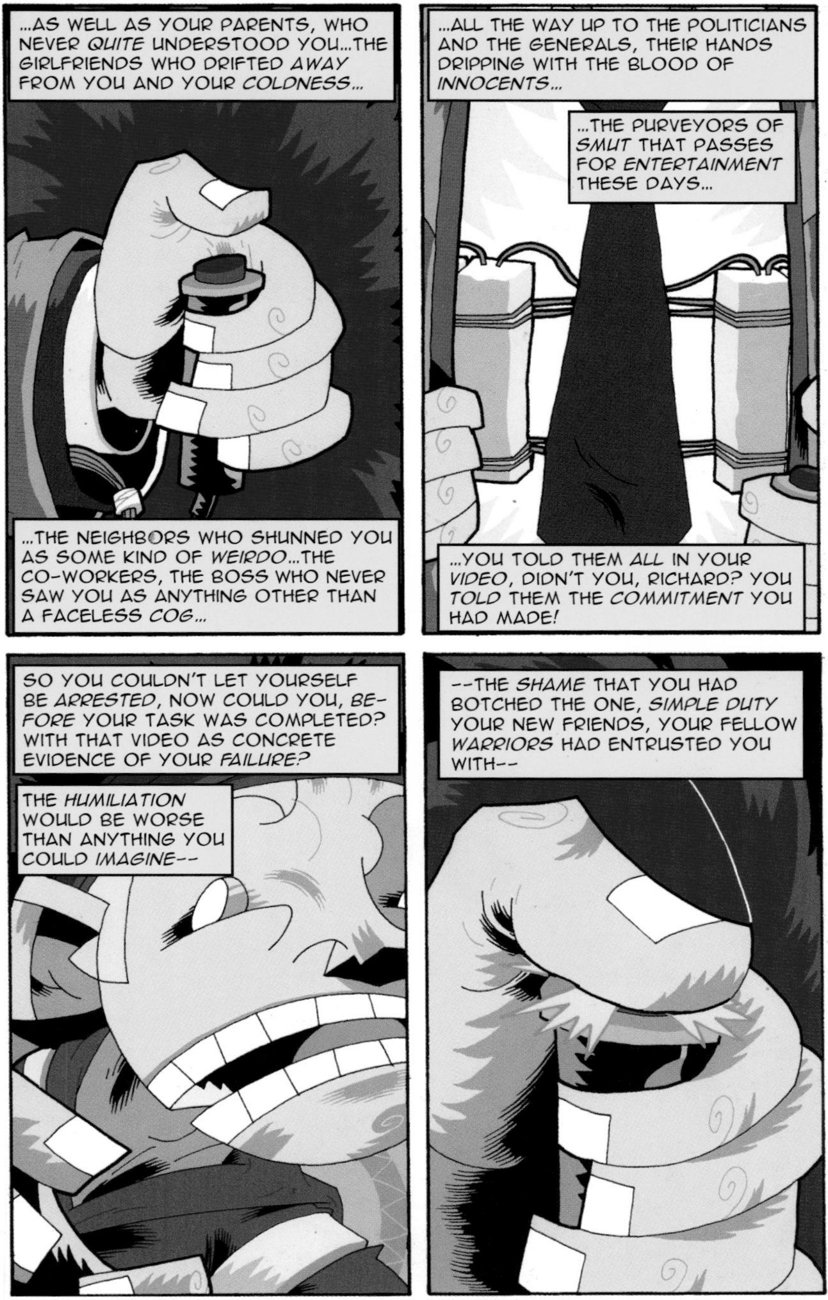
...AS WELL AS YOUR PARENTS, WHO NEVER *QUITE* UNDERSTOOD YOU...THE GIRLFRIENDS WHO DRIFTED *AWAY* FROM YOU AND YOUR *COLDNESS*...
...THE NEIGHBORS WHO SHUNNED YOU AS SOME KIND OF *WEIRDO*...THE CO-WORKERS, THE BOSS WHO NEVER SAW YOU AS ANYTHING OTHER THAN A FACELESS *COG*...
...ALL THE WAY UP TO THE POLITICIANS AND THE GENERALS, THEIR HANDS DRIPPING WITH THE BLOOD OF *INNOCENTS*...
...THE PURVEYORS OF *SMUT* THAT PASSES FOR *ENTERTAINMENT* THESE DAYS...
...YOU TOLD THEM *ALL* IN YOUR *VIDEO*, DIDN'T YOU, RICHARD? YOU *TOLD* THEM THE *COMMITMENT* YOU HAD MADE!
SO YOU COULDN'T LET YOURSELF BE *ARRESTED*, NOW COULD YOU, *BE-FORE* YOUR TASK WAS COMPLETED? WITH THAT VIDEO AS CONCRETE EVIDENCE OF YOUR *FAILURE?*
THE *HUMILIATION* WOULD BE WORSE THAN ANYTHING YOU COULD *IMAGINE*--
--THE *SHAME* THAT YOU HAD BOTCHED THE ONE, *SIMPLE DUTY* YOUR NEW FRIENDS, YOUR FELLOW *WARRIORS* HAD ENTRUSTED YOU WITH--

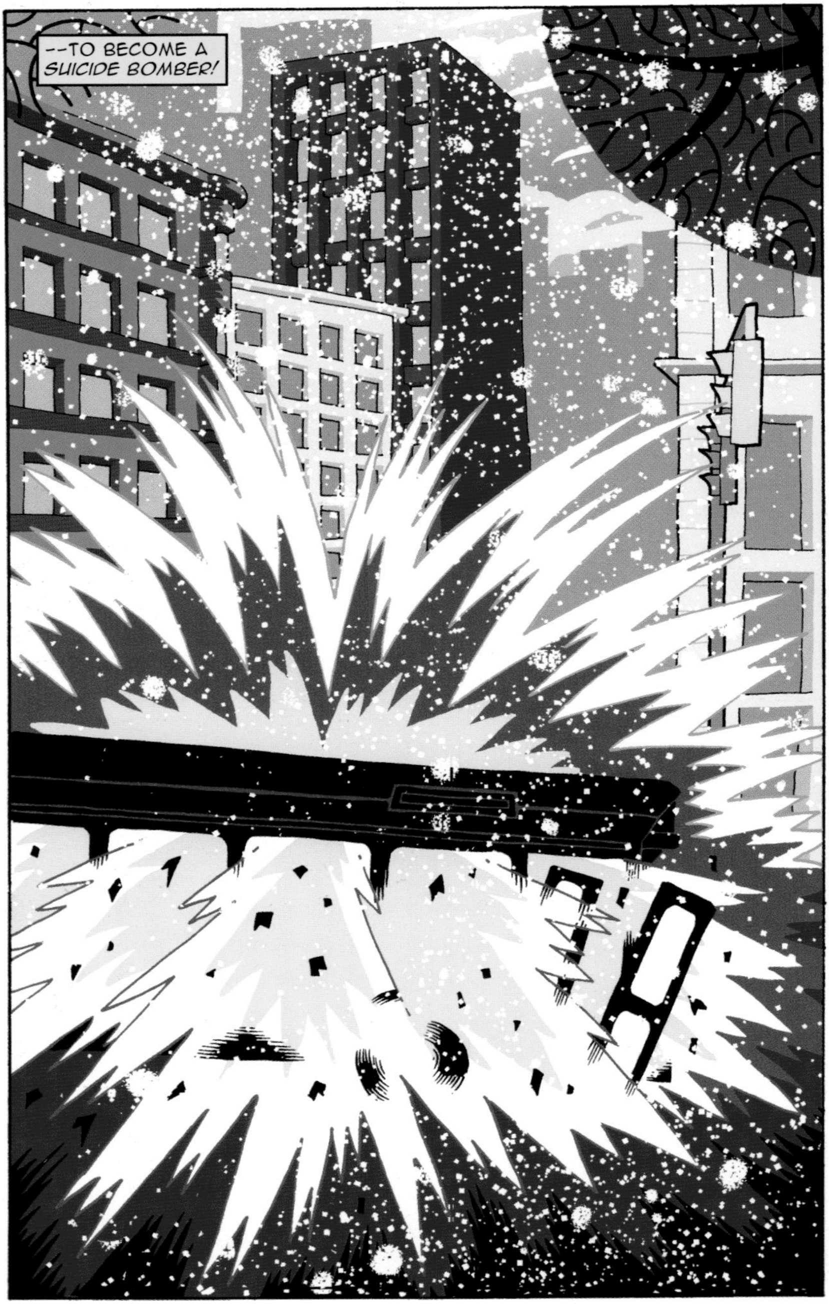
--TO BECOME A SUICIDE BOMBER!

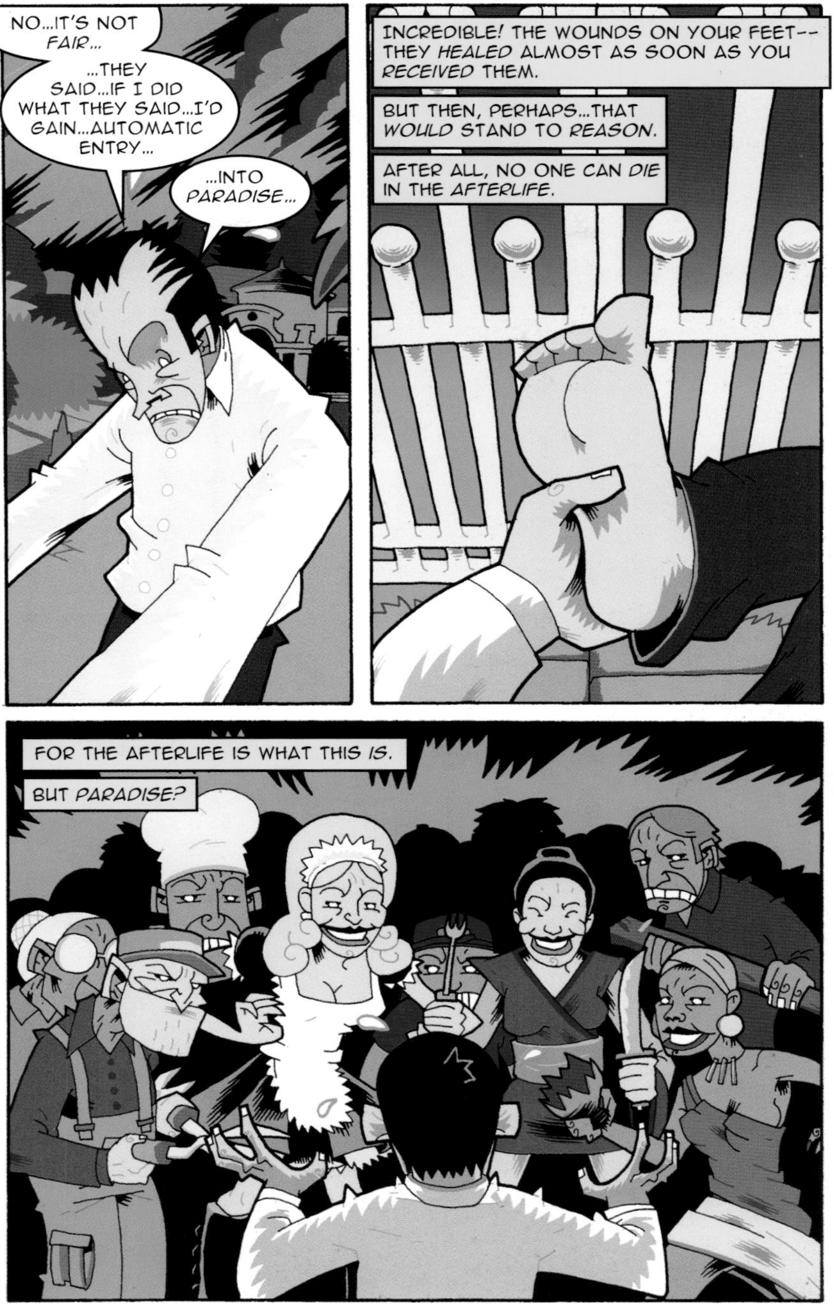
NO...IT'S NOT FAIR...
...THEY SAID...IF I DID WHAT THEY SAID...I'D GAIN...AUTOMATIC ENTRY...
...INTO PARADISE...
INCREDIBLE! THE WOUNDS ON YOUR FEET-- THEY HEALED ALMOST AS SOON AS YOU RECEIVED THEM.
BUT THEN, PERHAPS...THAT WOULD STAND TO REASON.
AFTER ALL, NO ONE CAN DIE IN THE AFTERLIFE.
FOR THE AFTERLIFE IS WHAT THIS IS.
BUT PARADISE?

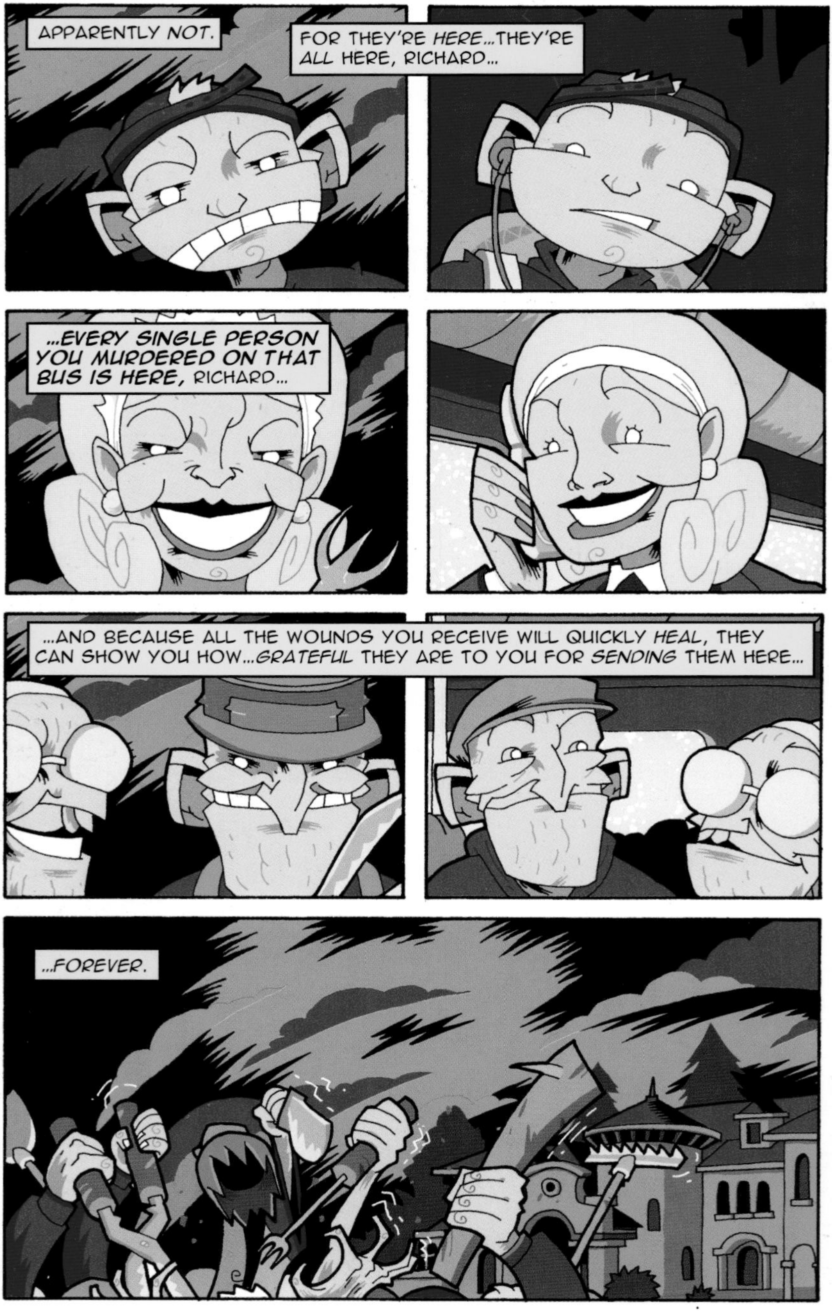
APPARENTLY NOT.
FOR THEY'RE HERE...THEY'RE ALL HERE, RICHARD...
...EVERY SINGLE PERSON YOU MURDERED ON THAT BUS IS HERE, RICHARD...
...AND BECAUSE ALL THE WOUNDS YOU RECEIVE WILL QUICKLY HEAL, THEY CAN SHOW YOU HOW...GRATEFUL THEY ARE TO YOU FOR SENDING THEM HERE...
...FOREVER.

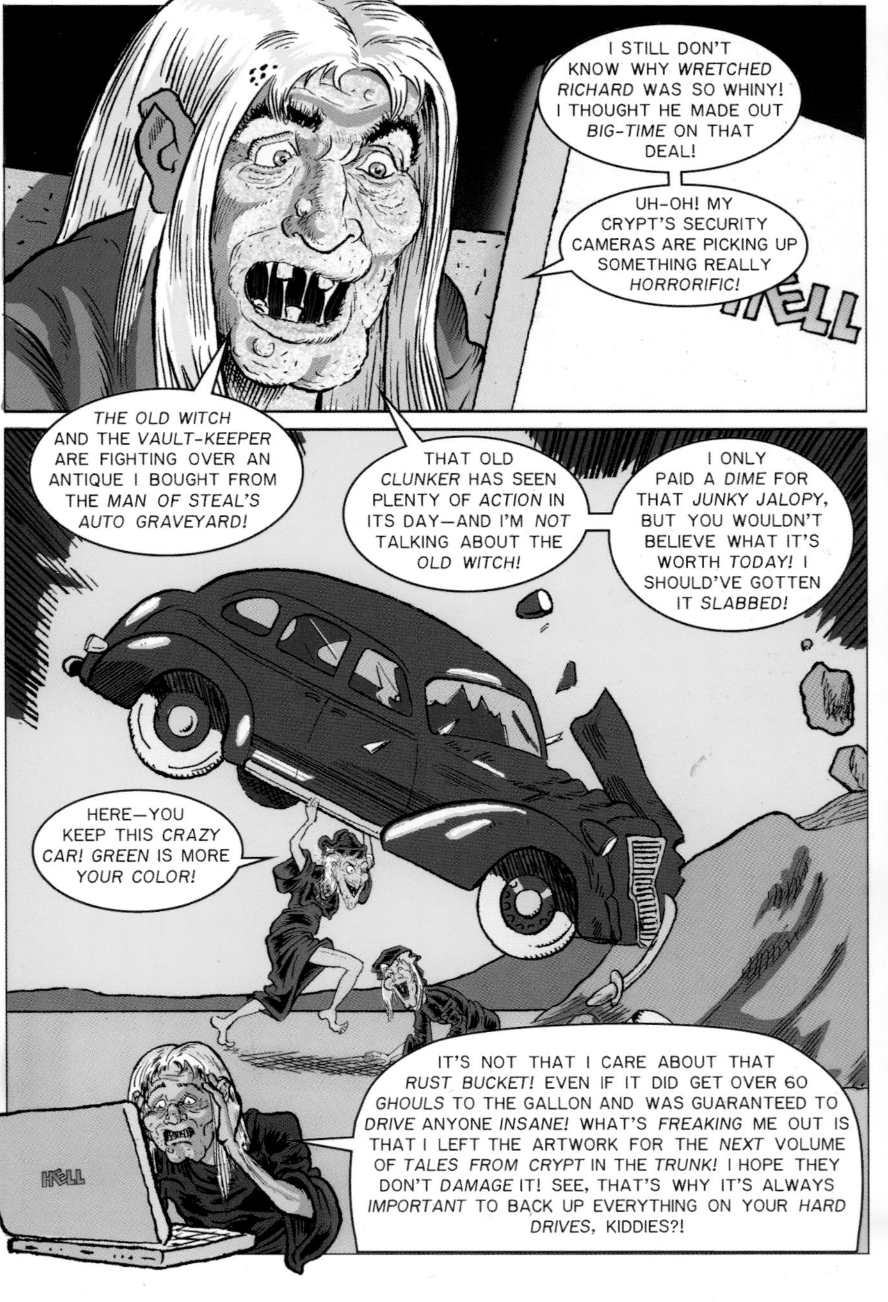
I STILL DON'T KNOW WHY WRETCHED RICHARD WAS SO WHINY! I THOUGHT HE MADE OUT BIG-TIME ON THAT DEAL!
UH-OH! MY CRYPT'S SECURITY CAMERAS ARE PICKING UP SOMETHING REALLY HORRORIFIC!
THE OLD WITCH AND THE VAULT-KEEPER ARE FIGHTING OVER AN ANTIQUE I BOUGHT FROM THE MAN OF STEAL'S AUTO GRAVEYARD!
THAT OLD CLUNKER HAS SEEN PLENTY OF ACTION IN ITS DAY—AND I'M NOT TALKING ABOUT THE OLD WITCH!
I ONLY PAID A DIME FOR THAT JUNKY JALOPY, BUT YOU WOULDN'T BELIEVE WHAT IT'S WORTH TODAY! I SHOULD'VE GOTTEN IT SLABBED!
HERE—YOU KEEP THIS CRAZY CAR! GREEN IS MORE YOUR COLOR!
IT'S NOT THAT I CARE ABOUT THAT RUST BUCKET! EVEN IF IT DID GET OVER 60 GHOULS TO THE GALLON AND WAS GUARANTEED TO DRIVE ANYONE INSANE! WHAT'S FREAKING ME OUT IS THAT I LEFT THE ARTWORK FOR THE NEXT VOLUME OF TALES FROM CRYPT IN THE TRUNK! I HOPE THEY DON'T DAMAGE IT! SEE, THAT'S WHY IT'S ALWAYS IMPORTANT TO BACK UP EVERYTHING ON YOUR HARD DRIVES, KIDDIES?!

"HERE'S A SNEAK PEEK AT 'EXTRA LIFE' FROM *TALES FROM THE CRYPT* NO. 3..."

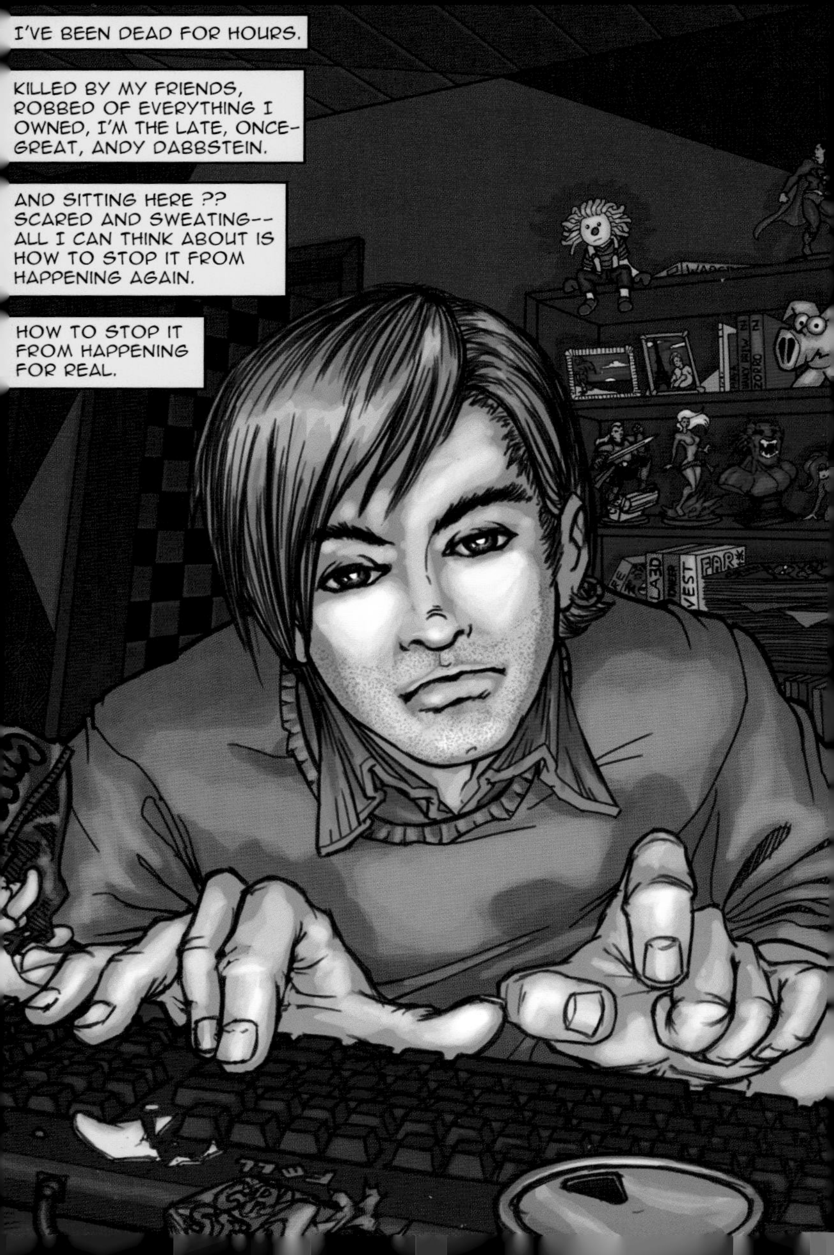

I'VE BEEN DEAD FOR HOURS.
KILLED BY MY FRIENDS, ROBBED OF EVERYTHING I OWNED, I'M THE LATE, ONCE-GREAT, ANDY DABBSTEIN.
AND SITTING HERE ?? SCARED AND SWEATING-- ALL I CAN THINK ABOUT IS HOW TO STOP IT FROM HAPPENING AGAIN.
HOW TO STOP IT FROM HAPPENING FOR REAL.

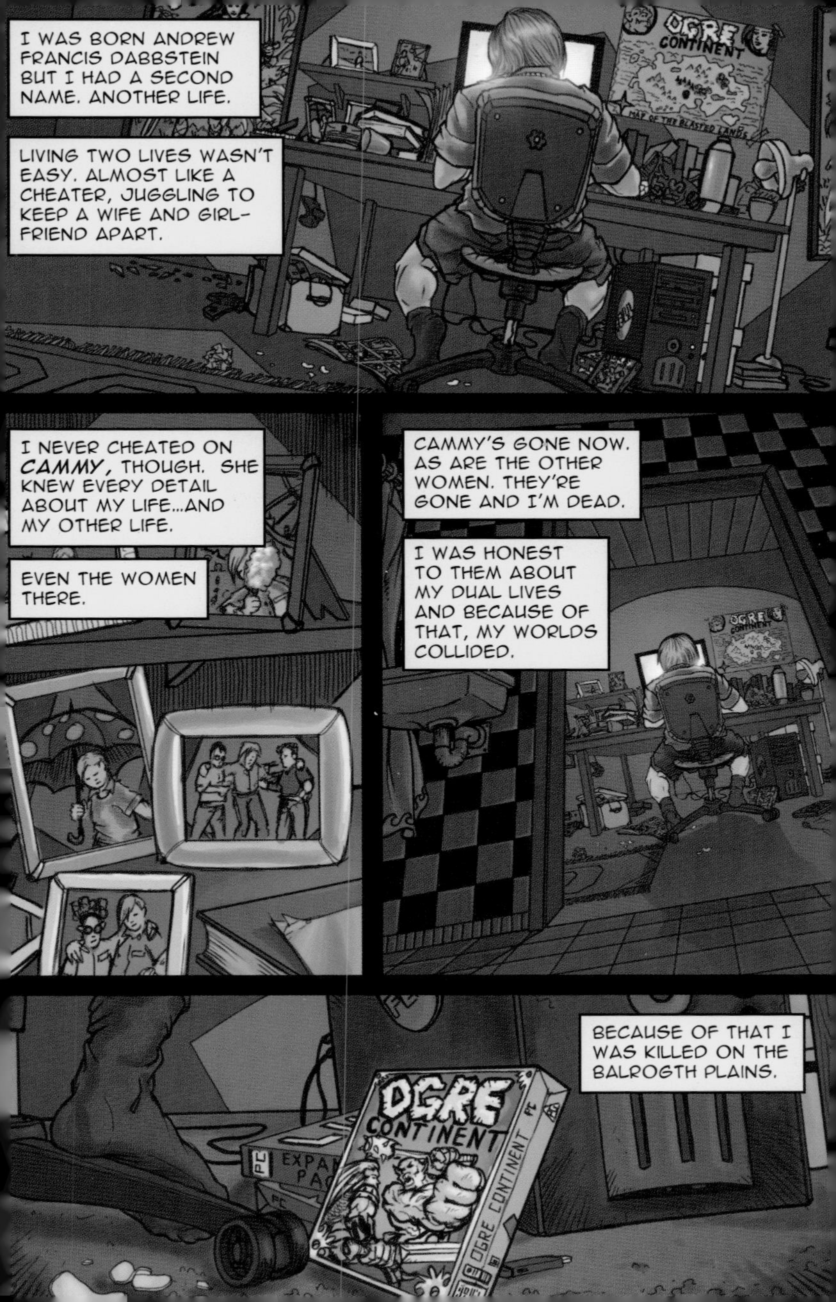
I WAS BORN ANDREW FRANCIS DABBSTEIN BUT I HAD A SECOND NAME. ANOTHER LIFE.
OGRE CONTINENT
MAP OF THE BLASTED LANDS
LIVING TWO LIVES WASN'T EASY. ALMOST LIKE A CHEATER, JUGGLING TO KEEP A WIFE AND GIRL-FRIEND APART.
I NEVER CHEATED ON CAMMY, THOUGH. SHE KNEW EVERY DETAIL ABOUT MY LIFE...AND MY OTHER LIFE.
EVEN THE WOMEN THERE.
CAMMY'S GONE NOW. AS ARE THE OTHER WOMEN. THEY'RE GONE AND I'M DEAD.
I WAS HONEST TO THEM ABOUT MY DUAL LIVES AND BECAUSE OF THAT, MY WORLDS COLLIDED.
BECAUSE OF THAT I WAS KILLED ON THE BALROGTH PLAINS.
OGRE CONTINENT
PC
OGRE CONTINENT
PC

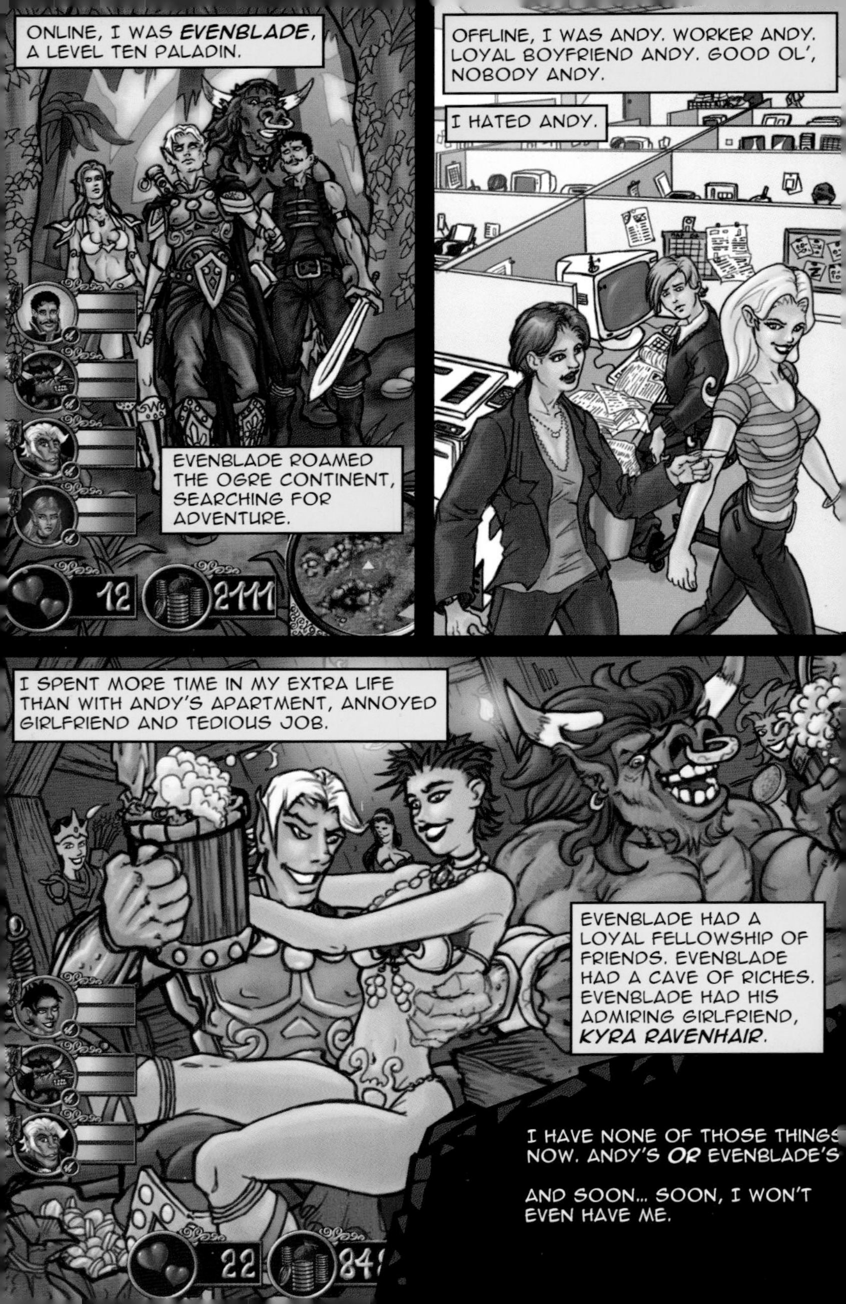
ONLINE, I WAS ***EVENBLADE***, A LEVEL TEN PALADIN.
EVENBLADE ROAMED THE OGRE CONTINENT, SEARCHING FOR ADVENTURE.
12
2111
OFFLINE, I WAS ANDY. WORKER ANDY. LOYAL BOYFRIEND ANDY. GOOD OL', NOBODY ANDY.
I HATED ANDY.
I SPENT MORE TIME IN MY EXTRA LIFE THAN WITH ANDY'S APARTMENT, ANNOYED GIRLFRIEND AND TEDIOUS JOB.
EVENBLADE HAD A LOYAL FELLOWSHIP OF FRIENDS. EVENBLADE HAD A CAVE OF RICHES. EVENBLADE HAD HIS ADMIRING GIRLFRIEND, ***KYRA RAVENHAIR***.
22
I HAVE NONE OF THOSE THINGS NOW. ANDY'S ***OR*** EVENBLADE'S.
AND SOON... SOON, I WON'T EVEN HAVE ME.

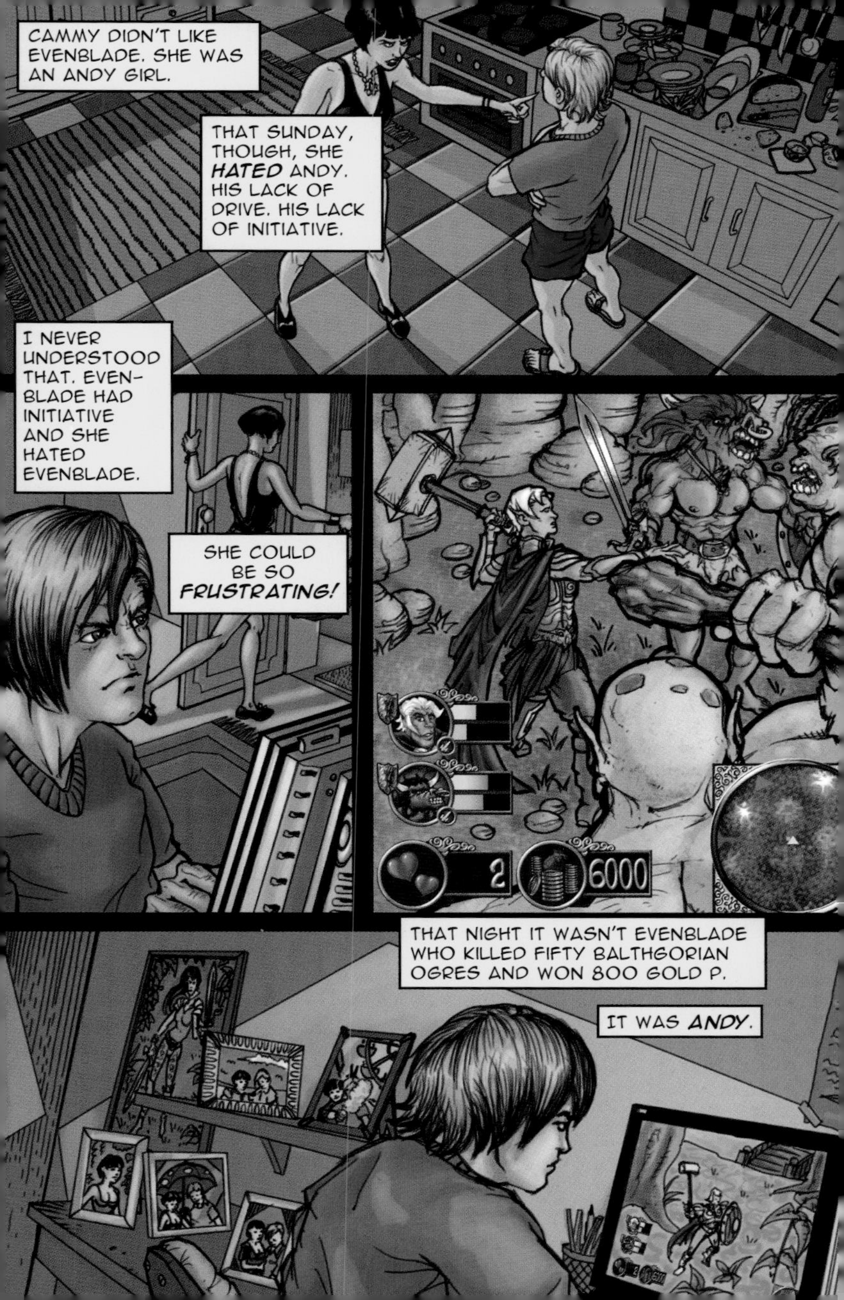
CAMMY DIDN'T LIKE EVENBLADE. SHE WAS AN ANDY GIRL.
THAT SUNDAY, THOUGH, SHE *HATED* ANDY. HIS LACK OF DRIVE. HIS LACK OF INITIATIVE.
I NEVER UNDERSTOOD THAT. EVEN-BLADE HAD INITIATIVE AND SHE HATED EVENBLADE.
SHE COULD BE SO *FRUSTRATING!*
2
6000
THAT NIGHT IT WASN'T EVENBLADE WHO KILLED FIFTY BALTHGORIAN OGRES AND WON 800 GOLD P.
IT WAS *ANDY*.

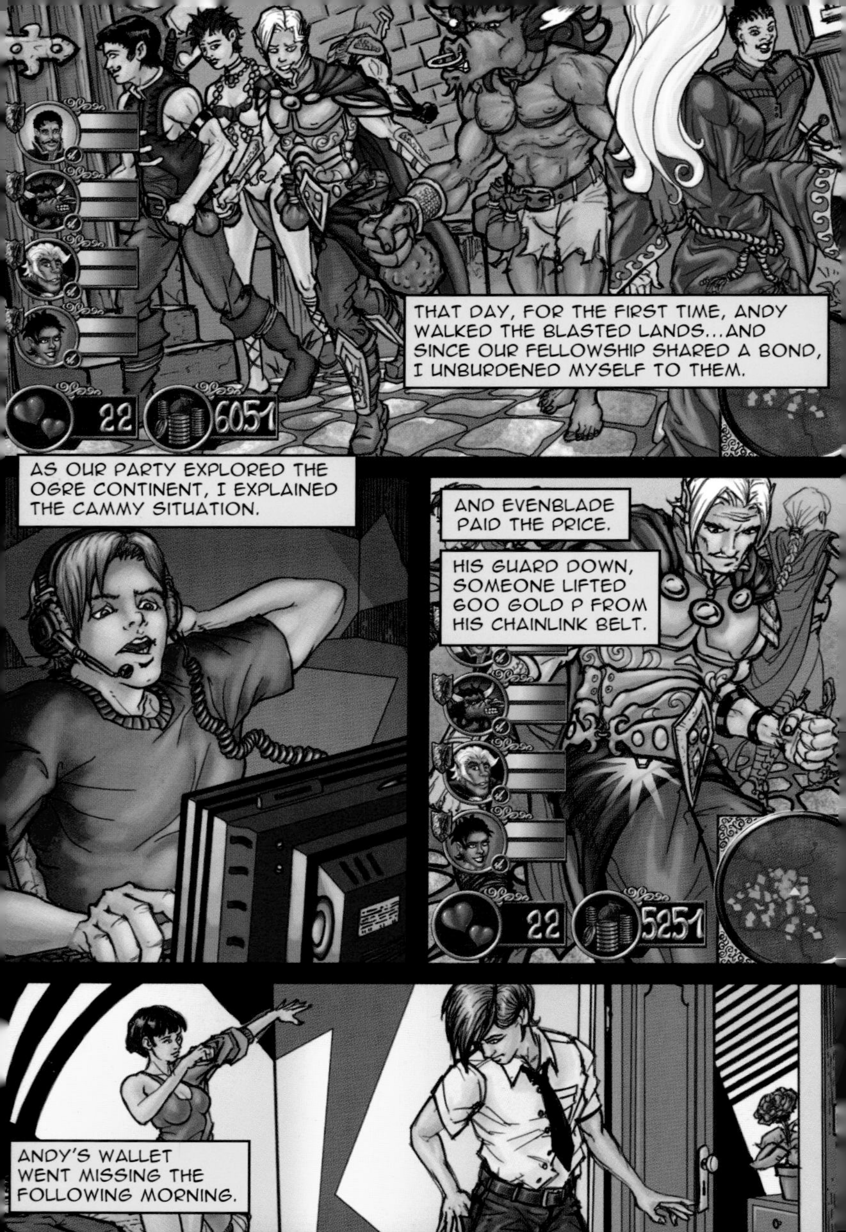
THAT DAY, FOR THE FIRST TIME, ANDY WALKED THE BLASTED LANDS...AND SINCE OUR FELLOWSHIP SHARED A BOND, I UNBURDENED MYSELF TO THEM.
22
6051
AS OUR PARTY EXPLORED THE OGRE CONTINENT, I EXPLAINED THE CAMMY SITUATION.
AND EVENBLADE PAID THE PRICE.
HIS GUARD DOWN, SOMEONE LIFTED 800 GOLD P FROM HIS CHAINLINK BELT.
22
5251
ANDY'S WALLET WENT MISSING THE FOLLOWING MORNING.

“DON’T MISS TALES FROM *TALES*
THE CRYPT NO. 3, ‘EXTRA LIFE’”

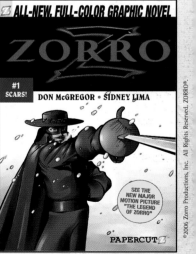

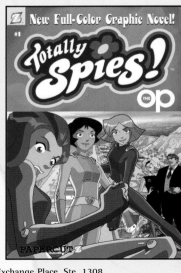

WATCH OUT FOR PAPERCUTZ™

Hi, it's me, good ol' Jim Salicrup again with another jam-packed edition of the Papercutz Backpages. We've got more unbelievably shocking news, so I hope you're sitting down. Last time, we revealed that Papercutz had obtained the exclusive rights to create and publish all-new TALES FROM THE CRYPT comicbooks and graphic novels, and we're still feeling the shockwaves from that bombshell announcement! This time around, we're trumpeting the return of yet another world-famous comicbook title-CLASSICS ILLUSTRATED!

We'll fill you in on why that's such an awesome big deal in the following pages, but right now I need a moment to take it all in. You see, even though I've been in the world of comics for thirty-five years, I'm still very much the same comicbook fan I was when I was a kid! And if my partner, Papercutz Publisher, Terry Nantier, were to magically go back in time, and tell 13 year-old Jim Salicrup that he was going to one day be the editor of NANCY DREW, THE HARDY BOYS, TALES FROM THE CRYPT, and CLASSICS ILLUSTRATED, he'd think Terry was out of his mind!

Let's get real. Back then I'd see CLASSICS ILLUSTRATED comics in their own display rack, apart from all the other comicbooks, at my favorite soda shoppe in the Bronx. Each issue featured a comics adaptation of a classic novel-that's why they called it CLASSICS ILLUSTRATED. But unlike other comicbooks, these were bigger, containing 48 pages per book; cost a quarter, more than twice as much as a regular 12 cent comic; and stayed on sale forever, as opposed to the other comics which were gone in a month. Clearly, these comics were something special.

Bah, I can take a gazillion moments, but this is still way too humungous an event for my puny brain to fully absorb, so I'm going to give up trying and accept that we here at Papercutz must be doing something right to be entrusted with Comicdom's crown jewels! So no more looking back--time to focus on the future. That means doing everything we can to make sure these titles live up to their proud heritage, while gaining a whole new generation of fans. As usual, you can contact me at salicrup@papercutz.com or Jim Salicrup, PAPERCUTZ, 40 Exchange Place, Ste. 1308, New York, NY 10005 and let us know how we're doing. After all, we want you to be as excited about Papercutz as we are!

Thanks,

Jim

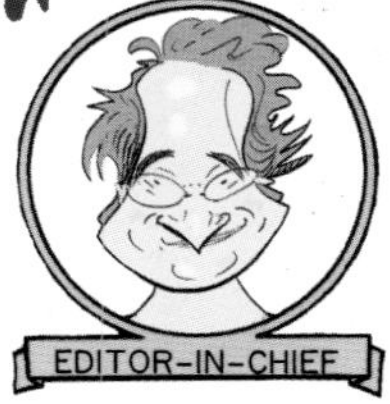
EDITOR-IN-CHIEF

CLASSICS
Illustrated

**Featuring Stories by the
World's Greatest Authors**

Returns in two new
series from Papercutz!

   The original, best-selling series of comics adaptations of the world's greatest literature, CLASSICS ILLUSTRATED, returns in two new formats--the original, featuring abridged adaptations of classic novels, and CLASSICS ILLUSTRATED DELUXE, featuring longer, more expansive adaptations-from graphic novel publisher Papercutz. "We're very proud to say that Papercutz has received such an enthusiastic reception from librarians and school teachers for its NANCY DREW and HARDY BOYS graphic novels as well as THE LIFE OF POPE JOHN PAUL II...*IN COMICS!*, that it only seemed logical for us to bring back the original CLASSICS ILLUSTRATED comicbook series beloved by parents, educators, and librarians," explained Papercutz Publisher, Terry Nantier. "We can't thank the enlightened librarians and teachers who have supported Papercutz enough. And we're thrilled that they're so excited about CLASSICS ILLUSTRATED."

Upcoming titles include The Invisible Man, Tales from the Brothers Grimm, and Robinson Crusoe.

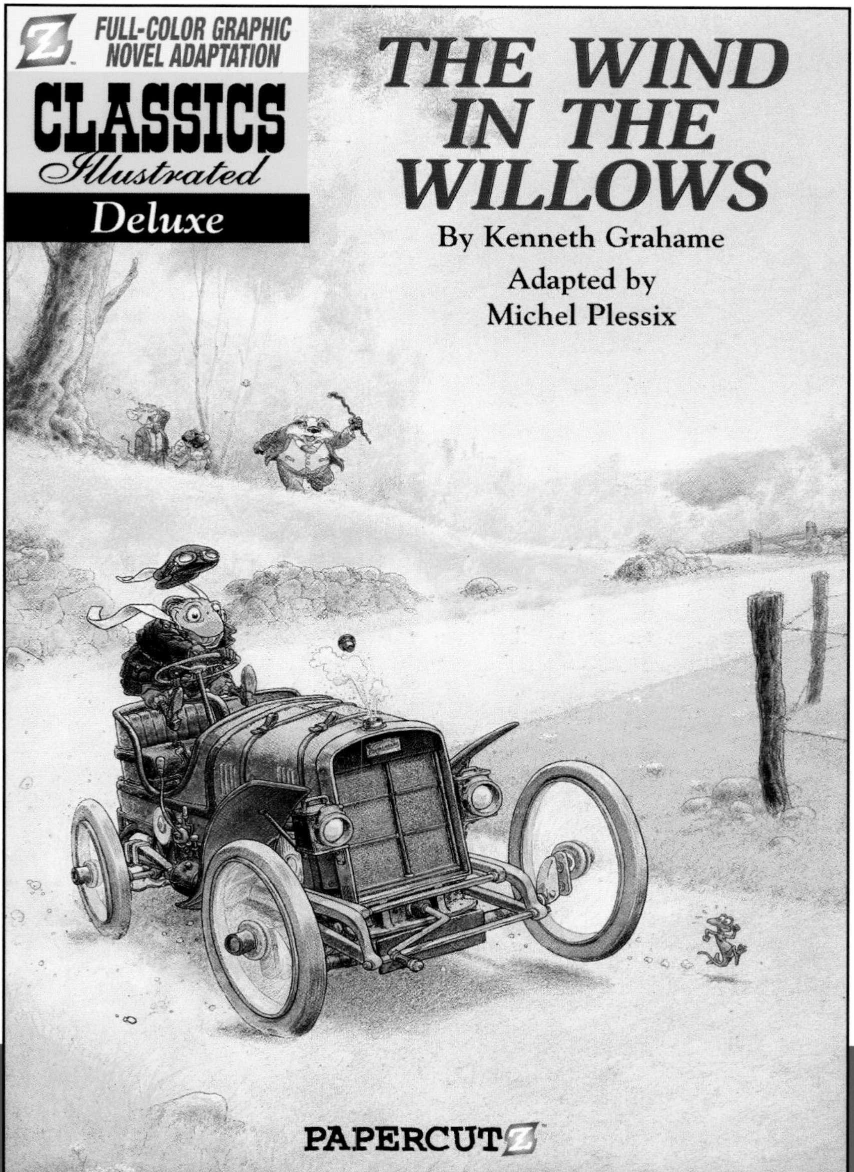
FULL-COLOR GRAPHIC NOVEL ADAPTATION
CLASSICS
Illustrated
Deluxe
THE WIND IN THE WILLOWS
By Kenneth Grahame
Adapted by
Michel Plessix
PAPERCUTZ

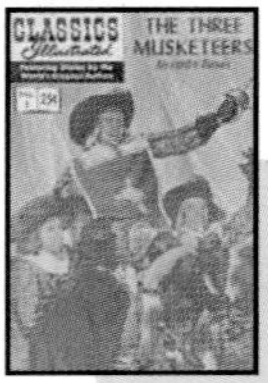
CLASSICS
THE THREE MUSKETEERS
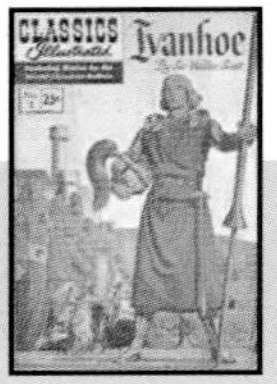
CLASSICS
Ivanhoe
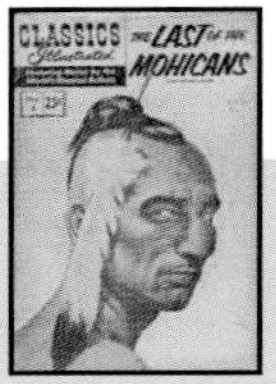
CLASSICS
THE LAST OF THE MOHICANS
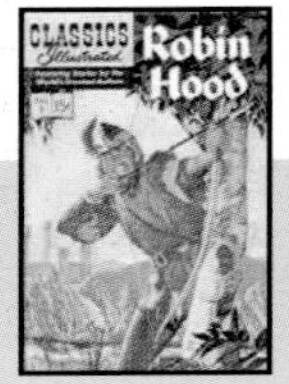
CLASSICS
Robin Hood
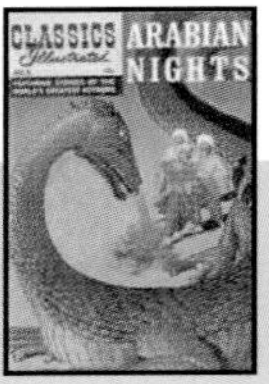
CLASSICS
ARABIAN NIGHTS
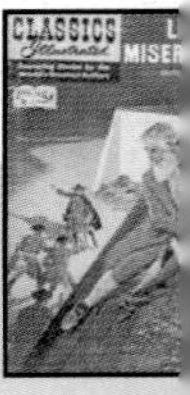
CLASSICS

A Short History of CLASSICS ILLUSTRATED...

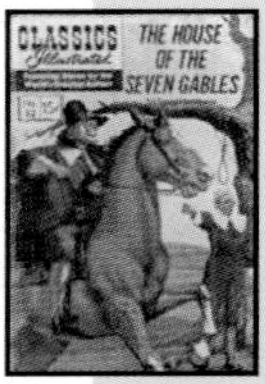
CLASSICS
THE HOUSE OF THE SEVEN GABLES
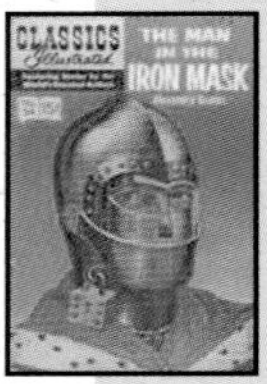
CLASSICS
THE MAN IN THE IRON MASK
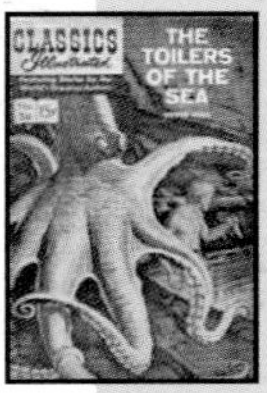
CLASSICS
THE TOILERS OF THE SEA
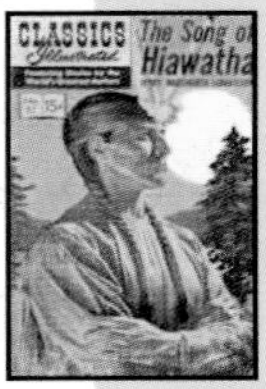
CLASSICS
Hiawatha

William B. Jones Jr. is the author of Classics Illustrated: A Cultural History, which offers a comprehensive overview of the original comic-book series and the writers, artists, editors, and publishers behind-the-scenes. With Mr. Jones Jr.'s kind permission, here's a very short overview of the history of CLASSICS ILLUSTRATED adapted from his 2005 essay on Albert Kanter.

CLASSICS ILLUSTRATED was the creation of Albert Lewis Kanter, a visionary publisher, who from 1941 to 1971, introduced young readers worldwide to the realms of literature, history, folklore, mythology, and science in over 200 titles in such comicbook series as CLASSICS ILLUSTRATED and CLASSICS ILLUSTRATED JUNIOR. Kanter, inspired by the success of the first comicbooks published in the early 30s and late 40s, believed he

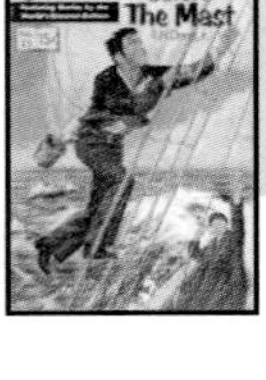
CLASSICS
Two Years before The Mast
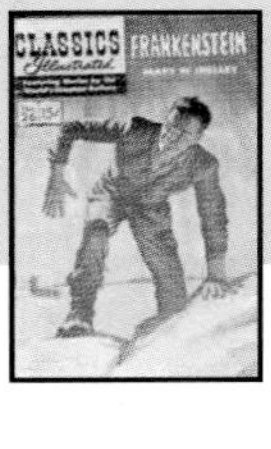
CLASSICS
FRANKENSTEIN
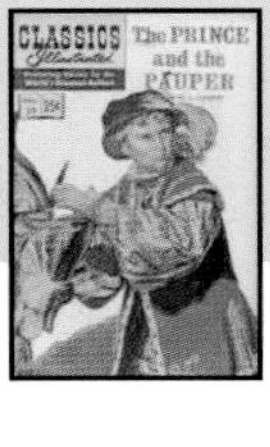
CLASSICS
The PRINCE and the PAUPER
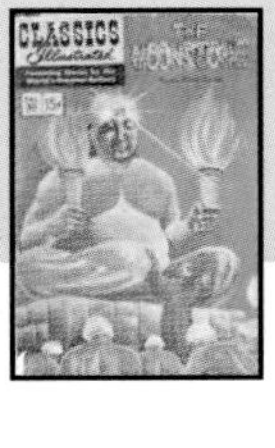
CLASSICS
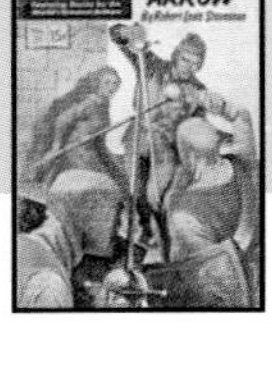
CLASSICS
THE BLACK ARROW
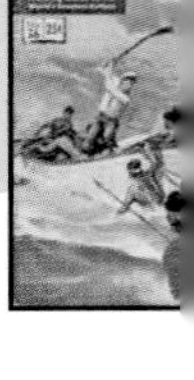
CLASSICS

DON QUIXOTE

CLASSICS
Rip Van Winkle

CLASSICS Illustrated
UNCLE TOM'S CABIN

CLASSICS Illustrated

CLASSICS Illustrated
The CORSICAN BROTHERS

CLASSICS Illustrated
OLIVER TWIST

could use the same medium to introduce young readers to the world of great literature. CLASSIC COMICS (later changed to CLASSICS ILLUSTRATED in 1947) was launched in 1941, and soon the comicbook adaptations of Shakespeare, Stevenson, Twain, Verne, and other authors, were being used in schools and endorsed by educators.

CLASSICS ILLUSTRATED was translated and distributed in countries such as Canada, Great Britain, the Netherlands, Greece, Brazil, Mexico, and Australia. The genial publisher was hailed abroad as "Papa Kassiker." By the beginning of the 1960s, CLASSICS ILLUSTRATED was the largest childrens publication in the world. The original CLASSICS ILLUSTRATED series adapted into comics 169 titles; among these were Frankenstein, 20,000 Leagues Under the Sea, Treasure Island, Julius Caesar, and Faust.

Albert L. Kanter died, March 17, 1973, leaving behind a rich legacy for the millions of readers whose imaginations were awakened by CLASSICS ILLUSTRATED.

CLASSICS Illustrated
THE PRAIRIE

CLASSICS Illustrated
WUTHERING HEIGHTS

CLASSICS Illustrated
BLACK BEAUTY

CLASSICS Illustrated
WESTERN STORIES

TWENTY YEARS AFTER

CLASSICS Illustrated
GREAT EXPECTATIONS

CLASSICS Illustrated
Kidnapped

CLASSICS Illustrated
DAVID COPPERFIELD

CLASSICS Illustrated
TOM SAWYER

CLASSICS Illustrated
THE SPY

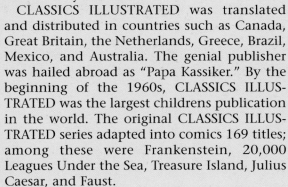

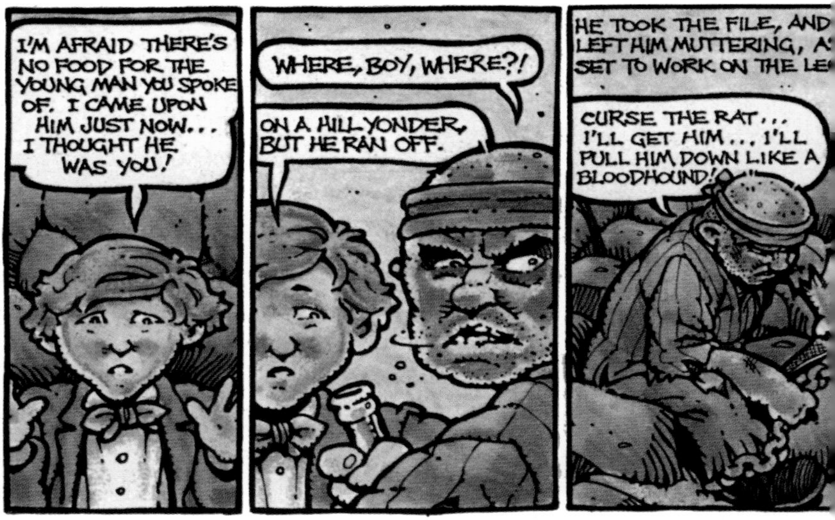
I'M AFRAID THERE'S NO FOOD FOR THE YOUNG MAN YOU SPOKE OF. I CAME UPON HIM JUST NOW... I THOUGHT HE WAS YOU!
WHERE, BOY, WHERE?!
ON A HILL YONDER, BUT HE RAN OFF.
HE TOOK THE FILE, AND LEFT HIM MUTTERING, SET TO WORK ON THE
CURSE THE RAT... I'LL GET HIM... I'LL PULL HIM DOWN LIKE A BLOODHOUND!

CLASSICS ILLUSTRATED was re-launched in 1990 in graphic novel/book form by the Berkley Publishing Group and First Publishing, Inc. featuring all-new adaptations by such top graphic novelists as Rick Geary, Bill Sienkiewicz, Kyle Baker, Gahan Wilson, and others. "First had the right idea, they just came out about 15 years too soon. Now bookstores are ready for graphic novels such as these," Jim explains. Many of these excellent adaptations have been acquired by Papercutz and will make up the new series of CLASSICS ILLUSTRATED titles.

The first volume of the new CLASSICS ILLUSTRATED series presents graphic novelist Rick Geary's adaptation of "Great Expectations" by Charles Dickens. The bittersweet tale of one boy's adolescence, and of the choices he makes to shape his destiny. Into an engrossing mystery, Dickens weaves a heartfelt inquiry into morals and virtues-as the orphan Pip, the convict Magwitch, the beautiful Estella, the bitter Miss Havisham, the goodhearted Biddy, the kind Joe and other memorable characters entwine in a battle of human nature. Rick Geary's delightful illustrations capture the newfound awe and frustrations of young Pip as he comes of age, and begins to understand the opportunities that life presents.

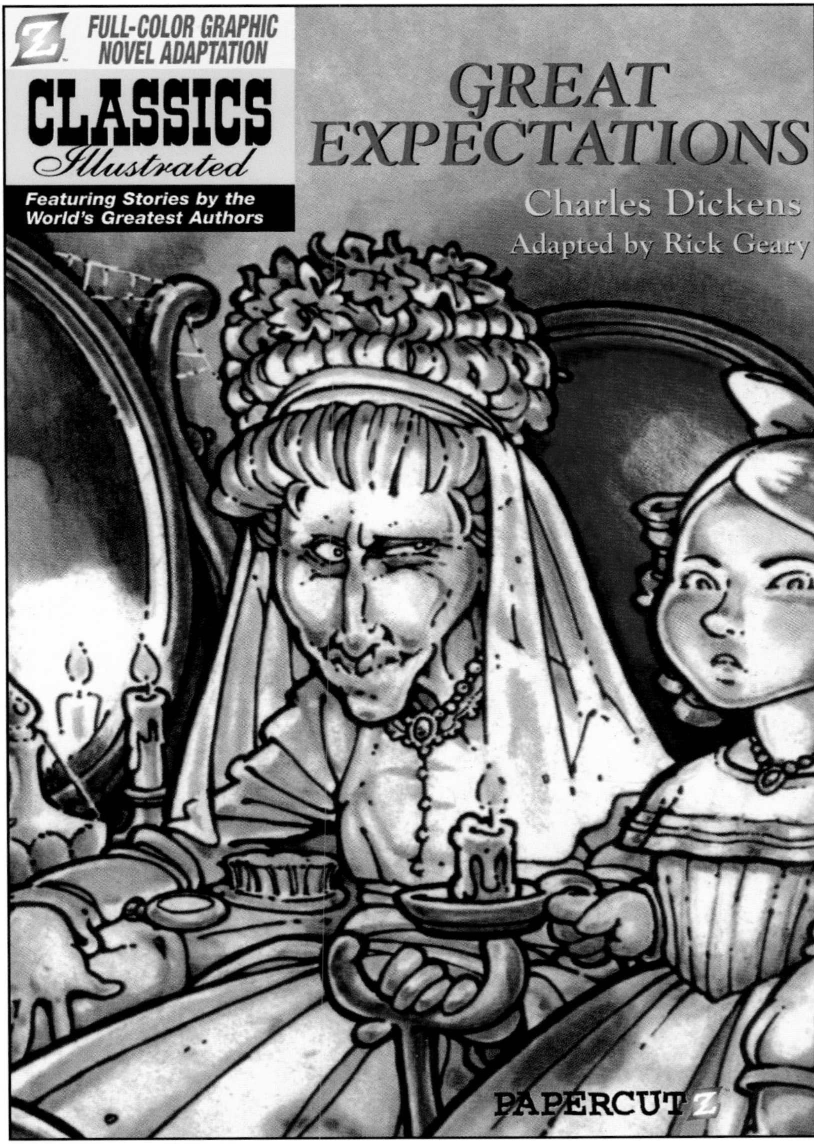

FULL-COLOR GRAPHIC NOVEL ADAPTATION
CLASSICS Illustrated
Featuring Stories by the World's Greatest Authors
GREAT EXPECTATIONS
Charles Dickens
Adapted by Rick Geary
PAPERCUTZ

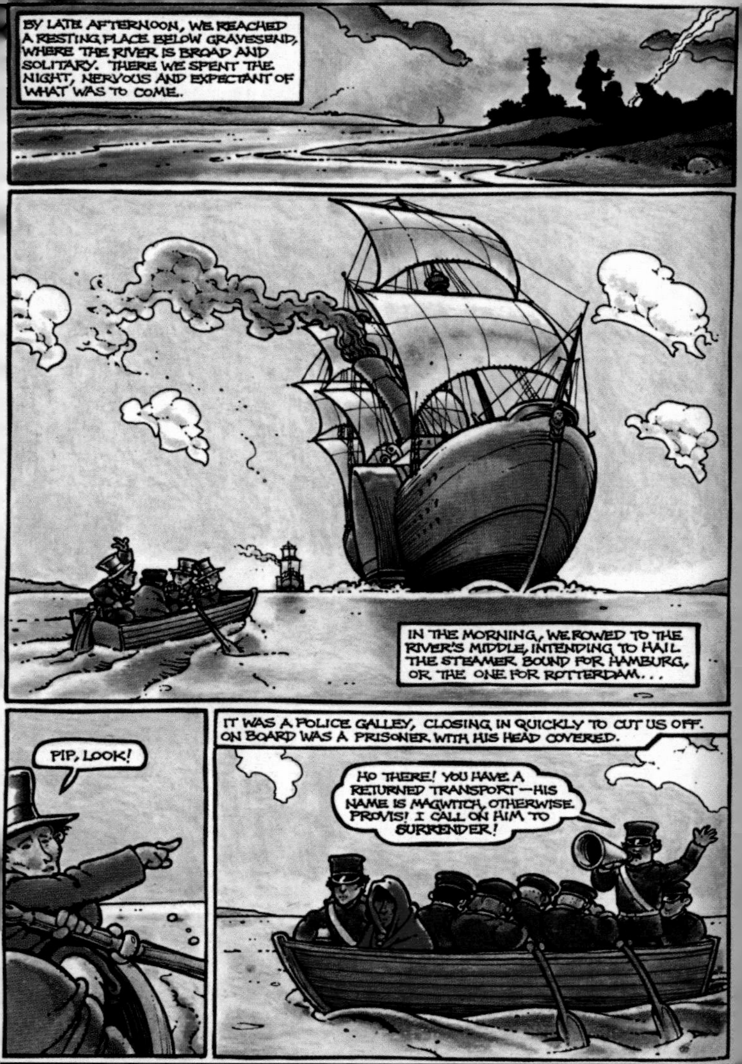
BY LATE AFTERNOON, WE REACHED A RESTING PLACE BELOW GRAVESEND, WHERE THE RIVER IS BROAD AND SOLITARY. THERE WE SPENT THE NIGHT, NERVOUS AND EXPECTANT OF WHAT WAS TO COME.
IN THE MORNING, WE ROWED TO THE RIVER'S MIDDLE, INTENDING TO HAIL THE STEAMER BOUND FOR HAMBURG, OR THE ONE FOR ROTTERDAM...
PIP, LOOK!
IT WAS A POLICE GALLEY, CLOSING IN QUICKLY TO CUT US OFF. ON BOARD WAS A PRISONER WITH HIS HEAD COVERED.
HO THERE! YOU HAVE A RETURNED TRANSPORT—HIS NAME IS MAGWITCH, OTHERWISE PROVIS! I CALL ON HIM TO SURRENDER!

Iere are two preview pages of CLASSICS ILLUSTRATED #1 "Gre
Expectations" by Charles Dickens, as adapted by Rick Geary. (CLA
ICS ILLUSTRATED will be printed in a larger 6 1/2" x 9" format, s
he art will be bigger than what you see here.)

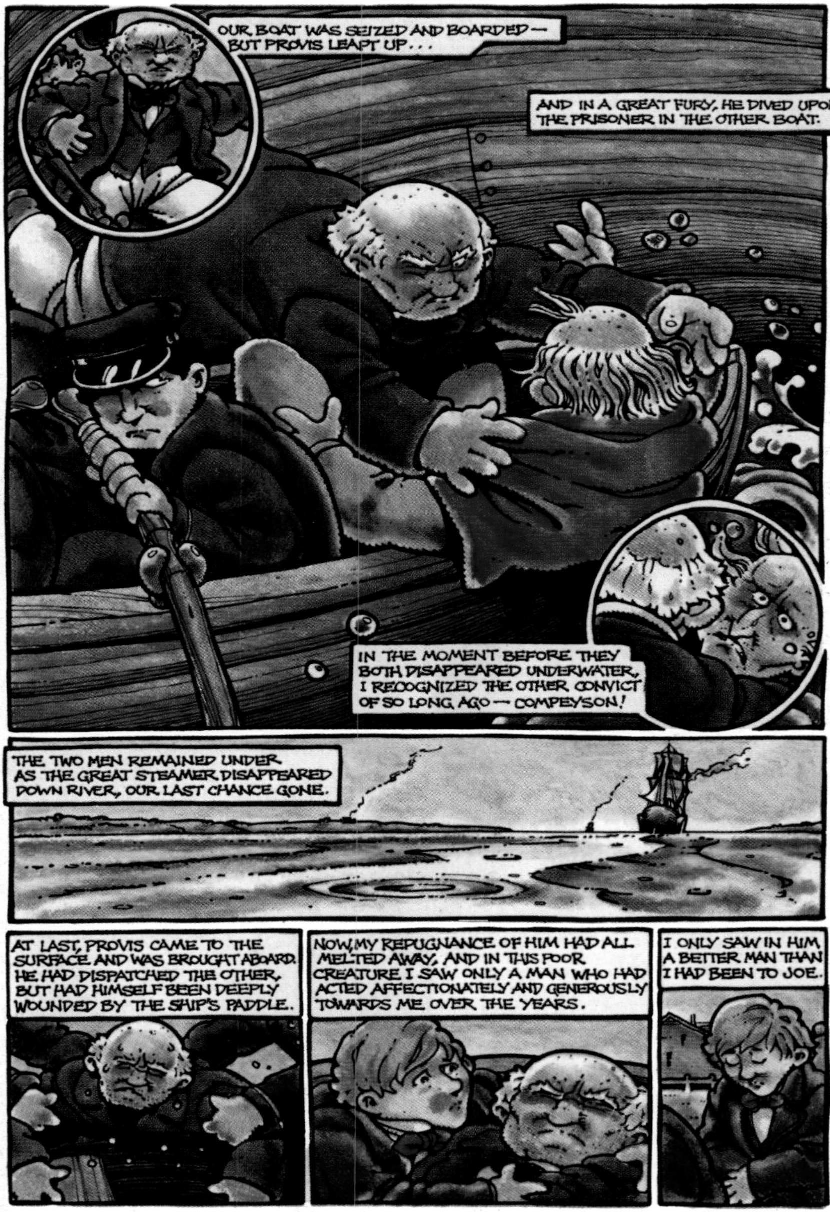
OUR BOAT WAS SEIZED AND BOARDED — BUT PROVIS LEAPT UP . . .
AND IN A GREAT FURY, HE DIVED UPON THE PRISONER IN THE OTHER BOAT.
IN THE MOMENT BEFORE THEY BOTH DISAPPEARED UNDERWATER, I RECOGNIZED THE OTHER CONVICT OF SO LONG AGO — COMPEYSON!
THE TWO MEN REMAINED UNDER AS THE GREAT STEAMER DISAPPEARED DOWN RIVER, OUR LAST CHANCE GONE.
AT LAST, PROVIS CAME TO THE SURFACE AND WAS BROUGHT ABOARD. HE HAD DISPATCHED THE OTHER, BUT HAD HIMSELF BEEN DEEPLY WOUNDED BY THE SHIP'S PADDLE.
NOW, MY REPUGNANCE OF HIM HAD ALL MELTED AWAY, AND IN THIS POOR CREATURE I SAW ONLY A MAN WHO HAD ACTED AFFECTIONATELY AND GENEROUSLY TOWARDS ME OVER THE YEARS.
I ONLY SAW IN HIM A BETTER MAN THAN I HAD BEEN TO JOE.

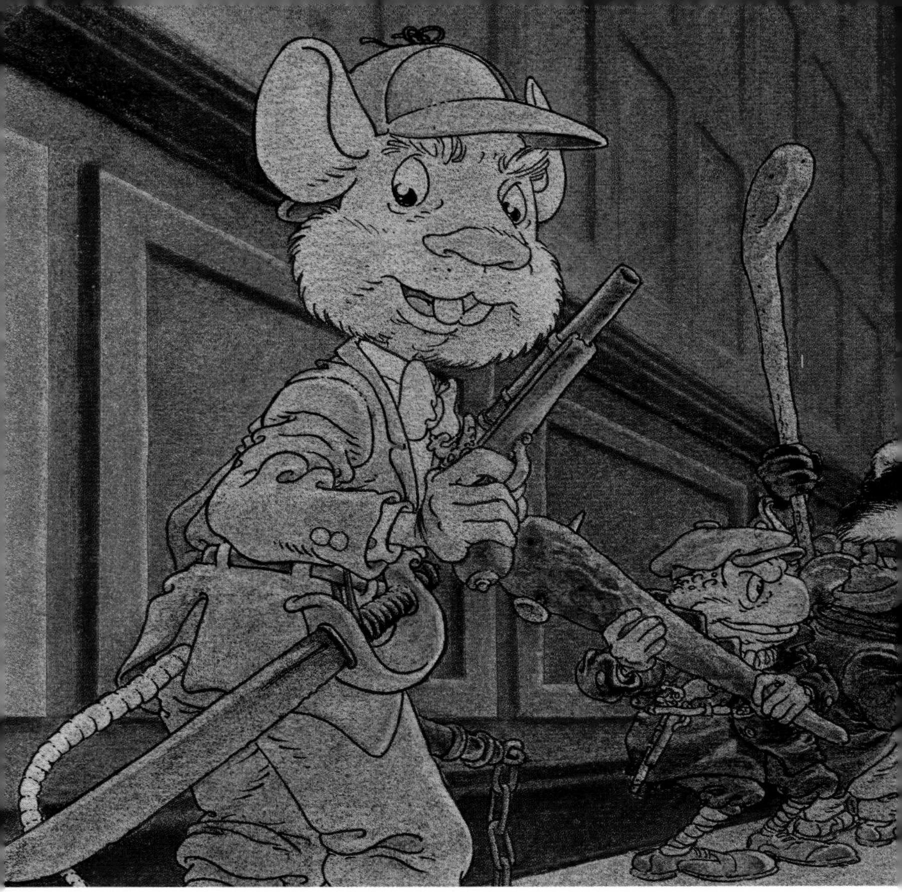

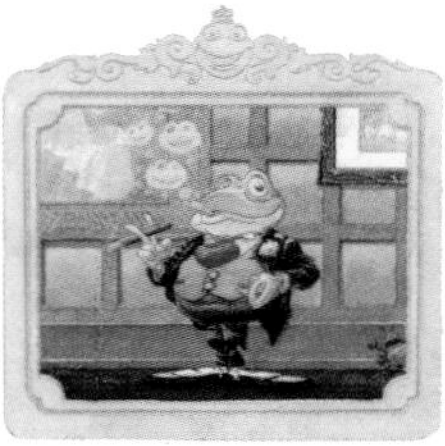

Papercutz has also obtained rights to all-new adaptations of the classics, by some of the world's finest graphic novelists. These new adaptations devote three-to-five times as many comics pages as the previous series to more fully capture the depth of the original novels. These adaptations will run as a separate series entitled CLASSICS ILLUSTRATED DELUXE. "While educators are thrilled that we're bringing back CLASSICS ILLUSTRATED, comic art fans are going to appreciate just how beautiful these books are," Jim opines.

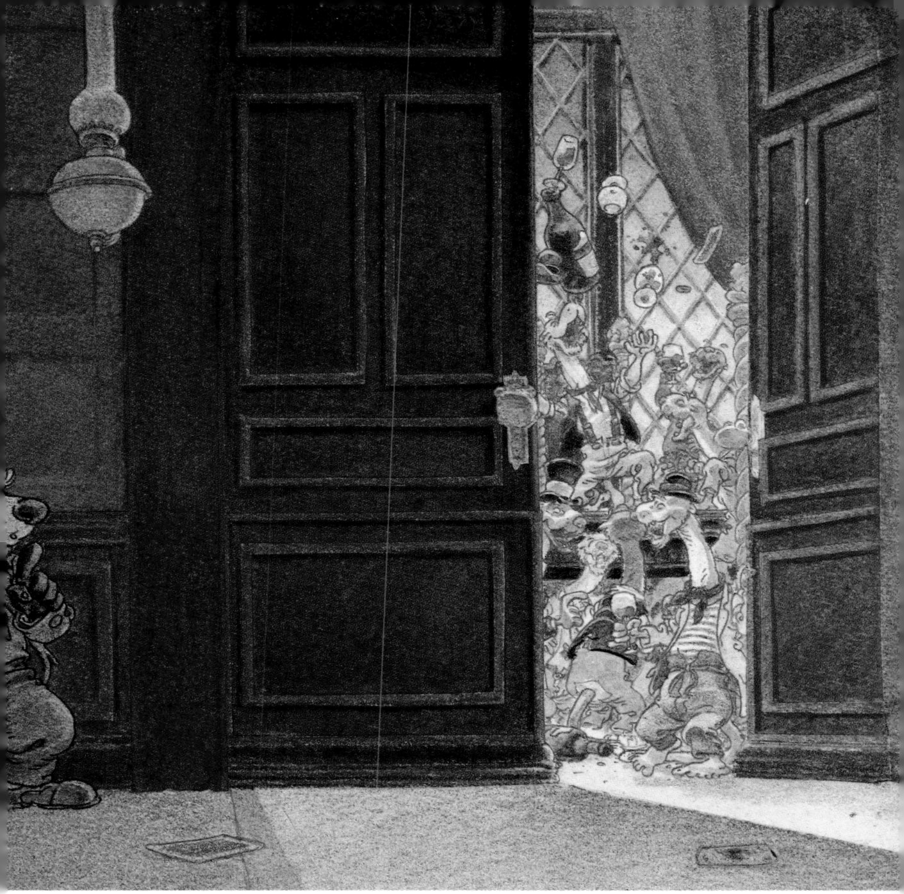

CLASSICS ILLUSTRATED DELUXE #1 presents graphic novelist Michel Plessix's lush adaptation of "The Wind in the Willows" by Kenneth Grahame. The artwork is in aquarelle, with thin, precise, detailed lines. In "Wind in the Willows," Plessix breathes life into Mole, Rat, and Toad (of Toad Hall) as they picnic on the riverbank, indulge in Toad's latest fad, and get lost in Wild Wood. The pacing is masterful: each panel lingers just long enough to make you appreciate the simple pleasures of life. Originally published in four volumes, Papercutz is proud to collect the entire series, for the very first time, in one affordable volume.

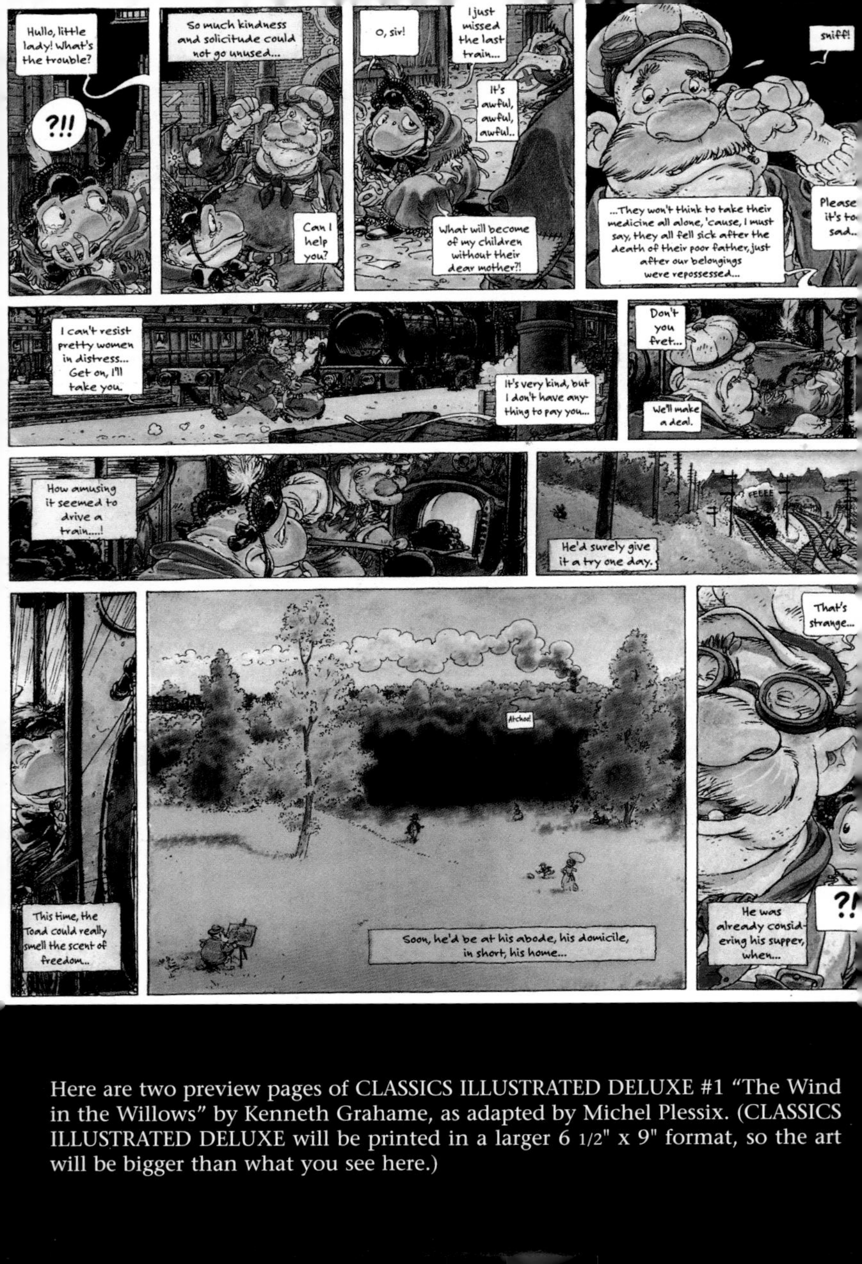

Hullo, little lady! What's the trouble?
?!!
So much kindness and solicitude could not go unused...
Can I help you?
O, sir!
I just missed the last train...
It's awful, awful, awful..
What will become of my children without their dear mother?!
sniff!
...They won't think to take their medicine all alone, 'cause, I must say, they all fell sick after the death of their poor father, just after our belongings were repossessed...
Please it's to sad...
I can't resist pretty women in distress... Get on, I'll take you.
It's very kind, but I don't have any-thing to pay you...
Don't you fret...
We'll make a deal.
How amusing it seemed to drive a train....!
He'd surely give it a try one day.
This time, the Toad could really smell the scent of freedom...
Atchoo!
Soon, he'd be at his abode, his domicile, in short, his home...
That's strange...
?!
He was already consid-ering his supper, when...

Here are two preview pages of CLASSICS ILLUSTRATED DELUXE #1 "The Wind in the Willows" by Kenneth Grahame, as adapted by Michel Plessix. (CLASSICS ILLUSTRATED DELUXE will be printed in a larger 6 1/2" x 9" format, so the art will be bigger than what you see here.)

There's a train following us when we should be alone on the track...
The police! His goose was cooked!
POW
POW
POW
Mercy! I lied to you.
?
I'm not the washerwoman that I seem to be...I'm a dangerous criminal who has just daringly escaped from the most loathsome, rotten, nauseating dungeon on earth!
Nobody's perfect...
Oh, kind sir! If you only knew what I've had to endure!
There wasn't even any sour-orange jam for breakfast...!
What did you do?
Ooohhh, nothing very much...I only borrowed something without permission. But you know how people are once you touch their dear property!
Yep. In any case, no one gives me orders when I'm on my own engine.
Especially the police.
Now you pile on the furnace with all the coal you can shovel!
Sir, yes sir!
A pitiless pursuit got underway.
Mmoooo!
Well, aren't we spoiled!
Alas, weighted down by the cars, they didn't have a chance.
It's no use! They're catching up!
Then, there's no other choice!
HEY?!
WHAT ARE YOU DOING?!!

PAPERCUTZ Feedback

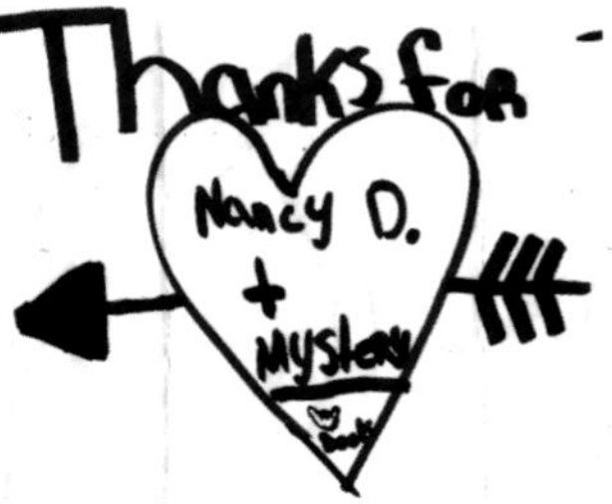
Thanks for
Nancy D.
+
Mystery

Dear Sirs:
I am sending you a thank you note from a student. I bought NANCY DREW, HARDY BOYS, and ZORRO at Comic Con in San Diego this summer. I can not keep these books on the shelf. Students check them out from the shelving cart before I ever get to put them away. The best part of the Papercutz series of books is that my reluctant readers are READING! I was tentative about getting graphic novels, comicbooks, in the library, but no more.
Keep up the good work. I need more HARDY BOYS and NANCY DREW books in the library, so write and draw faster.
Thank you,
Laura Boston
Librarian
Briarmeadow Charter School
Houston, TX

Thanks for your letter, Laura. While our main goal is to produce the most entertaining graphic novels we possibly can, it's also great to hear that our Papercutz graphic novels are helping kids improve their reading skills. We've heard similar reports from many other librarians and from many teachers as well. We're thankful for the support we've been given, and that's one of the reasons we're launching CLASSICS ILLUSTRATED. While everyone is sure to enjoy these comic art adaptations of stories by the World's Greatest Authors, they're especially compelling for reluctant readers.